Also by Blaize Clement

Curiosity Killed the Cat Sitter

DUPLICITY DOGGED THE DACHSHUND

The Second Dixie Hemingway Mystery

BLAIZE CLEMENT

St. Martin's Paperbacks

This is a work of fiction. All of the characters, organizations and events portrayed in this novel are either products of the author's imagination or are used fictitiously.

DUPLICITY DOGGED THE DACHSHUND

Copyright © 2007 by Blaize Clement.
Excerpt from *Even Cat Sitters Get the Blues* copyright © 2007 by Blaize Clement.

ISBN: 0-312-94770-4
EAN: 9780312-94770-5

Printed in the United States of America

St. Martin's Press hardcover edition / March 2007
St. Martin's Paperbacks edition / November 2007

St. Martin's Paperbacks are published by St. Martin's Press, 175 Fifth Avenue, New York, NY 10010.

10 9 8 7 6 5 4 3 2 1

Acknowledgments

As always, many thanks to The Thursday Group—Greg Jorgensen, Kate Holmes, Clark Lauren, and Janet McLaughlin—who heard a lot of this book as fast-scribbled scenes written during our weekly Improv Writing Class. For their support, information, and friendship, I am blessed.

Thanks to Barry DeChant, aka the famous "Bonzo," for letting me join one of his classes for future clowns, many of whom will work in hospices and children's hospitals. The world is enriched by their wise humor and generosity of heart, as it is by clowns all over the country. For general crime-scene information, a big thank-you to Sarasota County Sheriff's Department Crime Scene Technician Lora Garrett; to Dr. Reinhard W. Motte, Miami-Dade County Associate Medical Examiner; and to Homicide Detective Chris Ioreo of the Sarasota County Sheriff's Department.

For this and every other book in the Dixie Hemingway Mystery Series, I have gratefully used information provided by numerous Web sites, newspapers, magazines, and books, most notably *The New Natural Cat* by Anitra Frazier with Norma Eckroate, and nature articles by Kat Wingert in the *Siesta Key Observer*.

And finally, many thanks to my dream team: Marcia Markland, the world's best editor, and her assistant, Diana Szu; and to my agent, Annelise Robey, and her cohorts at the

Jane Rotrosen Agency. In a time when many writers are wearing invisible black armbands for their dead faith in the publishing world, Marcia, Diana, and Annelise have been unfailingly loyal and supportive.

DUPLICITY
DOGGED THE
DACHSHUND

1

It was a few minutes past six when I got to the Powells' house on Monday morning. A pinkish-gray sky was beginning to be brushed with apricot plumes, and wild parakeets were waking and chattering in the branches over the street. It was the last week of June, a time when everybody on Siesta Key was slow and smiling. Slow because June is so hot on the key you may keel over dead if you hurry, and smiling because the snowbirds had all gone north and we had the key to ourselves. Not that there's anything wrong with snowbirds. We *like* snowbirds. We especially like the money they spend during season. But the key goes back to being a quiet laid-back place when they leave, and we all go around for weeks with sappy smiles on our faces.

I'm Dixie Hemingway, no relation to you know who. I used to be a deputy with the Sarasota County Sheriff's Department, but something happened a little over three years ago that made the department afraid to trust me with certain parts of the population. Now I take care of pets while their owners are away. I go in their homes and feed them, groom them, and exercise them, which works out well for all of us. They don't ask a lot of questions, and I don't run the risk of doing something I'll regret.

Siesta Key is an eight-mile barrier island that sits like a tropical kneecap off Sarasota, Florida. Running north and south, it lies between the Gulf of Mexico on the west and

Sarasota Bay on the east. Our powdery white beach is made of quartz crystal that stays cool even when the sun sends down lava rays, and it magnetizes poets and painters and mystics who believe it's one of the planet's vortexes of energy. Lush with hibiscus, palms, mangrove, bougainvillea, and sea grape, Siesta Key is home to about seven thousand sun-smacked year-round residents and just about every known species of shorebirds and songbirds and butterflies. In the bay, great bovine manatees with goofy smiles on their faces move with surprising grace, eating all the vegetation in their path and keeping the waterways clear. In the Gulf, playful dolphins cavort in the waves, and occasional sharks keep swimmers alert.

There are other keys off Sarasota, but they tend to look down their proper noses at Siesta. She's the slightly rebellious daughter whose conservative family is always afraid she'll do something to embarrass them. Nubile maidens dance on her beach while drummers sound down the sun, tourists young and old shed their inhibitions and thread her streets with bemused smiles on their faces, and the natives don't overly concern themselves with the histories of some incredibly wealthy residents who have no discernible talents.

I wouldn't live anywhere else.

Judge and Mrs. Hopewell Powell had just left for their annual three-week vacation in Italy, putting Mame, their elderly miniature dachshund, in my care. Mame had a more formal official name, but when she was a puppy she had been such an inquisitive little snoop that Judge Powell—he wasn't a judge anymore, but he'd sat on the Florida Supreme Court so long that everybody still called him Judge—had begun to sing, "Put the blame on Mame, boys, put the blame on Mame," and the name had stuck. They still sang the song to her, and until lately Mame would stand on her hind legs and wave her front paws in the air as if she were dancing.

Siesta Key only has one main street, Midnight Pass Road, so you either live on the Gulf side or the bay side. The Powells lived near the north end, in an exclusive bayside neighborhood called Secret Cove. Secret Cove is actually a one-lane bricked street that traces an irregular north-south ellipse squeezed between Midnight Pass Road and the bay. Mossy oaks, pines, sea grape, bamboo, palm, and palmetto hide it from Midnight Pass Road, maintaining the illusion of an area unspoiled by human habitation. Live oaks form a canopy over the lane, and frequent signs warn that the street is for residents only; outsiders will presumably be drawn and quartered. In the event two cars meet, occasional bulges in the street allow the less expensive car to back up and pull aside.

A thick wild preserve fills the inside of Secret Cove's oval, and more wild thickets separate its dozen or so houses. Narrow inlets intrude on the bay side, where scattered houses have boat docks and spectacular water views. The Powells lived on the waterless front side near the southern end where the street loops back on itself. The house was modest for the area: two-story pinkish stucco, red barrel-tile roof, attached double garage facing the street, a front door the color of eggplant, and a yard full of pebbles and tropical foliage growing so fast you could almost see it move. On the key, the unwritten rule is that the more green stuff you have surrounding your property, the less of it you have covering your yard. Places that are practically in a wilderness therefore have pebble or shell instead of grass.

Mame was behind the glassed front door watching for me. She barked to let me know that while I might have a key to her door, it was still her house.

I love those little dogs. Every miniature dachshund I've ever known has been affectionate and up for anything. You want to go for a walk? A miniature dachshund will head for the door with his tail wagging. You want to sit and watch TV? He'll sit with you and look hard at the screen. You want to play Fetch-the-stuffed-Wal-Mart-toy? He'll run after it as many times as you throw it. Except for a tenacious streak that makes them determined to explore anything that takes their fancy no matter how much you may try to talk them out of it, dachshunds are among the most amenable pets in the world.

Mame was an auburn longhair with a face blanched by age. In people years, she was pushing ninety, which made it problematic to leave her alone. But the Powells were pushing ninety too, in people years, and there comes a time when you have to make hard choices, and they'd made theirs. They wanted Mame to be at home, not in a boarding kennel, and they didn't want anybody staying in the house with her.

I squatted to talk to her through the glass before I unlocked the door.

"Hey, Mame, can I come in?"

She stopped barking, but that's all. In times past, she would have reared up on her hind legs and excitedly waved her front paws at me. Now arthritis and sadness made her simply watch me unlock the door and punch in the access code.

When I was growing up, nobody ever locked their doors on the key. But as more people moved here and we learned to be afraid, we began installing dead bolts and night latches. Now, thanks to slick salesmen and a general uneasiness about the world, a lot of people have security systems. After I've unlocked a door with my key, I have to hurry inside and punch the appropriate code on the keypad or an alarm will go off at the security company. If I'm too slow, they will call, and I have to give them my name, my security code name, which differs at each house, and my security code number.

I keep my clients' security codes in a little black book that I guard as if it held vital secrets to the planet's survival. To make it even more difficult for a potential code thief, I have given each client my own personal pseudonym. Anybody reading my little codebook will therefore not find a security code listed for Judge Powell. Instead, he's listed as Flip Wilson—as in "Here come da judge, here come da judge!" It may be a goofy way to keep records, but it works for me.

After I punched in the appropriate code, I knelt to pet Mame and let her lick my hands. Then I got her leash for her morning walk. Old dachshunds don't absolutely need walking, but I thought it was good for Mame to begin her day with a little adventure.

As Mame and I got to the end of the driveway and started to step into the narrow street, Conrad Ferrelli's silver BMW came tearing toward us down the tree-darkened lane, going so fast that I grabbed Mame and jumped back. I recognized the car because I sometimes took care of Conrad's Doberman pinscher, Reggie. I couldn't actually see Conrad, but I saw the silhouette of Reggie's triangular head, with his ears cocked up.

I liked Reggie. I liked Conrad Ferrelli. I liked his wife, Stevie. And so as the car drew even with me, I waved and smiled. I may have even chirped, "Hey!"

The car disappeared around a curve, its license plate winking in the shadows, and I led Mame out into the street as if nothing unusual had just happened.

Dumb, dumb, dumb.

I heard the roar of Conrad's car as it pulled onto Midnight Pass Road and sped south toward Crescent Beach and the village. His breakneck speed seemed odd, but then Conrad wasn't known for being a conformist. People sucked up to him for his money, but when his back was turned they snickered and elbowed one another because of the way he dressed. He wasn't exactly a cross-dresser, but he was a weirdly flamboyant dresser. His preferred getup was a pair of wild flowered skorts worn with a tailored coat and tie and mismatched transparent plastic slippers, maybe turquoise on one foot and yellow on the other. And he always, without fail, wore huge garish clip-on ear bobs.

Since I come from a long line of people who marched to the beat of their own drums, I'd always sort of admired Conrad for wearing whatever he damn well pleased.

That's why I waved at Conrad's car. That's why I probably said, "Hey!"

That's my excuse.

Mame and I walked slowly, because her legs were short and she was so old. We stopped to let her do her doggie business. We stopped to let her sniff at a tree. We stopped to watch a great egret take flight. At the place where the lane curves sharply to form its bayside stretch, one of my Keds had come untied, and I knelt to tie it, releasing the leash briefly to use both hands. Mame suddenly took off into the forested area, nose stretched, tail straight out, moving as if she'd dropped half her years. I made a grab for the leash but missed it. I called to her, but she ignored me and disappeared. I called again and heard a rough scratching sound behind the trees.

Mame was digging at something, and when a dachshund finds a place it wants to dig, you can't change its mind. The word *dachshund* means *badger dog* in German, and the scent of a rabbit or a field mouse triggers their badger-seizing instincts. Mame couldn't actually tunnel into an animal's underground home, of course, but she could have fun thinking she might. In a way, I was pleased for her. At her age, this might be her last hunt. But I couldn't let her dig willy-nilly in that thicket because all kinds of unfriendly critters live in places like that. I called a few more times, even though I knew it was useless, and then gritted my teeth and stepped into the dark morass of ferns, potato vines, saw grass, and palmettos under the trees.

I found Mame next to a long funky-smelling mound of pine needles and dead leaves at the base of a live oak dripping with Spanish moss. She was growling deep in her throat and tugging on something with her teeth. Gingerly, bracing myself for a rat's tail or a baby snake, I leaned to see what she'd found. When I saw what it was, I let out an involuntary yelp.

She had a human finger in her mouth. The finger was attached to a hand. The finger was grayish blue, and so was the hand. The hand disappeared about mid-palm under the loose mulch.

I grabbed Mame's leash and tried to jerk her back, but

she stiffened her front paws and arched her head to resist me. She didn't let go of the finger, and the hand came out higher, up to the wrist.

I whispered "Mame!" as if she and I were complicit in some kind of crime and I didn't want anybody to hear. She growled. It was her finger and she wasn't giving it up.

Grimacing, I lightly smacked the top of her nose.

"Let go, Mame! No!"

She growled again and shook her head angrily, but she didn't let go. The shaking loosened the hand, creating a ring of space between wrist and pine needles.

I smacked her nose again, harder. "Mame, no! Let go!"

Along with knowing this was one of the most bizarre things I'd ever done, fighting with a dog over a corpse's finger, was the uneasy knowledge that we were at the scene of a crime. Mame had already disturbed the covering by digging in the loose mulch, and I was trampling on it and possibly obliterating valuable evidence. There was also the possibility that whoever had covered the body was watching from behind a tree.

I squatted over Mame, took her determined jaws in both hands, and forced them open. Mame snarled and tried to snap at me, but the dead finger slid out and the hand flopped on the ground. Rigor mortis sets in quickly in a dead body, especially in hot weather, but this one was still limp. Which meant it hadn't been dead long. Which meant the killer might still be lurking nearby.

In the murky light, I could see it was a man's hand, large, with long fingers and manicured fingernails. Through the dark dry matter around the wrist, I caught a glimpse of gold. Mame thrashed and growled low in her throat, so angry I knew that if I let her jaws go she would nip at me. Quickly, I moved one hand to grab her collar. Keeping that arm stiff to hold her away, I felt for a pulse on the man's blue wrist with my other hand. No doubt about it, he was dead, and the color of his skin said he'd died of asphyxiation. I jerked my hand away and duck-walked backward, still stiff-arming Mame's collar while I scrambled in my pocket for my cell phone to dial 911.

When the dispatcher answered, I gave her my name and location.

"I'm out walking a dog, and she just dug up a dead body."

"Your dog dug up a body?"

"Not the whole body, just a hand."

Mame snarled over her shoulder and barked for good measure, sounding like a dog five times her real size.

It must have impressed the dispatcher, because she said, "Somebody will be right there, ma'am, but stay on the phone with me, okay?"

I knew she wanted to keep me talking until a deputy arrived in case I was reporting a crime I'd committed myself. Also, the investigating officer would want to know how I'd come upon the body, and the dispatcher didn't want me to leave the scene.

I said, "I won't disconnect, but I'm going to put the phone down because I need to calm the dog."

Before she could tell me what she thought about that, I laid the phone on the ground so I could use both hands on Mame. I not only wanted to calm her, I wanted to get us both back to the street. Keeping her collar in one hand, I stroked her head with the other and talked softly to her.

"Good girl, Mame, good girl. You're a very good girl, and everything's okay."

That's what we all want to hear, that we're good and that everything's okay.

I kept repeating it, and she gradually stopped snarling and decided not to bite me. But when I turned her around to pick her up, her eyes were full of reproach. I had hurt her feelings and she wasn't going to forgive me easily. I didn't blame her. I *never* hit an animal, any more than I would hit a child, and I despise people who do. No matter how people may try to justify it, any time a large person uses physical punishment on a small vulnerable body, it's despicable abuse.

But here the first time I'd caught Mame with a corpse's

finger in her mouth, I'd smacked her nose. Both of us were going to have to readjust our opinions of me.

I picked up the phone and carried Mame to the street, stepping out of the thicket just as a green-and-white patrol car cruised toward us. I told the dispatcher the deputy had arrived and turned off the phone. The patrol car pulled to a stop and the driver got out. When I saw who it was, I took a deep breath. Deputy Jesse Morgan recognized me at about the same time. I imagine he had to suck up a bit of air too. The last time we'd met had been over another dead body, in circumstances no less peculiar than this one.

He was crisp and neat in his dark green shorts and shirt, his waist bulging with all the paraphernalia of a law-enforcement officer, his muscular legs covering the ground in a confident stride. Only the diamond stud in one earlobe indicated that he had a life apart from keeping Siesta Key safe.

He nodded to me with that impassive face that all law-enforcement officers cultivate.

"Miz Hemingway."

I nodded back. "Deputy Morgan."

"You called about a body?"

"The dog smelled it and ran over and started digging. She had a hand pulled out before I knew what it was." I pointed toward the thick trees and underbrush. "The body is under that big oak."

He stepped into the thicket, walking as if he wasn't at all concerned about poisonous snakes or spiders or fire ants. I could see his dark green back through the branches, saw him stop and stand a moment with his hands on his hips, saw him kneel for a few seconds, and then stand and turn to walk back to me, talking on his phone as he came. When he stepped onto the street, his face was unreadable. I wasn't surprised. Only once or twice in our acquaintance had I caught him in a smile.

"What time did you find it?"

"Not more than ten minutes ago."

"You called as soon as you saw it?"

"I had to fight the dog first. She wouldn't let go of the finger. If it has tooth marks, they're from Mame."

His mouth turned down a bit. "She chewed on the finger?"

"I wouldn't say she chewed on it exactly, more like clamped her teeth down and held on."

He looked hard at Mame, who returned his look with an imperious tilt of her nose. It took a lot more than a uniformed deputy to intimidate Mame.

He said, "I used to have a dachshund. They're stubborn little guys."

"That's just it; she doesn't know she's little."

He didn't slip up and smile, but his eyes warmed a bit and he nodded. Another car drew up, and Deputy Morgan walked over to meet Sergeant Woodrow Owens. Mame squirmed in my arms and I put her down. Like a little guided missile, she headed straight back toward the thicket. I had the leash this time, so I pulled her back and glared at her, feeling like an embarrassed parent whose child is showing unflattering traits in public.

2

As he passed by with Deputy Morgan to go look at the body, Sergeant Owens flapped his hand at me. A tall, lanky African-American with droopy basset-hound eyes and a slow drawl that sounds like he just swallowed a mouthful of warm buttered grits, Sergeant Owens is the man who once looked me in the eye and told me I was too fucked up to continue as a law-enforcement officer. He understood why and was sympathetic, but he couldn't have a deputy who was liable to go apeshit every now and then. I don't hold it against him. I'd have done the same thing in his position.

I sat down on one of the cypress logs edging the lane and trapped Mame between my knees. In a few minutes Sergeant Owens came out and squatted beside me.

"You okay, Dixie?"

"Yeah, I'm good."

"Haven't seen you since that other business."

I nodded. "That other business" had been a few months back when I had gone in a house to feed a cat and found a murdered man in the kitchen. I had ended up nearly getting killed myself, but in an odd way it had been good for me. I had thrown off a sick sense of victimhood and done what I needed to do to defend myself. I'd also stopped being afraid that I might be truly crazy. Now I was pretty sure I wasn't much more neurotic than the average person.

I said, "I left shoe tracks by the body, and there are probably some dog hairs there too."

"I'll tell the crime techs. I've called Lieutenant Guidry. I imagine he'll want to talk to you."

"Guidry will be handling this?"

I didn't like how my voice went up an octave when I said that or how my heart did an annoying little tap dance. Guidry had been the homicide detective on the case where I'd found the murdered man in the cat's house, and there had been times when I'd hated him with a fine and pure venom—mostly because he had usually been right and also because he had forced me to move out of the dark web I'd spun round myself. I was much stronger now, and I had to admit that Guidry had a lot to do with why. Even so, I wasn't ready for any kind of relationship with a man, and it irked me that my body didn't seem to know that.

I said, "I need to take the dog home."

Sergeant Owens stood and reached to give me a hand up. Keeping Mame's leash short, I dusted off my cargo shorts and pointed toward her house. "It's just down the road there. I won't be long."

"Take your time. We'll be here awhile."

I knew what he meant. Nothing is rushed at a crime scene. Crime technicians would walk shoulder to shoulder around the area looking for anything a killer might have dropped. They would photograph the mound and the protruding hand. They would photograph my tracks and Mame's. They would look for any other tracks, for fibers, for hair, for anything that might point to the identity of the person or persons who had covered a dead body with soil and duff. They would take several measurements of the exact location of the body from the base of the tree and from other markers. Only then would they uncover the corpse.

As I carried Mame home, she looked over my shoulder toward the brambly woods as if I'd deprived her of the most fun she'd had in a dog's age. We met two unmarked cars, with a van from the Crime Scene Investigation Unit close behind. They pulled close to the cypress logs along the edge of the street, but they still blocked the single-car lane. Secret Cove residents were going to be pissed.

At Mame's house, I carried her straight to the bathroom and scrubbed my hands several times with antiseptic soap. Then I gave Mame a bath, wrapped her in a big beach towel, and brushed her teeth with poultry-flavored toothpaste. Every time I thought of that dead finger in her mouth, I said "Bleh!" and went over her molars again. For good measure, I gave her a Greenie to make her breath sweet again. I was a little tempted to chew one myself.

While she chewed on her Greenie, I took her out to the lanai to brush her dry in the early sunshine. I talked to her while I pulled my brush through her ear fringes and down her trousers and inside her forearms, telling her how beautiful she was and what a good girl she was, but my mind kept straying to what was happening at the crime scene. Mame seemed preoccupied too, chewing her Greenie with her eyes half closed as if my voice was background music to the images in her head.

When she was all dry and gleaming, I put her on the floor and pulled some hair from the grooming brush to put into a plastic bag. In the kitchen, I got out a twenty-pound bag of organic senior kibble and measured a half cup into her bowl—all a miniature dachshund needs for good health and a shiny coat. I added a Jubilee Wafer to keep her joints supple and gave her fresh water in a clean bowl. Mame wagged her tail and followed me to the front door to let me know we were friends again.

At the front door, I took her face in both hands and kissed the tip of her nose.

"I'll be back tonight, okay?"

Mame swallowed the last of her Greenie and licked my hands with a chlorophyll-green tongue. People say dogs live only in the moment, that they don't have memories of the past. I don't believe that for one second. I was sure Mame remembered everything that had happened, but I didn't mention it. Some things are best left unsaid.

I walked down the street to the crime scene, where more cars edged the lane and yellow crime-scene tape had been stretched around the trees. A deputy from Community Policing stood beside the crime-scene tape.

I said, "I'm Dixie Hemingway. I was with the dog that found the body this morning. I brought some of the dog's hair for the techs."

She took the plastic bag and looked at the silky russet hairs inside.

"Irish setter?"

"Long-haired dachshund."

"I'll give it to them."

"Is Lieutenant Guidry here?"

She tilted her head toward a group of people standing behind an ambulance. "He's over there."

"I imagine he'll want to get a statement from me."

She nodded and strode to the clump of officers. They all turned and looked at me, and then they parted and Lieutenant Guidry stepped through the gap.

Gosh.

Nobody should look that good, especially not somebody in law enforcement. Most law-enforcement men look like they've gained twenty pounds since they bought their last suit, but since they don't have the time or money to buy new clothes every time they gain weight, they just keep cramming their expanding guts into old pants and letting their jacket sleeves strain at the armpits. Half of them wear Thom McAn shoes and black socks that haven't faded the same way, so one is darker than the other.

Not Guidry. Some Italian designer kept him supplied with the kind of easy free-hanging jackets and pants that only the very rich can afford. The kind of things that wrinkle because they're made of natural breathable fibers from countries where people live in yurts or alpaca tents. Poor people get stuck with complicated clothes made of crap left over from oil refining, synthetic stuff you can wad up and run a truck over and it won't wrinkle. He wore leather sandals and no socks, and anybody looking at the leather could tell it was the best damn leather money could buy. Guidry was either independently wealthy and just working as a homicide detective for kicks, or some rich woman dressed him.

Not that I cared. Neither he nor his clothes were any of my business, and I never wasted a second thinking about him. Truly.

Guidry is olive-skinned, probably late thirties or early forties—old enough to have acquired permanent parentheses around his mouth and fine white laugh lines fanning at the corners of his eyes. His hair is dark with a sprinkling of silver at the sides, close-cropped to show a shapely skull and nice ears. He has gray eyes, a beaky nose, and even white teeth. I didn't know anything about his personal life, or care, but he had mentioned once that he'd been married in the past and didn't have any children. Okay, he didn't mention it until I asked a leading question. I don't know why I asked. I didn't really care one way or the other.

Today he wore an oatmeal linen jacket with the sleeves pushed up his tanned forearms. His pants were linen too, brown and nicely wrinkled, and his knit shirt was a dark salmon pink. I absolutely hate it when a man looks better than I do. As he approached I was acutely conscious of my rumpled khaki shorts and of my bralessness. My sleeveless T was black knit. You couldn't see through it, but men have a kind of X-ray vision that always alerts them when a woman isn't wearing a bra.

We shook hands, formal as if we were meeting for the first time. Neither of us mentioned what had happened the last time we were together. I don't know why he didn't mention it, but I had almost got killed then, so it wasn't something I wanted to talk about.

He said, "I understand your dog found the body."

"She's not my dog, but I'm taking care of her. She must have smelled it from the street, and she ran to it and tried to dig it up. She bit on a finger."

He didn't look surprised. Dogs can smell dead bodies from a long way away, and they're always drawn to them. That's why rescue teams use cadaver dogs to find dead bodies trapped under wreckage.

"Break the skin?"

I shrugged. "I'm not sure."

Dead bodies don't bleed and I hadn't looked that closely.

I said, "I gave the crime techs some hair from the dog for comparison."

"You didn't see or hear anything in the area before you found the body?"

"Not a thing."

"Any cars, people?"

"There was one car earlier, but it was somebody who lives here."

"Name?"

"Conrad Ferrelli. At least it was his car. I didn't actually see the driver."

He seemed surprised. "You know Conrad Ferrelli?"

"I've taken care of their dog several times."

His gray eyes were watching me. "Something bothering you?"

"The car was going awfully fast."

"Wait here."

He stooped under the crime-scene tape and went over to talk to the Medical Examiner. The crime-scene technicians joined them, and from time to time they all glanced at me. I shifted from foot to foot, thinking uneasily of Conrad Ferrelli's speeding car.

Guidry came back to me. "They're ready to uncover the body. Come see if you know who it is."

I followed him to the tree where the techs were kneeling beside the body, gently brushing soil away from the head. The techs blocked my view of the face, and as I waited I looked toward a rustling in the surrounding greenery. Conrad Ferrelli's Doberman pinscher stood beside a tree trunk, a thin shaft of light sharply defining the rust markings on his muzzle and throat. His dark eyes looked puzzled and wary.

I said. "Oh, no."

The Medical Examiner looked up. "Ms. Hemingway?"

I pointed toward Reggie. "That dog belongs to the Fer-rellis."

I squatted on the ground and stretched my hand toward Reggie. Behind me, I heard Guidry say, "Everybody stay where you are and be quiet."

I could see Reggie clearly now. He wore a pale dangling necktie—probably one of Conrad's—but he didn't have a collar or a leash.

I said, "Reggie hi, boy, that's a good boy, good Reggie, come here, Reggie, come on, Reggie."

He raised his ears but he didn't move. I crooned to him some more, while the people behind me stayed silent and still as statues. I stretched my hand toward him, palm up, and sent him mental images of my hand holding kibble, of my hand stroking his head, of my hand patting him with love. I've always done that with animals, and I'm convinced they get the pictures exactly the way I send them. I can't prove it, and lots of people think it's a nutty idea, but as long as animals respond to it, I'll keep doing it.

Reggie lowered to his front elbows, a look on his face that I could only describe as ashamed. Still hunkered low, I slid my feet in his direction, moving in tiny increments while I crooned sweet phrases to him and sent him mental messages of our happy connection. Somebody shouted in the street, and I sensed Guidry leaving the tree to go shush the people beyond the crime-scene tape.

It seemed to take hours, but it was probably no more than a couple of minutes until I got close enough to get a firm grip on the necktie.

"Good boy, Reggie. That's a very good boy. Sweet Reggie, you're a good, good boy."

I carefully moved my hands over his body, feeling for broken bones or swelling, watching his face for signs of pain. He didn't seem hurt in any way, but I could feel fine tremors under his skin. When I sensed that he was calm enough to follow me, I led him around the group of forensics people to the Community Policing Officer. Then I went back to look at the dead body. So far as I was concerned, it had already been identified.

3

The forensics people resumed their careful work, brushing humus away from the corpse's head, watching each spoonful they removed, exquisitely mindful that valuable clues could be mixed with the rotted leaves and bark. My breath was shallow and fast, filled with dread for what I was about to see. The techs' hands stopped moving, and a ripple of silent shock seemed to run around the circle of people bending over the body. When they pulled back to let me see the uncovered face, I felt the same shock.

Not because the jaw had dropped in the automatic reaction of death, or because the eyes were wide and staring. Those things were expected. What was unexpected was the fool's grin slashed with bright red lipstick on the blue-tinged face.

They all looked up at me as if for explanation as well as identification.

I said, "That's Conrad Ferrelli."

Guidry gave a curt nod, managing to thank me and dismiss me with one gesture.

"I don't need to tell you not to divulge anything about the lipstick."

Of course he didn't. Innocent people would come forward to make false confessions. Guilty people would give false alibis. Citizens would call with leads and misguided information. That angry lipsticked leer was knowledge that only the killer and the homicide investigators would have. And me.

I turned to go. I didn't want to stay to see the rest of the uncovering. I didn't want to find out how Conrad had been suffocated. That was something only the homicide investigators and the killer should know.

Guidry caught up with me. "You know Mrs. Ferrelli, right?"

"Why?"

"Her dog has to be taken home. I was thinking it would be easier for her if you came with me."

"You mean if I told her."

"That too."

"What is it with you? Every time you get assigned to investigate a murder, you end up making me do all your dirty work."

"I wouldn't say *every* time, and I'm not making you do anything. You can refuse. You can let the woman open her door and find a total stranger standing there with her dog. You can let a total stranger break the news that her husband's dead."

I glared at him. The last thing in the world I wanted to do was tell Stevie Ferrelli that she was a widow, but Guidry had a point.

The Ferrilli house was just around the bend, the first one at the southern end of the waterside properties, but it seemed more respectful to arrive in a car than go straggling down the street leading a dog by a necktie.

I said, "We'll have to take my car."

The Community Policing Officer was kneeling beside Reggie, talking softly to him, and when I took the end of the necktie he came without resisting. Guidry followed us down the lane to Mame's driveway and my Bronco. Reggie balked a bit at getting into the back but finally obeyed. With Guidry in the passenger seat, I looped a right to the bay and drove past a few shuttered houses that looked closed for the summer.

The Ferrellis' tall cypress house was on the edge of an inlet, with a curving drive sweeping across the front. The house had weathered silver gray, and near-black Bermuda shutters on its slim windows gave it a coy look, like an island woman with demurely lowered eyelashes. A louvered breezeway separated a wide carport from the house, and a sparkling white Scarab 35 Sport rocked gently at a wooden dock.

I parked in front of the entrance, went to the back of the Bronco, and looped a cotton leash around Reggie's neck. He was tense, holding his neck stiffly arched as I led him up the steps to the door. Guidry rang the bell, and I laid my hand on top of Reggie's head while we waited.

Stevie opened the door, her face showing a mixture of apprehension and irritation, as if she didn't appreciate unexpected people at her door so early in the morning. She was about forty, with the lean high-cheekboned beauty I always associate with generations of money. She was barefoot, in white linen shorts and a high-necked black sleeveless knit top, her dark hair loosely twisted into a comb at the back of her head. When she saw Reggie, her mouth made an O of surprise, and then she looked quickly at Guidry,

I remembered the feeling, the dark curtain slowly descending so that color and light become dingy, the brain screaming that what you're about to hear can't be true, even though you already know before you hear it that it is.

I said, "Stevie, it's about Conrad."

She covered her own mouth, but I knew it was mine she wanted to shut up.

Guidry said, "Mrs. Ferrelli, I'm Lieutenant Guidry of the Sarasota County Sheriff's Department. May we come in?"

Mutely, she stood aside, and Guidry and I stepped into space that soared to a high cathedral ceiling, with a glass wall at the back overlooking the bay. We walked over dark tile to stand awkwardly on a rug where caramel leather sofas and chairs formed a grouping.

Stevie said, "Has Conrad had an accident?"

Guidry said, "I think you'd better sit down, ma'am."

She sat, suddenly and heavily, as if her legs had suddenly given way. I slipped the cotton leash off Reggie, and he trotted to her, instinctively going to give comfort. She touched his neck with trembling fingers.

Guidry said, "Mrs. Ferrelli, when did you last see your husband?"

She seemed to shrink inside her skin. I wanted to rush to her and comfort her, but I stayed quiet.

She said, "Tell me what's happened. Why are you here?"

Guidry said, "We found the dog in the wooded area beside the street. Apparently, your husband was attacked while he was walking him."

She shook her head. "No, there must be some mistake. Conrad takes Reggie to the beach. He doesn't walk him on the street."

Guidry's voice was gentle but firm. "He was in the wooded area by the street."

She looked to me, as if I might have better news.

"Dixie? Is Conrad hurt? Is it bad?"

I said, "Stevie, I'm sorry. He was killed."

She reacted the way civilized women do, first with disbelief and irrational insistence that it was all a case of mistaken identity, then with controlled despair, with shuddering tears, with questions, and finally with gradual acceptance and the ability to give Guidry names to call, people to notify.

There should be some kind of cosmic rule that news like that only comes when you're alone, totally removed from civilized strictures, so you can fling yourself on the ground and howl like a wild dog. So you can beat your fists on hard surfaces and break your own bones. Civilization forces us to push our grief into our chests where it turns into a sustained moan.

I left her with Guidry and went into the kitchen where a coffeemaker was steaming on the counter, two clean coffee mugs sitting beside it. I poured coffee into one of the mugs and carried it back to the living room for Stevie. She looked up at me with blank eyes when I set it on the table next to her. Guidry got up and handed me a coaster from a stack on the coffee table, and I lifted the mug and reposi-

tioned it on the coaster. We were like fussy hosts taking
care of a guest's needs.

I went back to the kitchen and put out fresh water and
dried food for Reggie, noting with approval that the food
was what I had recommended, the same natural diet that
Mame ate but for younger dogs. Reggie heard the plinking
sound of kibble hitting his dish and trotted into the kitchen
to wolf it down. I watched him closely, looking for any indication of swallowing problems or pain when he chewed.
He seemed okay, and when he finished he looked up at me
and wagged his docked tail.

I knelt to slip the necktie from his neck. It was peach-
colored silk. Undoubtedly expensive. I could imagine Conrad putting it on him that morning, thinking it looked cool,
or thinking it was funny, or thinking God knew what, since
Conrad didn't think like anybody else.

I said, "You had a bad morning, didn't you? I'm so sorry."

He lowered his rear end to the floor and sat with his
head tilted, his dark eyes looking at me with such intelligence it seemed he might begin to speak. Too bad he
couldn't. He was the only witness who could tell us who
had accosted Conrad and killed him.

I washed and dried Reggie's food bowl and put it where
it belonged. I folded the tie and put it on the shelf next to
the bag of kibble, all my tidiness to make me feel I was in
control of something, the same way Guidry's fussiness
with the coaster had been.

When I went back to the living room, Guidry was gently
questioning Stevie, going softly but firmly into personal
matters that seemed to rattle and annoy her. She said Reggie slept in the breezeway between house and carport, and
that Conrad always got up early and took him to Crescent
Beach to run. No, she hadn't heard his car leave that morning, but she never did because she was asleep. When Conrad came home after running with Reggie on the beach,
she was usually up and they had breakfast together unless
one of them had an early appointment. No, she hadn't been
worried that he wasn't home yet because it was still early.

As beautiful and rich as she was, Stevie had a childlike, vulnerable quality, and she looked up at me as if I might rescue her.

I pretended not to know what was happening. A man had been murdered and Guidry had to find the person who'd done it. No matter how irrelevant his questions might seem, he had to ask them.

I said, "Stevie, I fed Reggie and put out fresh water for him. Would you like me to come back tonight?"

She and Guidry both looked surprised, but I knew she would need me, even if she didn't.

Stevie took a deep breath. "Please."

I said, "I'll let myself out."

I went outside and got in my Bronco and headed for Midnight Pass Road, taking the route that avoided the crime scene. In spite of my horror at what had happened to Conrad, and my empathy for Stevie, I had a schedule to keep and I was already over an hour behind. Cats were waiting to be fed and groomed and played with, a few birds were waiting for fresh paper in their cages and fresh seed in their feeders, a lone guinea pig was waiting for food and fresh cedar shavings.

As I turned onto Midnight Pass Road, I saw two middle-aged female power walkers leaning over a cardboard box on the sidewalk on the Gulf side of the street. The box had a hand-lettered sign saying FREE KITTENS, and the women had the sappy *Awwww* grins that people get when they see the baby form of anything. I resisted an urge to stop and rant about the stupidity of putting out kittens to broil in the heat. It was still early. Maybe the kittens would be rescued before the sun was fully up. If nobody rescued them, maybe whoever had put them out would take them inside. In my rearview mirror, I saw the women turn and begin their brisk elbow-swinging walk again. They had probably ruined their heartbeat goal by pausing to look at the kittens, but maybe seeing something that makes you say *A-wwww* is better for the heart than exercise.

I was halfway to a Siamese cat's house when I remembered that Guidry had ridden to Stevie's house with me. I felt a wicked grin coming on at the thought of him walking back to his own car. In those Italian leather sandals. With his linen jacket getting sweaty across the back, and his forehead getting moist from the heat. . . .

I slapped the steering wheel. What was wrong with me? I had just witnessed a gruesome homicide scene. I had just learned that a sweet funny man who had shown me kindness had been killed. I had just watched his widow crumble in stunned grief. And yet here I was thinking about Guidry's body slicked with perspiration.

Then came the thought I'd been avoiding, postponing it with domestic puttering, feeding the dog, washing dishes, grousing about kittens left in the heat, imagining Guidry's sweat. I couldn't put it off any longer. Conrad's killer had been driving the car I'd seen that morning. He had got a good look at me. And because I'd waved and smiled and said "Hey!" he had every reason to think I'd got a good look at him.

For the rest of the morning, I went through the motions like a robot, doing what had to be done and trying to give every pet the attention it needed. But all the time my mind was on the driver of Conrad Ferrelli's car. He wouldn't be dumb enough to keep the car. He had probably already parked it in front of some not-yet-open office complex or strip center.

He must have been hiding in the bushes and stepped out as Conrad and Reggie passed by. But Doberman pinschers are highly protective dogs, and Reggie would have attacked anybody hurting Conrad. Unless the killer had lured Conrad into the trees and killed him out of Reggie's sight. But how could he have done that and then put Reggie into Conrad's car? And when had he stopped and let Reggie out? Or had Reggie escaped? In either case, the dog would have headed home, cutting through the wooded area to reach his street.

By eleven o'clock, the temperature was climbing toward 100 degrees, and I felt like somebody was sticking the sharp point of a knife into the center of my brain. The lovebird still on my list could wait awhile longer. I needed coffee and food, in that order.

I drove straight to the Village Diner, where I've eaten the same breakfast so many times nobody even asks me what I want. When they see me come in, Tanisha, the cook, starts making two eggs over easy with extra-crisp home fries and a biscuit. Judy, the waitress who is a close friend even though she and I never see each other anyplace except the diner, grabs a coffeepot and has a full mug ready for me by the time I sit down. This morning, I hustled to the ladies' room and splashed cold water on my face and scrubbed animal off my hands before I took the booth where Judy had put my coffee. I drank half of it in one glug, and she was instantly back to refill it.

If Judy were a dog, she'd be a beagle. She's neat and compact, with golden-brown hair, hazel eyes, and a scattering of gold freckles over her nose. She works efficiently and cheerfully, and she's ever ready to yap and take off after something that catches her fancy. Unfortunately, she has always gone after the wrong game, because they've all turned out to be sorry sons-of-bitches who didn't appreciate her intelligence or her smart mouth.

She said, "Lord, girl, you're red as a beet! You been standing in the sun?"

"Now and then."

"How come?"

I took a deep breath, dreading what she would say when I told her. "A dog I was walking this morning found a dead body, and I was there when they uncovered it."

Judy frowned and squinted at me, her eyes taking on a suspicious look.

"Terrific. You found another dead body."

"I didn't find it, a dog found it. I had to call nine-one-one and hang around until they uncovered it."

"I hope this time you'll stay out of it and let the cops handle it."

"Of course I'm staying out of it!"

"Uh-hunh."

Tanisha rang the bell to signal that my food was ready, and Judy went off to get it. On her way back, she picked up a *Herald-Tribune* somebody had left on a table and put it down with my food.

"Here, read the paper and get your mind off that dead body."

She splashed more coffee in my mug and left me to mutter sweet nothings to my biscuit. I didn't look at the paper until I'd eaten every last morsel and Judy had filled my mug two more times. Then I skimmed the front page, where some old men in Washington had sent a company of young troops off to die for some ill-defined reason, turned to the inside pages where some old men from other countries had sent their young people off to fight for equally ill-defined reasons, and finally got to the comics, which is about the only thing that makes any sense. If I ran the world—and God knows I could do a better job of it than the yahoos doing it now—any leader who sent troops off to fight would have to march at the head of the ranks. That would bring about world peace in about four weeks.

After the comics, I turned the page and started to fold the paper for the next person to read. A photograph stopped me. It was a picture of Conrad Ferrelli and a man I recognized as Ethan Crane, an attorney I'd had some dealings with regarding a cat's estate. An accompanying article said Ethan Crane headed the board of directors of a new foundation funded by the Ferrelli Charitable Trust. Part of a drive to restore Sarasota's long association with the circus, the foundation's purpose was to create a retirement home for people who had dedicated a major portion of their professional lives to the circus.

Crane was quoted as saying, "It will be patterned after the Lillian Booth Actors' Home, but we'll begin on a smaller scale." Those who could pay would be charged according to their income. Those who couldn't pay would receive the same high standard of housing and assistance. Conrad was quoted too. "Circus people spend their lives giving laughter and cheer to the world. Their last walka-bout should be in comfort and dignity."

I folded the paper around the article so it would tear more cleanly and was ripping it out when Judy came with my check.

"Why're you vandalizing our communal paper?"

"It's after eleven. It's only vandalism if it's before ten."

"Uh-hunh. Say, who was that dead body?"

I held up the scrap of paper I'd torn out. "Conrad Ferrelli."

"That rich guy?"

"That's the one."

"So what're you going to do, put the picture in your dog scrapbook?"

Somebody at the booth in front of me asked her for more coffee, and she turned to pour it while I sat with my lips bunched together and feeling like an idiot. I didn't have a single good reason for keeping that picture. I wadded it up into a little ball, dropped it in my plate, and covered it with my napkin. I wondered if I had become somebody whose life was so empty that I might start collecting photographs of my rich clients. It was a depressing thought.

Judy stepped back to me. "You reckon the wife killed him?"

"Why do you think that?"

"It's always the wife that kills rich guys. Or the butler."

"They don't have a butler, and Mrs. Ferrelli is a nice woman. But I'm sure the detective will question her."

"That hunky detective?"

I took out bills and put them on the check. "He's not hunky."

She scooped up the money and stuck it in her pocket. "Oh, yeah, he's hunky all right."

I slid out of the booth and grabbed my backpack. "I've got to go take care of a lovebird. See you later."

She was busy gathering up my dirty dishes and only grunted good-bye. She knew she'd see me later. I'm dependable like that.

4

When my grandfather was a young man, he traveled through Florida on business and stumbled on Siesta Key. He spent a week here, and before he left he'd bought a piece of land on the edge of the Gulf. My grandmother was flabbergasted that he'd put them in debt for a thousand dollars for land that wouldn't even grow tomatoes, but he persuaded her to bundle up my two-year-old mother and come see the key for herself. They arrived just as the sun was setting. My grandmother stood on the dazzling white beach and watched openmouthed as a molten gold sun quivered itself into the water while banners of iridescent rose and turquoise and lavender streamed in the sky.

"I'm never leaving here," she said, and she didn't.

My mother was probably looking the other way, because she left as soon as she got the chance. My brother and I are like our grandparents. We're never leaving either.

I live in an apartment above a four-slot carport next to the frame house where Michael and I lived with our grandparents. I moved here after the earth cracked in my world and left me standing beside a jagged fissure that threatened to suck me in. Michael and his partner, Paco, live in the house, and except for a remodeled kitchen, they've left it pretty much the way it was. With Michael and Paco to remind me that I am loved, and the continuous roll of the surf to remind me that life never stops, I have survived the last few years. Barely.

A wide covered porch runs the length of my apartment, with a hammock strung in one corner and a table for eating and watching the waves break on the beach. French doors open into a small living room with a sofa and chair. A one-person breakfast bar separates the living room from a galley kitchen. My bedroom is just big enough for a single bed and a dresser. The bathroom is cramped too, but there's an alcove in the hall for a washer and dryer, and I have a big walk-in closet. I put a desk in one side of it, and that's where I take care of my pet-sitting business. The whole place has Mexican tiled floors and oyster-white walls. I wouldn't call it spartan exactly, but it's definitely no-frills.

It was nearing noon when I drove home down the twisting tree-lined lane. All the cars were gone from the carport, and only a few foolhardy seagulls wheeled in the blazing sunlight. The undulating sea glinted diamonds, and down on the beach wavelets slapped the white sand and stained it beige. I unlocked the French doors and went inside just long enough to go to the bathroom and wash my face. Then I came back out and dropped my weary self into the hammock in the shady corner of the porch. I'd been up since 4 A.M., and I was bushed. I fell asleep in seconds, rousing once to the sound of Michael and Paco's laughter downstairs and then falling even deeper asleep knowing they were home. I always instinctively relax when I know they're home, not even aware until then that I've been tense. That's how dependent I am on them. I hate to admit it, but it's true.

Michael is thirty-four, two years older than me, and he looks like the golden genie that would pop out of a magic lantern in an Arabian desert. He's a firefighter, like our father and his father before him, and he is probably the best human being in the world. Paco is also thirty-four, and he looks like the camel driver who would find the magic lantern. Slim, dark, and elusive, Paco is with the Sarasota County Special Investigative Bureau, which means he does stings, drug busts, and other undercover stuff, frequently in disguises so good he could pass right by me and I wouldn't know him. Both Michael and Paco are so good-looking that women tend to consider hanging themselves when they learn they're a unit, but they've been together twelve years and counting, which makes Paco my other brother. They're my best friends in all the world. They protect me, they feed me, they keep me sane. Mostly.

I slept until almost two o'clock, and woke up feeling rested, hot, and thirsty. I went inside and got a bottle of water from the refrigerator and drank it as I went down the hall to my office-closet to check phone messages. There were several. You'd think my business would fall off in the summer when all the seasonals leave, but it actually gets busier. Snowbirds usually stay put when they get here, so they don't need anybody to take care of their pets. Year-rounders, on the other hand, go traveling in the summer and leave their pets at home. I returned the calls, turned down a couple of jobs on the mainland because I work strictly on the key, gave two people my rates, scheduled a job for the following weekend with a pair of Persians, and made arrangements to go meet a couple of Lhasa apsos and get their information.

I take my pet-sitting business as seriously as I did being a deputy. In a way, the jobs are a lot alike. Whether you're taking care of pets or enforcing the law, you've been entrusted with lives, and I treat that with a lot of respect. I belong to a professional association of pet-sitters that has a code of ethics as strong as the AMA's. I'm bonded, licensed, and insured. When I take on a pet-sitting job, my clients sign an agreement detailing what they expect of me and what they agree in return. I get their vet's name and number, any medical conditions the pet has, along with medications or vitamins or special treatments needed. I get a complete history of illnesses, injuries, and allergies. If the client has a trusted relative or friend, I get the name and number to call in an emergency. I find out the pet's favorite foods, favorite toys, favorite games, even their favorite TV shows and favorite music. I have the owners show me where they keep the pet's food, litter, leash, and grooming equipment. In some cases, I agree to pay for any emergency medical treatment or any unexpected home repairs that may arise while the owners are away, and they reimburse me when they return. In other cases, especially with clients who know me well, they simply give me signed blank checks to use as needed. While I'm on duty, I keep meticulous records of what I did and when I did it. In other words, pet-sitting is my profession, and I treat it in a professional manner.

By the time I finished the calls, it was time to leave for my afternoon visits. I took a quick shower and put on fresh shorts, a clean T and clean white Keds, and slathered sunscreen on every inch of exposed skin. Except for our father's black eyelashes, Michael and I inherited our mother's blond coloring, so I fry after just a few minutes of sun. I grabbed my backpack, detouring through the kitchen on the way out to search for a banana or an apple. Except for breakfast an eternity ago, I hadn't eaten all day, and hunger was sucking in my stomach. My kitchen was like Mother Hubbard's cupboard. No cheese, no apples, not even a limp stalk of celery. All I found was a mostly empty package of whole almonds. I grabbed it and told my stomach I would give it dinner later.

By the time I was at the foot of the stairs, the almonds were all gone. I tossed the empty bag in the trash can and got in my hot Bronco. I really needed to go grocery shopping. I really needed to get my life organized. I really needed to get a life. There was fresh egret and gull poop on the hood of the Bronco. I needed to wash my car too. Jesus, if I did all the things I needed to do, I wouldn't have time for any of the things I *had* to do.

During the summer, afternoon rain clouds start scudding in from the Gulf around four o'clock. Like freewheeling blue aardvarks, they rumble and flick lightning tongues at golfers and swimmers and tennis players, indiscriminately loosing showers here and there to cool the air and make the foliage smile. To avoid mildew or getting struck by lightning, I try to walk all my dogs before the rains start. Then I repeat everything I've done in the morning except for grooming. Mornings are for grooming and walking and playing and feeding. Afternoons are only for walking and playing and feeding. Either way, I spend the same amount of time, about thirty minutes, at each house.

Morning or afternoon, my first stop is always at the Sea Breeze, a big pink gulfside condo where Billy Elliot lives. Billy Elliot is a greyhound that Tom Hale rescued from the fate that befalls dogs who don't win enough races. Tom's a CPA who has been in a wheelchair since a wall of lumber fell on him at a home-improvement store. Tom and I trade services. He handles my taxes and anything having to do with money, and I go by twice a day and run with Billy Elliot.

When I got there, Tom yelled at me to come sign some papers. I went in the kitchen where he works at a center table. Tom has a thick mop of curly black hair, round black eyes behind round rimless glasses, and a plump middle. He looks like the Pillsbury Doughboy, except cuter.

He said, "Sign this form for the state, and this one for the federal government."

I signed on the lines where he pointed, and he leaned back in his wheelchair and glared at me.

"Dixie, don't ever sign anything without reading it."

"I wouldn't know what I was reading anyway, and I trust you."

"Never trust anybody with your money."

"It's not my money. It's a cat's money. You promised me you would take care of it, and that's all I need to know."

He sighed. "How is the cat, by the way?"

"We should have that cat's life. He lives with people who spoil him rotten. He eats, he sleeps, he plays a little, he eats, he sleeps."

Tom grinned. "He's a damn rich cat. I've made a report for you, all the investments the cat has made, all his profits and expenses. Take it home with you for bedtime reading. I mean it, Dixie. I know you trust me, and I appreciate that, but you need to know what's going on. Too many people are too trusting when it comes to money, and I'm beginning to think half of the suckers live in Florida. I guess it's because we've got so many old people."

I narrowed my eyes at him. "That's a little ageist, don't you think?"

"Probably, but I've spent all week trying to help a sweet trusting great-grandmother who's a victim of identity theft. Somebody cleaned out her savings account and ruined her credit. I suspect she signed things she didn't read or gave out information just because somebody asked for it."

I stood up and grabbed the folder. "I don't do that."

"Good. Read those reports."

I promised I would, but we both knew I wouldn't. Sometimes you just have to trust people.

It was close to seven when I neared Secret Cove. The box of free kittens had been removed. Either they'd all been taken by kind Samaritans, or they'd all fried in the heat. At Mame's house, she was waiting behind the glass by the front door with the leash in her mouth and a determined gleam in her eye. I thought that was a good sign. She was old, but she had purpose, and when you really get down to it, that's the only thing that makes life worth living for any of us.

I hugged her hello and ignored the disappointed look she gave me when I put the leash back in the basket by the door. No way was I going to walk down that lane again today. Sheriff's cars were still at the crime scene, and I knew that's where Mame would want to go. I did a quick walk-through to make sure she hadn't had any accidents or done anything naughty. In Judge Powell's study, the rug beside his desk had two small wet spots on it. I poured club soda on the spots and blotted them dry.

Mame came and watched.

I said, "So your bladder isn't what it used to be. Whose is?"

She yawned and flapped her long ears as if the subject didn't even merit conversation.

When I took her out to the lanai for a sedate game of

fetch-the-ball, she played, but I could tell she had hoped to go chew on the finger again. At around seven-thirty, I changed the TV channel—Mame liked variety—set the timed night-light, and kissed her good-bye.

At the Ferrellis' house, the driveway was filled with cars. I parked in the street and went to the front door and rang the bell. A flint-faced woman with black hair cut in an angled bob answered the door with a lit cigarette in her hand. She gave me a snooty glare.

"Can I help you?"

"I'm Dixie Hemingway. Mrs. Ferrelli asked me to come by tonight."

She looked as if she didn't believe me, and turned to yell into the living room. "Stevie, did you ask somebody named Hemingway to come by?"

Instead of answering, Stevie came down the hall. "For God's sake, Marian, let her in!"

The woman shrugged and stepped aside, giving my rumpled shorts and T scathing looks as I went by.

Stevie said, "I'm sorry, Dixie. Things are a little bit out of control."

I said, "If I'm in the way—"

"Oh, no. God, no. You're probably the only person who *isn't* in the way."

She followed me across the living room, which was filled with people chatting and smoking and drinking cock-tails. They stopped talking when they saw me, staring as if I were an alien who had just flown in.

As we left the room for the kitchen, I heard the woman who'd answered the door say, "Stevie insisted on her com-ing in. Don't ask me why. You know how Stevie is."

In the kitchen, Reggie was lying on the floor in front of the sink, sprawled on the tile as if he were cooling his belly. I knelt to feel his black nose and touch him all over again, searching for bumps or painful places. He was okay, just not frisky. Like Mame, he was dealing with the trauma of the morning in his own way.

I got his leash from its place in the pantry and took him

out the back way, through the laundry room and breezeway and carport. I didn't want Reggie to go near the place where Conrad had been killed, so we walked north, toward the place where the street loops. Lights were on in the houses we passed, but they were like the lights at Mame's house—on timers to fool would-be burglars into thinking the owners hadn't left town.

At the loop, we turned and retraced our way back to the Ferrelli house. Stevie must have been listening for us, because she came in the kitchen as soon as we got back. She leaned on the kitchen counter and watched me get out Reggie's bowl and shake food into it. She watched Reggie fall on his kibble and chew enthusiastically. She seemed dazed, as if she were in someone else's house watching someone else's dog.

I said, "I'll come in the morning and take him for a walk. Is there anything else I can do for you now?"

"Dixie, tell me what happened this morning. How did you find Conrad?"

"I was walking the Powells' dog, their little dachshund, and she got away from me. She ran into the bushes by the road, and when I went in after her she was digging in a mound of leaves and pine needles. I saw that it was a body, and checked for a pulse. Then I called nine-one-one."

I didn't think she needed to know that her neighbor's dog had pulled on Conrad's dead hand.

"Did you try CPR? Did you do anything to save him?"

Her voice had risen to a shrill pitch, and she put both hands across her mouth as if to keep herself from screaming.

"Stevie, he had been dead for a while."

"How could you be sure?"

"I used to be a deputy. I know how to tell if a person is dead."

"The detective wouldn't tell me how he was killed. He said there would have to be an autopsy. Don't they know how he was killed?"

"They probably have a good idea, but that's the procedure. Until there's a formal autopsy, they can't be absolutely sure what caused a death, so they wait."

"They can surely see a bullet hole, can't they?"

Her eyes were wide and unfocused, and I had the feeling she was about to spin out of control.

I said, "Stevie, do you have anything you can take? Something to get you through the next day or two?"

She laughed bitterly. "God, Dixie, everybody in my living room has brought their drug of choice for me. I don't even take aspirin. I don't want to be drugged."

I could hear conversation from the living room. It sounded more like a business meeting than a gathering of the bereaved.

"Are those people in there family?"

She crossed her arms over her chest and hugged herself.

"Conrad's brother and his wife; she's the one who answered the door. I'm not sure who those other people are. Somebody Conrad was doing business with, I think. His brother brought them."

"Do you want them here?"

"Jesus, no. I just don't know how to get rid of them."

"Would you like me to do it?"

She looked hopeful. "Could you?"

"Wait here."

I grabbed a tray from a custom-built slot and walked briskly to the living room, where I started gathering up overflowing ashtrays and half-finished drinks.

I said, "Mrs. Ferrelli needs to rest now. She asked me to tell you good night. She'll be in touch tomorrow."

They all stared up at me with sullen expressions of outrage and shock.

The woman who had opened the door said, "Who the hell are you to tell us to leave? You're not Stevie's family."

I straightened from leaning over a table to pick up a crumpled napkin and gave her the look, the look that anybody who has ever been trained in law enforcement knows, the one that says, *Don't mess with me, bitch; don't even think about it.*

She flushed, and a tall bald man with sensual lips got up. Half of his hairless scalp was mottled with sun spots, the other half was covered with a livid birthmark that split his face in half.

"I think this is where I came in," he said.

The bitterness in his voice seemed to come from old injustices, old pain, old anger. Everybody looked up at him with apprehensive faces, but his entire visage suddenly altered, going from brooding darkness to urbane smoothness. He crossed the room with a large hand held out to me, his thick lips drawn back in a patronizing smile.

"I'm Denton Ferrelli, Conrad's brother. You're the dog-sitter, aren't you?"

He wore an expensive navy blue suit with the requisite white shirt and tie. Except for his bald head and the dark birthmark, he was like any well-educated rich man. But his voice was too icky-soft, like a scab that floats off in the bathwater, and either drugs or dislike for me had made his pupils contract to pinpricks.

Since both my hands were occupied with the tray, I ignored his proffered handshake.

"I'm Dixie Hemingway."

"Good of you to take care of Stevie. The family appreciates it."

My skin prickled at the slimy innuendo that Stevie was the dog I was there to take care of. He winked lazily, one maroon eyelid sliding over a milky yellow-green eye, giving his face the look of a heavy-lidded cobra. As he held my gaze, the tip of a fleshy gray tongue crept between his heavy lips and rapidly flicked back and forth. It was a peculiarly lewd gesture that left me feeling dirtied, as if he'd jacked off against me.

His expression hardened. "We'll be going now. Because we choose to, dog-sitter, not because you've told us to."

Everybody immediately got busy finding their purses or adjusting their crotches, depending on their sex, and generally working their way toward the front door. I stood with the tray full of cocktail glasses and watched them leave. The last person out was Denton Ferrelli. He turned before he closed the front door and did the lip-licking thing again. Denton Ferrelli might be a multimillionaire, but he was a crass bastard.

I opened the sliding glass doors to air out the smoke in the room, and took the tray into the kitchen. Stevie was standing exactly where I'd left her, with Reggie lying on her feet, pushing his body close against her ankles.

I said, "They're gone. I told them you'd be in touch tomorrow."

She buried her face in her hands and sobbed for a quick moment, as if she had an allotted amount of time for crying and didn't want to waste it.

When she raised her head, her face was wet.

I said, "Have you eaten anything today?"

"I guess. I don't know."

I suddenly realized what was missing from this house of mourning. In ordinary Florida neighborhoods, death automatically means neighbors bearing platters of fried chicken and bowls of potato salad. They bring deviled eggs and green Jell-O salad and red Jell-O salad and cookies and meat loaf. They bring it in a steady stream until the bereaved are inundated with gastronomic sympathy. Most of Stevie's neighbors had left for the summer, and her relatives had brought drugs. The rich really *are* different from everybody else.

I pawed around in her refrigerator and found eggs and butter. She watched me beat a couple of eggs in a bowl, watched me scramble them in butter in a skillet, and obediently sat down at the bar when I put them on a plate. Neither of us talked. I gave her a fork and a napkin and poured her a glass of wine from a bottle in the refrigerator. While she ate, I ran water in the sink and squirted dishwashing liquid in it to make it bubble. I washed the skillet, bowl, and beater and turned around to look at her. She had polished off the scrambled eggs and was sipping her wine.

She said, "You had something like this happen to you, didn't you?"

I leaned against the counter and wiped my wet hands with a dish towel. "Three years ago, my husband and our little girl were on their way home, and they stopped to get some things for supper. My husband was a deputy, and he had picked Christy up at day care when he got off duty. She was three years old."

I stopped and swallowed a lump in my throat. I had never told this before, not to somebody I didn't know well. I wasn't sure I could tell it now, but I knew I needed to say it. Not just for Stevie, but for myself too.

"I'm sure Todd was holding her hand when they walked across the parking lot, he was always careful with her. She was probably skipping along and telling him all the things that had happened that day, and he was listening to her like everything she said was the most important thing he'd ever heard. He was like that. With everybody."

My hands were bone dry but I kept drying them on the towel anyway. "A man driving across the parking lot turned into a parking place. He was ninety years old and almost blind, but he had a current driver's license. He lifted his foot to hit the brake, but instead he slammed it down on the gas. He hit Todd and Christy and three other people. They told me Todd and Christy died instantly, but I'm not sure if that's true."

I looked up to see tears rolling down Stevie's face. She whispered, "Oh, my dear God."

I said, "That's why I won't try to make you feel better about what's happened. I won't tell you to cheer up because Conrad's with Jesus now. I won't tell you that one day you'll stop hurting, because you won't. But one day you'll pick up your life and go on, because you'll have to."

She and Reggie walked with me to the front door. Before I went out, I said, "Stevie, Reggie wasn't wearing a collar when I found him this morning. Is that unusual?"

She smiled and shook her head. "He's so well trained to heel that Conrad always lets him run free."

"And the necktie?"

She shrugged. "That was just Conrad. He really didn't

like dog collars; he thought they were demeaning. He put
bandannas and neckties on Reggie. Every now and then a
necklace. A different drummer, you know."

"I put the tie on the shelf with the dog food."

She gave me a quick hug. "I'll see you tomorrow."

As I got in the Bronco, she and Reggie stood in the doorway and gazed after me with identical expressions of
stunned sorrow.

5

Before I pulled out of the driveway, I punched the CD button and let Patsy Cline's voice fill the car. Spend a few minutes with Patsy, and the world gets back in balance, especially after dark. Before noon it takes Roy Orbison to set things straight. They sort of balance out the day, which isn't surprising. Anybody who's ever given it any thought knows that Patsy and Roy are riding through eternity on the same soul train, blowing each other away with their heart truths.

It was near eight-thirty when I got home. Michael's prized grill was glowing, and the plank table on the deck was set. Michael was standing on the beach with his feet spread wide and his hands jammed in his pockets. An enormous orange sun hovered wetly above the horizon, pulsating like a living heart so its edges moved with its own heat. I walked down and stood beside him, both of us silent as sun and sea touched like lovers. The sea pulled the sun inside herself and left the sky smiling cerise and violet and peach. Michael and I let out held breaths. No matter how many times you watch that lovemaking, you never stop being awed by it.

He slung an arm over my shoulder, and we walked up the beach to the deck.

He said, "Are you hungry?"

"Are you kidding? I'm positively hollow."

He grinned with the pure joy that a master chef gets on

hearing that people want to eat. Michael works 24/48 at the firehouse, meaning twenty-four hours on duty, and forty-eight hours off. But always, whether he's at the firehouse or at home, he cooks. Like firefighting, cooking is Michael's way of saving people. To him, there's nothing so awful that a good meal won't make better.

I said, "Where's Paco?"

"Asleep. He has to work tonight, and he didn't get to bed until late this afternoon."

Vice cops work irregular hours, and for the last several weeks Paco had been leaving every night a little before ten and coming home late in the morning. Since an undercover cop's life can depend on secrecy, Michael and I never mentioned it, not even between ourselves. But it didn't take a super sleuth to deduce that he was working at some night job.

As much as he might enjoy having dinner with us, Paco exercises a good cop's judicious selfishness. Cops have to know what they absolutely require in order to function at their best, and not let anything keep them from getting it. A cop who needs sleep may accidentally kill somebody. A cop who goes too long without food may let his temper flare. A cop who needs to be alone and sort out the horror of something he's just seen may do something stupid. A cop who puts time with his family over his own needs won't be a good cop. He may not even be a living cop. Anybody too sentimental to be selfish ought to take up a different line of work than law enforcement.

I said, "I'll just be a minute. I have to go shower."

I ran up the stairs to my apartment and was naked by the time I got to the bathroom. I jumped in the shower to wash away the afternoon's heat and pet spit, slicked my wet hair back into a ponytail, ran lipstick over my mouth, and hopped around the closet pulling on underpants. I stepped into canvas mules and fought on a short dress with spaghetti straps and a built-in bra—surely the best invention ever—and was still damp and pushing everything into place when I clattered down the stairs to join Michael on the wooden deck.

He pulled out my chair with an unself-conscious gallantry that always makes me feel misty-eyed, and headed inside for the food. Paco met him at the door, groggy-eyed and cheek-creased, but alert.

Michael said, "Oh good, you're awake!" and moved inside with a little extra zip in his step that made me grin.

Paco gave my ponytail a gentle yank and slid into his chair. He was wearing the same outfit he'd been wearing every night since he started working at his mystery job: pleated khaki Dockers and a tucked-in black waffle-knit shirt with a collar and front pocket. The shirt was bulky, and you could see the bulge of its tail under his pants. My mind ran down all the night jobs that would require those clothes and came up with something like a motel night clerk. Not a sleazy motel where the night clerks could wear anything they wanted to, and not a premium motel where they wore suits. Maybe something along Tamiami Trail where families stayed.

Whatever it was, he didn't seem to be looking forward to it. He and I sat like slugs while Michael brushed olive oil on grouper fillets and slices of plantain and chayote squash. He squeezed lime juice on the grouper and laid everything on the grill along with a rack of corn on the cob. While that cooked, we all ate yummy cold avocado soup with teensy shrimp in it, and I told them how Mame had found Conrad Ferrelli's body. Except I left out the part about the lipstick smear on Conrad's face. Even to family, you don't divulge important secrets like that.

Michael got up once to turn the stuff on the grill and get hot French bread and orange butter, but he didn't ask any questions. Which made me nervous. Ever since we were kids, Michael has always known when I'm not being absolutely honest with him. When he thinks I'm holding out, he gets very quiet, like he was now. Paco was noncommittal too. He spooned up soup and listened intently, but he was as silent as Michael, and a couple of times I caught them exchanging enigmatic looks, the way parents do when they're listening to a child getting herself deeper and deeper into trouble.

When the fish and corn and plantains and chayote were ready, Michael served our plates at the grill and brought them to the table. He topped the grouper with mango salsa and added wine to my glass and his. Paco was sticking to iced tea.

I took a bite and moaned like a satisfied cat. We all ate silently for a few minutes, our taste buds too overjoyed for speech, and then Michael came up for air.

"Who's investigating the Ferrelli case?"

"Guidry. Guidry's investigating." I sounded like an echo chamber.

"Ah, Lieutenant Guidry. So did you tell Guidry everything you knew?"

"Sure."

"Uh-hunh. Did you tell him whatever it is you haven't told us?"

Paco looked across at him and quickly stopped himself from grinning.

I chewed and swallowed. I took a sip of wine. I shook my head.

"Not exactly."

He gave me a stern look.

"What's going on, Dixie? Why am I getting the feeling you're involved in something you shouldn't be?"

Like it might be my last meal, I took a second to enjoy the flavors in my mouth.

"It probably has something to do with the car I saw this morning."

Michael chewed somberly, looking steadily at me while I took another bite.

I said, "I saw a car driving fast this morning. It was Conrad Ferrelli's car, and his dog was in the backseat, so I thought Conrad was driving."

I took another bite and avoided Michael's stare.

"And?"

"And I waved hello."

Michael drank half his glass of wine, sort of compulsively, I thought.

He put the glass down and leaned toward me a tiny bit, the way he used to do when we were kids and he was getting ready to tell me he was going to kick my ass clear to Cuba if I didn't tell him the truth.

He said, "It's all over the news that Conrad Ferrelli was murdered this morning. They found his car in one of the beach-access parking lots. Are you telling me you saw the murderer leaving and you waved at him?"

"That's about the size of it."

He took a deep breath and chomped hard on a chayote slice.

"Did you tell Guidry you saw the car?"

"Sure."

"But you didn't tell him about waving to the driver, did you?"

I chewed and swallowed. I took a sip of wine. I shook my head.

"Not exactly."

"Dixie—"

"Don't lecture me, Michael. I wouldn't have waved if I'd known a murderer was driving the car."

Paco said, "She's right, Michael. You would have done the same thing."

I shot Paco a grateful smile, but his face was somber.

He said, "You have plenty of bullets for your thirty-eight?"

Michael slammed down his wineglass. "Come on, Paco, it's bad enough as it is."

"That's why she needs to get her gun out and keep it with her. She's in and out of empty houses all the time, and whoever killed Ferrelli may know it. She'll be a sitting duck if she's not prepared."

He was right, and I knew it. I had already thought about the thirty-eight.

I said, "It'll just be for a little while, Michael. They'll catch the guy."

"You call your detective first thing in the morning and tell him about this."

"He's not my detective, but I'll call him."

"Just promise me you'll stay out of this one, Dixie. I can't go through that again."

"Don't worry, I'll stay out of it."

He went silent again, and I couldn't blame him. I didn't believe me either. How could I stay out of it when I was already in it?

Paco stood up and stacked his dishes to carry inside. Before he picked them up, he put his arms overhead and stretched, tilting his head back and pulling his spine tall, twisting a bit to get vertebrae lined up right. When a healthy man as gorgeous as Paco stretches out in front of you, you might as well enjoy the sight even though he's as unattainable as one of the rings of Saturn. As he flexed his shoulders backward, his knit shirt snagged on something on his muscled chest, and a chunk of comprehension fell into my brain with a scary thunk. Paco wore a transmitter under that shirt.

I blurted, "I can see your nipples when you do that."

Startled, he jerked his arms down and gave me a puzzled look. Michael had the same incredulous look on his face, like *What the hell?*

I met Paco's gaze and saw his eyes shift as he realized my meaning.

He said, "Thanks, babe, I'll remember not to do that."

Michael stood up and started gathering dishes to take inside, shaking his head and muttering that all God's children had nipples, for God's sake, and what was the big deal? Paco and I didn't enlighten him. Michael worries enough as it is. He didn't need to know that Paco was going to some job every night to record information that would lead to somebody's arrest.

Up in my apartment, I locked the French doors and lowered the metal hurricane shutters that double as security bars. In the bedroom, I pulled my narrow bed away from the wall and opened the drawer built into its far side. The Sarasota County Sheriff's Department issues 9-millimeter Sig-Sauers to its officers. When an officer leaves the force, either through retirement or death, the department-issued gun has to be returned. But every law-enforcement officer has personal pieces for which he or she is lawfully qualified, and I had kept both Todd's and mine in a specially built case in the drawer under my bed.

The guns were all there, fitted into their felt-lined niches: Todd's 9-millimeter Glock and his Colt .357, along with my own Smith and Wesson .32 and a .38 that was my favorite. The .38 fit my hand the way it fit its niche in the case. I took it to the bar in the kitchen and cleaned and oiled it, finding as always a deep sense of satisfaction from the workmanship that went into making it, all the pieces sliding into one another so smoothly. When it was gleaming and ready to operate, I slid a magazine in the butt and got out two extra magazines to carry in my pocket. I put away the oil and polishing cloth and took the gun with me to the bathroom. I took a long shower and fell into bed with the .38 on the bedside table.

As usual, I dreamed of Todd and Christy. I dreamed of them every night, as if we had a standing dreamtime appointment to get together. This time I dreamed I went to heaven to get them and bring them home. I went to a big barred door and yelled for somebody to let me in, and God came down a long walk to look through the bars at me. He looked like Heidi's grandfather, with long white hair and a flowing white robe, but he had a wreath of leaves around his head like Caesar.

I said, "You can't keep them here. It's against the law."

He shook his head in a kind of pitying way, the way people do when they hear somebody say something incredibly stupid. "I'm above the law," he said. "You should know that."

I said, "Nobody's above the law, not even you."

"Ah," he said, "you still believe that, do you? That's your lesson to learn in this lifetime: the law isn't for everybody."

He turned his back on me and I clung weeping to the bars and shouted after him. "What about Todd and Christy?"

His voice floated back like a sigh. "They've already learned their lessons. Now they can reap their rewards."

I woke up with clenched fists, so angry I could have smashed someone. It's the same anger that has simmered under the surface for the past three years, the anger that makes the sheriff's department leery of letting me go back to work. I wish I could get rid of it, but it seems to have moved in to stay, like an undesirable relative that I can't shake.

The digital readout on the bedside clock showed 2:26. The red numbers lit the gun and gave it an eerie glow. I thought of Stevie Ferrelli sleeping for the first time without her husband, probably having her own dreams of loss. I thought of the killer who might believe I'd recognized him. I thought of all the places where I would be vulnerable: the early morning streets when I walked dogs, the houses where cats or gerbils or birds waited alone.

I turned over and tried to go back to sleep. I had to get up in an hour and a half, and I would need to be alert.

The killer could be anywhere, he could attack me at any time. Stevie had mentioned a bullet hole in Conrad, but she had also said that Guidry hadn't told her how he died. Had she been assuming a gunshot, or did she know? If Guidry hadn't told her, how did she know?

I sat up and looked at the clock. It was three o'clock, and I was wide awake. I got up and turned on lights, stuffed dirty clothes and Keds in the washer, shook in detergent, and turned it on. The homely sound of water gushing on my laundry at 3 A.M. was oddly comforting. Naked, I padded to the kitchen and started a pot of coffee. While it gurgled and spat and hissed, I turned on Roy Orbison, cranked the sound up, and to the tune of "Pretty Woman" pushed the vacuum cleaner around with a lot of balletic bending and swooping. There's nothing so empowering as running around vacuuming while Roy Orbison is singing and you're buck naked.

As small as my place is, the floors were dust-free by the time the coffee machine made its final sputter. I stored the vacuum away and went in the kitchen and looked out the window while I drank a cup of coffee. Roy Orbison had finished "Pretty Woman" and moved on to "Mean Woman Blues." I was alert. I was composed. I was a normal woman drinking a normal cup of coffee on a normal morning. I was so normal, if I'd had a donut I would have eaten it.

I rinsed my coffee cup, turned the pot off, and ambled down the hall. I tossed wet laundry in the dryer. I went to the bathroom and brushed my teeth and flossed them. I took a shower and slathered moisturizer and sunscreen all over myself. I pulled my hair into a ponytail and put on rosy lip gloss, being careful not to meet my own eyes in the mirror. In my office-closet, I stepped into lacy bikinis and new khaki cargo shorts. I put on a black satin racerback bra. I pulled on a stretchy black sleeveless top. I put on clean white Keds and laced them up. I dressed as carefully as if I were getting ready for an important date.

I might end up on a metal autopsy table that morning.

Or I might shoot somebody and *he* would end up on the table.

Either way, I wanted to look nice.

6

Before I raised the metal shutters, I dropped the spare magazines in my shorts pocket and got my backpack on. I held my car keys in one hand and my .38 in the other, and I stood to the side while the shutters folded into themselves and disappeared inside a cornice above the French doors. Nobody was on the porch, and I didn't see anybody when I went to the railing and looked over.

That predawn hour is my favorite time of day, a sensual time that always makes me pause to breathe in life. The sky was oyster-hued, the air silky smooth and tasting of salt and new beginnings. Mourning doves were waking in the trees lining the drive, calling to one another and making yearning answer. On the shore, wavelets kissed the beach and sighed like a passionate woman. In the distance, I could see dark humps of dolphins at play.

Holding my gun close to my thigh with my trigger finger pointed down the barrel, I walked down the stairs and scanned the darkness under the carport. A great blue heron lifted from the hood of the Bronco and sailed away making an irritated gargling sound. I got in the car and put the gun on the floor beside me, then sat with the motor running for a minute. This was nuts. I couldn't live like this. I couldn't go creeping around looking behind every door and examining every shadow. If the killer was out there waiting for me, he would find me. I wasn't going to be any safer for trying to see him before he got to me.

With that settled, I headed for the Sea Breeze to run with Billy Elliot. I parked in a visitor's spot by the front door, and put the gun in my pocket before I got out of the car. I wasn't going to go around scared, but I wasn't going to be unarmed either. The lobby was deserted that early in the morning, and the muted whine of the stainless-steel and mirrored elevator taking me to the second floor was the only sound. Tom was still asleep when I got to his condo, but I could hear Billy Elliot's nervous toenails on the tiled foyer. I unlocked the door and knelt to hug him and whisper good morning. Then I clipped on his leash and we took the elevator downstairs. Like thieves leaving a heist, we skittered silently across the shiny tile of the lobby to the glassed front door.

Billy Elliot needs a hard morning run the way some people need caffeine before they can think, and the Sea Breeze parking lot is a perfect substitute for his old racetrack. Cars park in the middle and around the perimeter of the asphalt, leaving a wide oval where we can run. I always try not to hamper his style with my inferior two-legged sprint, but no matter how hard I run, he still strains against the leash. In his dreams, he probably streaks around a track shouting hosannas because he doesn't have to drag along a poky blond woman.

As we came out of the condo and trotted into the parking lot, I noticed a dark wannabe monster truck—a small pickup raised on ridiculously huge tires—idling with its lights off at the edge of the lot. I gave it a second glance because it was the kind of show-off vehicle that flaunts Confederate flags and semiliterate bumper stickers, not the sort of vehicle that people living at the Sea Breeze drive. Then Billy Elliot pulled me in the other direction, and I turned away from the truck and followed him, not hitting my full stride yet because it takes a minute or two for my muscles to get the message that it's not a bad dream, they really do have to run like hell that early in the morning.

Billy Elliot strained at the taut leash until we got to the end of the line of cars parked in the middle of the lot. As we turned into the open area, I let the leash play out to its full extent and began running in earnest. Behind me, the pickup pulled out of its spot, drove to the exit into the street, and sped away, its indistinct form looking like a prehistoric monster in the darkness. It was still without lights, which meant the driver was either extremely unaware or had been in the parking lot for some illicit purpose. Neither is unusual in Florida.

It was around 6 A.M. when I worked my way to Secret Cove and Mame's house. Everything about her was listless, including the way her tail drooped. I knelt beside her and inspected her ears and felt her nose. She wasn't feverish, and she didn't have any sign of infection in her eyes or ears. No limping and no sore spots. But she wasn't feeling well, and most of the food I'd given her the day before was still in her bowl.

I considered calling her vet and asking if holding a dead man's finger in her mouth yesterday could have given Mame indigestion, but I didn't want that piece of gossip to fly all over the key. Besides, I knew what the real problem was. Mame was almost at the stage when she would want to crawl off to hide and face her death alone. It's the way animals handle the end of life. Perhaps humans should do the same.

I led her out the side door of the lanai and let her squat in a circle of Asiatic jasmine in the backyard. We played fetch-the-ball for a few minutes, but she walked stiffly after it, and I got the feeling she was indulging me. I lifted her to the table on the lanai and brushed her auburn coat until it gleamed. Long-haired dachshunds don't really need to be brushed every day unless they're shedding, but I do it anyway because they like it. Besides, I like it for myself. There's nothing like grooming a pet to get you calm and centered. Mame raised her nose and closed her eyes, with a dreamy look that caught at my heart. Her world was closing in, moments of satisfaction coming in smaller and smaller bits.

By the time I left her, she had perked up enough to trot behind me to the door. She even wagged her tail when I kissed her nose good-bye. I think she did it to make me feel better.

Lights were on at Stevie's house, and she opened the door before I rang. Her long dark hair was hanging free, and she was dressed a lot like me, shorts and a sleeveless top. She looked pale and tired but a lot more focused than she'd been when I left her last night.

She said, "I've already walked Reggie and fed him, but would you mind coming in for coffee?"

It was more request than invitation, so I followed her to the kitchen, where she gestured toward a table in a windowed alcove.

"There are some bran muffins if you'd like one. We have a cook twice a week, and she bakes up goodies when she's here and freezes them."

Bran muffins didn't sound like goodies to me, but I sat down and took one from a basket and broke off a chunk. Stevie slid two mugs of coffee on the table and took a chair opposite me.

She said, "I lay awake all night thinking about what Conrad would want me to do. He would want me to be strong. He would want me to take charge. So that's what I'm going to do. Because if I don't, Denton will."

The muffin tasted healthy but blah. I took a sip of coffee to wash it down.

I said, "Denton gave me the creeps last night. Is there something wrong with him?"

"Nothing except innate meanness. He and Marian are both despicable people."

"Stevie, I'm sure Lieutenant Guidry asked you, but is there anybody you know who had a grudge against Conrad?"

Her lips firmed in unconscious resistance. I waited, knowing that silence is often the best way to encourage somebody to tell what they're reluctant to say.

She said, "About a year ago, a man showed up here claiming to be Conrad's cousin. He said his father and Angelo Ferrelli were brothers, that they grew up in the same village in Italy. He claimed his father had originated Madam Flutter-By, and that Angelo had stolen it. He wanted money."

I blinked at her, wondering if the muffin had made me stupid. "Stevie, I understood about three words you just said: cousin, brothers, and money. The rest was Greek. Or maybe Italian."

"Sorry, I guess I always assume everybody knows who Angelo Ferrelli was. He was Conrad's father—Denton's too, of course, although not spiritually, like Conrad. Angelo Ferrelli was a famous clown with the Ringling Circus. He was known as Madam Flutter-By."

I must have still looked blank. She said, "I have a picture of him."

She got up and left the room. While she was gone, I wadded the rest of my muffin in a paper napkin. Stevie came back and set a framed photograph facing me on the table.

I did a double take, and Conrad's androgenous way of dressing suddenly made sense. Madam Flutter-By wore crisp white trousers and a matching cutaway coat, but the coat nipped in at the waist and its long skirt fanned out like a woman's peplum. It also had exaggerated leg-o'-mutton sleeves with black ruching at the wrists. He wore a close-fitting hat with a crown curiously rounded to give the suggestion of a prim librarian's bun. His face was stark white, with only five marks on it: two curving high on the cheekbones like long black tears, two arched above his eyes like blackbirds in flight, and one between the painted brows in a black teardrop. The only color was a wide bright-red mouth.

I thought of the red grin slashed on Conrad's face and felt ice running up my spine.

"Tell me again about that man's claim."

"His name was Brossi. He said his father was Angelo's brother and that Angelo had stolen Madam Flutter-By from his brother when they were boys in Italy. He wanted money."

I still didn't get it, so she explained it slowly, the way you'd explain long division to a three-year-old.

"The name Madam Flutter-By is registered, like a patent or a trademark. The makeup, that white face with the distinctive black marks and red lips, can't be used by any other clown. If his likeness is used in any way, his estate gets paid, the same way Disney gets paid if somebody runs a Mickey Mouse cartoon on TV or puts a Mickey Mouse face on a kid's lunch box or watch face. There were Madam Flutter-By films, Madam Flutter-By charms, and oil paintings and coffee mugs and pillows and thousands of other things with his face or form on them. They're collector's items today."

"So if that guy Brossi was telling the truth—"

"If he was telling the truth, his father should have got some of the money Angelo made."

"But Angelo was the one who actually made the idea work. His brother must not have had Angelo's talent, or he would have become famous himself."

"That's what Conrad said, among other things. Mostly, he said his father had created Madam Flutter-By, that nobody else had ever done the act, and that Brossi was a fraud. But I'm not sure if he could be positive about that. It was so long ago, and in some little place in Italy. Who knows who first came up with the act?"

"Do you know where Brossi went?"

"He didn't go anywhere. He owns a telemarketing firm here in Sarasota."

I said, "Did you know Madam Flutter-By?"

"No, but I knew Angelo Ferrelli. He had already retired from the circus when I met him, but he was a lovely man. Highly intelligent, cultured, witty. Conrad is a lot like him. Was. Conrad adored him. Denton was ashamed of him. Of course, Denton was ashamed of Conrad too."

I tried to think of a way to say it tactfully and couldn't, so I just said it. "Was Denton embarrassed by the way Conrad dressed?"

She grinned. "He hated it. Marian too."

"Is that why Conrad did it?"

"No, Conrad just liked wearing that crazy stuff. Growing up in a circus family, I guess it seemed normal to him. Sometimes I thought he could have been a little more sensitive to Denton's feelings about it, but it was a point of pride with him. You know, to be who he was, no matter what other people thought about it. He was that way when I met him."

"Where was that?"

She looked startled for a moment, as if she'd opened up something she hadn't intended. "We were both in drama at Yale."

Since my education consisted of two years of community college and six months at the police academy, that sentence alone exposed a social chasm between us. It also meant that Stevie could be a very good actress, pretending grief for a husband she'd killed herself. But I didn't think so.

I said, "When Brossi came—"

"Conrad practically threw him out of the house, and the man told Conrad he would be sorry. What he actually said was *One day you will see me again and be sorry.*"

"You didn't tell Lieutenant Guidry about this?"

"I didn't think about it until just now. Brossi never contacted Conrad again, or at least not so far as I know."

"If Brossi raised the issue now that Conrad's gone, what would happen?"

"Now he would be dealing with Denton. I don't know what Denton would do."

"Brossi's the only person you know of who had reason to hate Conrad?"

"He's the only one."

The truth lay on the table between us, as tasteless as the bran muffins. Denton Ferrelli had hated Conrad too. Maybe he had settled old scores with his brother.

"Stevie, I saw Conrad's car yesterday morning, with Reggie in the backseat. It went past when I was leaving the Powell house and turned onto Midnight Pass Road. I thought Conrad was driving, but he couldn't have been because just a few minutes later I found his body."

"But Reggie wouldn't have got in the car with a stranger."

"Exactly."

She stared at me with unfocused eyes. "You think Denton killed Conrad, don't you?"

"I think he may have had something to do with it."

I didn't need to remind her that Denton and Marian formed a duo. One of them could have killed Conrad while the other drove his car away with Reggie inside. I could see on her face that she had already figured that out for herself, but she didn't want to believe it was possible.

Her eyes suddenly blazed with tears. "I feel like I'm in a bad dream that won't stop."

"Stevie, is there anything I can do?"

"There's one thing. Wait a minute."

She hurried out again, and came back carrying a long swallowtail coat on a padded hanger. The coat was made of squares of satin and velvet in brilliant stained-glass colors, with wide red satin lapels and fist-sized plastic chrysanthemums for buttons.

"Conrad was going to wear this at a meeting to explain the details of the new retirement home to the circus community. He was looking forward to it so much . . ." She fought back tears and turned to me with steely control. "It should be returned to the people who made it. Somebody else should have a chance to enjoy it."

It was an oddly irrelevant thing to be concerned about right then, but I understood. When the mind has been shattered, it scrambles to find familiar things to do, little details to obsess over, bills to pay, appointments that must be canceled.

I took the coat from her. For so much material, it was surprisingly light.

I said, "Did the Metzgers make this?"

"You know them?"

"They have a couple of cats I take care of sometimes."

"You'll explain to them? Why Conrad can't wear it? And tell them Conrad loved the coat."

"I'll tell them, Stevie."

If Stevie Ferrelli didn't know her husband's murder was front-page news, she was still in shock.

7

Before I pulled out of Stevie's driveway, I put in a call to Guidry at his office, noting as I did that my phone showed three little batteries on its face, a gentle reminder to charge it. I got his mailbox and left a message that I had information about Conrad's murder. He called back while I was brushing a black Persian named Inky. When the phone buzzed, Inky gave me an annoyed frown and jumped off the grooming table. Even before I looked at the caller ID, I knew it had to be either Guidry or Michael or Paco, because nobody else has my cell number.

I said, "Hello, Guidry."

"You said you had information?"

"Two things. Denton Ferrelli was ashamed of his brother and hated his involvement with circus people. Also, they have a cousin, or a man who claimed to be a cousin, who came to see Conrad about a year ago demanding money. Conrad threw him out, and the guy told him he would be sorry. He runs a telemarketing firm here. Name is Brossi."

"Who told you that?"

"Stevie Ferrelli. While we were drinking coffee. There's something else too. Not exactly information, just something I forgot to tell you yesterday. About seeing Conrad's car before Mame found the body."

"Mame?"

"The dog. Not Conrad's dog, another dog."

"So what did you forget?" Guidry sounded like he might be talking through his teeth, so I hurried.

"I waved hello to him. To the driver of the car. I thought it was Conrad because I saw Reggie in the backseat. Reggie is Conrad's dog—was—so I waved. And I think I said *Hey!*"

The line was silent a moment.

"You're telling me the killer probably thinks you got a good look at him."

"Yeah."

"Okay. Anything else?"

I took a deep breath. "That's all."

"You sure?"

"Yeah."

"Okay. I'll talk to you later. In the meantime, be careful."

He clicked off and left me holding a dead phone.

I said "Damn!" but under my breath, because I don't like to cuss in front of my animals. I dropped the phone in my pocket next to the .38 and coaxed Inky back for the rest of his grooming. But our rhythm was off, and it wasn't very satisfying to either of us.

Josephine and Will Metzger's street is only about a mile from the verdant beauty of Secret Cove, but the people who planned it must have decided to uphold the virtues of ugly. There's not a tree in sight, and its sun-bleached frame houses squat gracelessly behind salty bald yards. It was about ten-thirty when I parked in the Metzgers' shell driveway and walked to the front door, holding Conrad's coat high above my shoulder so the tails wouldn't drag.

In their younger days, Josephine and Will had been aerialists with the Ringling Circus, but after they'd both broken and rebroken most every bone they had, the glamour of flying through the air without a net had lost its allure. Now they had a business making clown costumes. Will had a workshop over the garage where he made custom-designed clown shoes, while Josephine and a string of short-term helpers sewed baggy suspender pants and swallowtail coats made of outlandish polka dots and plaids.

Josephine's newest helper, an impossibly young mother named Priscilla, answered the door when I rang. I had never heard Priscilla speak, and I didn't know whether she was mute or just painfully shy. She didn't speak this morning either, but gave me a sweet smile with black-lipsticked lips. Priscilla had bright pink hair cut in a feathery halo and wore at least a half dozen rings around the rim of each ear. A diamond stud flashed at the edge of one nostril, and more diamonds, or reasonable facsimiles thereof, decorated her long emerald fingernails. A couple of gold rings flashed at her navel. Low-rider white Levi's sat on her narrow hips, and her cropped top hugged breasts the size of tangerines. Her shoes had soles a good four inches thick, with heels slightly higher, so that she tilted forward at a precarious angle. If it hadn't been for the fading yellow bruise high on her right cheekbone, she would have looked like any other teenager trying out a new identity.

She led me down the hall to a large square room that always made me feel like a visitor in an off-brand church. Sunlight streamed through ceiling-high windows, and bolts of fabric stacked on deep shelves absorbed the sound of two sewing machines that faced each other like dueling altars. A cloth tailor's dummy stood in the corner wearing a red-and-yellow-plaid cutaway with zoot-suit lapels and formal tails. A playpen sat next to Priscilla's sewing center, with a big-eyed baby girl clutching its mesh sides and doing bouncy knee bends.

Josephine was at an ironing board steaming open a seam. She looked up long enough to grin at me and then went back to steaming. Like her neighborhood, Josephine had given up on pretty a long time ago. Her long gray hair straggled over her shoulders, and not a smidgen of powder or blush colored her face. She didn't even bother to wear her bridge anymore, just flaunted all the gaps between her teeth.

She said, "'Cilla, do you see somebody in this room that looks like Dixie Hemingway? You remember her, the one we haven't seen in so long I can't remember. Could it be that she has come to see us?"

I hung Conrad's coat on a metal clothes rack and helped myself to a stick of chewing gum from a selection in a hat box on a table.

I said, "It's been several weeks, hasn't it?"

"You been busy with your cats and dogs, I guess."

"I really am, Jo. About all I do is get up and walk dogs and clean kitty litter, and then it's time to go back and do it all over again."

"Well, we love you anyway, even if we never hardly see you."

I chomped down on the gum and tasted its sweet juices flowing over my tongue. I hadn't chewed gum since high school, and I wondered why I'd ever stopped. The baby gave me a toothless grin, and I went over and fluffed the blond floss on the top of her head.

I said, "Have you heard about Conrad Ferrelli?"

"About a million times. His brother sending his coat back?"

The baby squealed and bounced her bottom up and down, looking up at me with wide trusting eyes.

I said, "His wife sent the coat back. But she said to be sure and tell you how much Conrad loved it."

"Then why's she sending it back?"

Resisting the urge to pick the baby up, I said, "So somebody else can wear it."

"I was hoping she'd bury him in it."

I couldn't tell if she meant she was glad Conrad was dead, or if she meant she'd like him to spend eternity wearing the coat she'd made for him. The baby lost her balance and plunked down hard on the playpen's padded floor. She began to cry, and Priscilla jumped up and came to calm her. Feeling slightly guilty for overstimulating the baby, I moved out of the way and stood beside the cloth dummy. My chewing gum seemed to be getting stringy and sticking to my back teeth. All the sweet juiciness in it was gone too.

I said, "Why did you think his brother would send the coat back?"

Josephine cast an evaluative eye toward Priscilla and the baby, then picked up the garment she was steaming and shook it out.

"Denton Ferrelli hates the circus and everybody connected to it. He didn't want Conrad to give all that money to build a home for circus people. If he has his way, it won't happen now."

The baby stopped crying and Priscilla went back to her sewing machine. Josephine looked up with an approving glint in her eye. Josephine was not one to pay somebody for time spent placating a crying baby.

I said, "I thought the circus retirement home was a done deal."

"Done except for being done. Denton Ferrelli did everything he could to put a stop to the clown school Conrad built, but that wasn't anything compared to the retirement home. Now that Conrad's gone, we think the home probably won't happen."

By *we*, I assumed she meant the circus community.

The baby had found a pacifier and curled up with it in her mouth. Priscilla looked relieved and bent over her work. She looked young enough to be doing junior high homework, but anybody that careful with a baby gets high marks from me.

I said, "I didn't even know there was a clown school."

"You think people just get born clowns? People train, they train damn hard. You see some clowns onstage doing a skit that takes maybe five minutes, you better know they've probably spent fifteen hours planning every move. It's choreographed, just like a dance."

I wallowed the gum around in my mouth and wished I hadn't started chewing it. I felt like a cow chewing her cud. Whatever a cud is.

"Do you know anybody except his brother who had a problem with Conrad?"

"You think it was a circus person that killed him?"

From her sewing center, Priscilla stopped stitching and raised her head and looked at me. The baby's eyes were at half mast, and she was making little humming sounds to herself. I tucked the gum into the back corner of my gums and started working my way toward the door.

"I didn't say that."

"Well, it wasn't, I can tell you that. Every clown in this town loved Conrad Ferrelli, and so did all the other circus people. He was one of us, you know."

I'd never looked at Conrad that way, but now that I thought about it, I supposed the way he dressed was a way of being a clown. The baby's eyes closed all the way, and I was a little disappointed that I didn't get to wave bye-bye to her. It's enough to make Superman puke, what a pushover I am for babies.

In the Bronco, I wadded a tissue around the used gum and tossed it in the trash bag before I headed for the diner. I waved to Judy when I came in the door, then made a quick detour into the ladies' room. Tanisha had left the kitchen and was with another woman at the sinks, both of them wide as Volkswagens. When I was little, I always hoped I'd wake up one morning with satiny chocolate skin like theirs. It was a major disappointment when my grandmother broke the news that I would always be plain vanilla.

Tanisha and my brother are the best cooks in Florida. When it comes to pastries, Tanisha's got Michael beat hands down because he doesn't bake at all. Tanisha would probably have a slightly smaller butt if she didn't, but then she wouldn't be Tanisha.

She gave me a dimpled smile when I came in and pulled a brown paper towel from the dispenser. She said, "This here's my sister Diva."

"Hi, Diva, I'm Dixie."

Diva turned off her faucet and shook water from her fingertips. She and I grinned at each other, but we didn't shake hands. Women don't shake hands in the restroom. I'll bet men don't either. I can't imagine them turning from a urinal to shake somebody's hand. Ick.

Diva had on a khaki skirt made of enough material to cover a truckload of oranges. She also wore a waffle-knit black shirt with a collar and front pocket. Her shirt wasn't tucked in but hung loose over her enormous hips. I knew that shirt. It was a twin to the one Paco wore every night when he left on his current undercover job.

Tanisha handed her sister a paper towel and said, "Me and Diva was just talking about how she ought to kick her husband's sorry ass out."

Diva giggled. "It's the truth. He don't do nothing but get my butt wet, and I can do that myself in the tub."

I didn't even want to think about how he got her butt wet. I was more interested in what she was wearing.

I said, "Where do you work, Diva?"

She wadded her damp paper towel and tossed it in the bin on the wall. "Well, that's the thing. That no-call thing has really cut down on work, you know? I used to could pull in maybe twelve–thirteen dollars an hour, what with them giving a dollar for every sale on top of the seven dollars an hour. I mean, that's good money, you know, and they paid the dollar bonuses in cash. But now they got that no-call list, and we can't hardly call nobody, so I'm back to seven dollars an hour, period. I can't live on that. I got bills to pay."

Tanisha walked to the door and pulled it open. "Your old man don't work! He don't help pay them bills. What's that got to do with it?"

Diva headed for the door, heaving a sigh that made her bosom expand alarmingly. "Yeah, I know, but what if I get laid off? Where else am I gonna make even seven dollars an hour?"

At the door, she looked back and smiled at me. "Nice to meet you."

"Thanks, you too."

The door shut behind them, and I headed for a stall. Now I knew Paco was working as a telemarketer. Half of me wished I didn't know that much about his undercover work, and the other half wished I knew a lot more. He was going every night to a job where people made unwelcome telephone solicitations to people's homes. He was wearing a wire. What the heck was he hoping to pick up? It didn't make any sense.

I scarfed down my usual eggs and home fries and biscuit. I drank my usual three cups of coffee. I thought my usual thoughts. Except now my usual thoughts were crowded with some unusual ones that had to do with Paco's undercover job and the person who'd been driving Conrad Ferelli's car. Josephine had said Conrad Ferrelli's brother hadn't wanted him to give money to support a retirement home for circus professionals. Maybe he had killed Conrad to stop him from putting millions into that foundation. Maybe Denton Ferrelli wanted the money for himself.

Exhaustion finally made me pay my tab and drive home. I'd had less than four hours sleep last night, and I needed a nap bad.

Michael and Paco were both gone when I got home. Michael had started his twenty-four-hour shift that morning at eight, and Paco was off making drug busts or something.

As soon as I unlocked the French doors, all the little hairs on my body stood up in alarm. Something was different—a subliminal foreign scent or a rearrangement of the air. I pulled my .38 out of my pocket and held it stiff-armed, ready to blow an intruder away, and moved slowly forward. Nobody in the living room, nobody hiding behind the bar in the kitchen, nobody in the bedroom. I flattened myself against the wall in the hall and then sprang into the doorway of the office-closet. Nobody there. My clothes weren't tumbled, my desk wasn't messy. Down the hall to the bathroom, where I repeated the move into the doorway. Nobody in the shower, nobody behind the door. I retraced my steps, still certain somebody had been in my apartment.

In the office-closet, I lifted the loose tile that covers a floor safe and peered inside. The only articles I kept in the safe were a diamond ring that had been my grandmother's, and a living trust giving my half of the beachfront property to Michael. They were both there. In the bedroom, I pulled my bed out and opened the drawer on the wall side where I keep the guns. They were all there.

So I was being paranoid. So I was imagining things. Going without sleep will do that.

I dropped my gun back in my pocket, went out to the porch, and fell into the hammock. The world spun and I spun with it, down into a dreamless velvety black sleep.

I woke up groggy and dry-mouthed and went into the kitchen for a bottle of cold water. I drank half of it while I looked hopefully in the refrigerator for a gift from the fruit fairy, like a surprise peach or a fresh bag of oranges. All I found was a dried-up lime and a hard mystery fruit that might have begun life as a succulent apricot but got overlooked and went wrong. I apologized to both the lime and the mystery fruit and tossed them in the kitchen wastebasket. I really needed to go grocery shopping.

I drank more water while I went down the hall to the office-closet, where my answering machine's little red light was flashing. I hit PLAY and listened to a woman explain in excruciating detail that she'd called to ask about my fees because she and her husband were going to Cleveland to visit their son, but they weren't sure when they could go because the son was buying a new house and was busy packing, so they would have to wait until—"

The machine cut her off and I gave it a nasty smile of approval.

A new voice clicked on, and I stopped smiling. It was a man's voice, deep and menacing. He spoke only two words.

"You're next."

I set the water bottle on the desk and replayed the message. It still said the same thing. I told myself it was a joke, somebody trying to scare me. I played it again. It was somebody trying to scare me, but it didn't sound like a joke.

I drank the rest of the water and carried the empty bottle to the kitchen. I stood a minute looking out the kitchen window at the treetops, and then I went down the hall to the bathroom and took a shower. I took extra time with my hair and lipstick. I even put on a slim skirt and heels. I was going to question Ethan Crane, and I wanted to look like the kind of woman who should get answers.

Ethan Crane's office was jammed into Siesta Key's business section, otherwise known as the Village, in a stucco building gently crumbling around the edges. I had been there only once before, when he had given me the depressing news that a woman had left a considerable living trust to her cat, with me as trustee. In spite of his crummy office, I remembered him as both surprisingly handsome and surprisingly efficient.

The gilt paint on the glass door was still flaking, still proclaiming ETHAN CRANE ESQ., ATTORNEY AT LAW, even though it had originally been painted for the grandfather of the man who now held the office. Built to withstand flood tides and hurricanes, the building had a flight of worn wooden stairs leading directly from the front door. I took them with what I hoped was a measured tread, letting my heels click on each step to alert the people upstairs that somebody was approaching.

I needn't have bothered. Nobody was in the secretary's office. Her desk was bare except for a gooseneck iMac, and her chair had been neatly pushed in as if she were gone for the day. Across the hall, Ethan Crane was asleep, tilted back with his feet on his desk and his mouth open. A herd of elephants wouldn't have waked him.

I rapped on his open office door, and his eyelids flickered. I rapped again, and he snapped to attention, jerking his feet off the desk and bringing his chair upright so fast he almost launched himself into space.

He yelled, "Jesus!"

Smiling sweetly, I walked forward with my hand out. "Mr. Crane, I don't know if you remember me. I'm Dixie Hemingway."

He recovered well, got to his feet in one graceful thrust, and leaned over the desk to shake my hand. Even sleep-rumpled, he was still as handsome as I remembered him. Tall, jet black hair brushing the collar of a crisp white shirt, prominent cheekbones, eyes the color of bittersweet chocolate, eyelashes so thick and black they made his eyes look rimmed with kohl, a strong nose and broad jaw, even white teeth. He gave me a politician's smile as he adjusted his tie and got himself in professional mode.

8

I said, "I take care of Conrad Ferrelli's dog. I suppose you know what happened to Conrad."

His face sobered. "Oh, God, yes, I'm sick about it. Conrad was a great guy. It's just inconceivable that somebody would—"

"I know about the retirement home Conrad was funding. Will those plans still go forward now that he's dead?"

He frowned. "Why would you ask that?"

"People in the circus community think it won't. They say Conrad's brother will put a stop to it. Is that true?"

His voice got a frosty edge. "Ms. Hemingway, I don't see what any of this has to do with pet-sitting."

Although I hadn't been invited, I sat down in one of the rump-sprung leather chairs facing his desk.

"I saw Conrad's killer driving away in Conrad's car. I thought it was Conrad, so I waved to him. I was only a few feet away, and he could see me clearly. This afternoon somebody left a message on my answering machine that said *You're next*. I think the killer thinks I can identify him."

"And you can't?"

"All I actually saw was Conrad's dog in the backseat."

He gave me a look meaning *So?*

"Look, everybody says Denton Ferrelli hated the circus and everything connected to it. I think he might have killed Conrad to stop it."

He sat down behind his desk. "That's a serious accusation."

"I'm not asking you to decide if he's the killer, I'm just asking you to tell me how the Ferrelli money will be used for the circus home."

He fiddled with a gold-capped pen for a moment and then laid it down decisively.

"Angelo Ferrelli set up several philanthropic trusts. Each is an independent nonprofit with its own charitable focus and its own fiduciary and organizational responsibilities. One makes grants to environmental causes, one to health initiatives, one to education and the arts, one to community enrichment. They're all under the discretionary trusteeship of a trust company that Angelo headed until his death. Then Conrad took over."

Being too mathematically challenged to balance a checkbook, most of what he said sailed over my head, but I thought I got the main idea.

I said, "Which one of the trusts is funding the circus retirement home?"

"Actually, none of them. Conrad formed a separate foundation for that. His idea was to have each of the trusts contribute to it as a part of its own philanthropic purpose. The trust devoted to health issues will provide money for the medical care of the residents, the education trust will provide funds for continuing-education classes, and so forth."

"So what's Denton's role in the plan?"

"Denton is chairman of the board of the trust involved in community development. They fund building projects that improve a community's economy and living standards. Their official statement of purpose is to provide jobs and create good communities."

He seemed to stop himself from saying what its unofficial purpose was. He got up and went over to a wall of bookshelves where an undercounter refrigerator had been fitted.

"Would you like a cold drink? Water?"

"No, thanks."

He leaned over and opened the door, giving me an opportunity to see the outline of a butt as toned and shapely as his shoulders. He popped the tab on a Diet Sprite and took a drink as he walked back to his desk.

"Denton's board of directors is composed of bankers and financiers and politicians. Late last year, they brokered a deal between Sarasota County and some investment realtors for a large tract of gulfside land. The plan was to put a parking lot and dock for a casino boat there. They were going to build an administration building, a ticket office, the whole works. Denton even talked the state engineering department into agreeing to dredge a mooring for the boat. They claimed it would give jobs to a lot of people, plus bring in money people won on the casino boat. To sweeten the whole plan, some state senators and lobbyists in Denton's pocket were pushing hard to get Indian land casinos declared illegal."

He took another pull on the Sprite and gave me a half smile. "Like my people might actually get a break now and then."

"You're Indian?"

"One-quarter Seminole, just enough to make me pay attention to the fact that the state never recognized Indian nations or made treaties with them."

I looked at his high cheekbones and square jawline. He was one fine-looking Seminole.

He said, "Anyway, when Conrad got wind of Denton's casino-ship deal, he went ballistic. It was not only in direct opposition to about a hundred environmental standards of the trusteeship, it smelled in a lot of other ways as well. Casino boats are unlicensed, unregulated, unscrutinized. They operate in international waters where anything goes, including money laundering. Conrad used his power as head of the trusteeship company and put a stop to it. Instead, he directed that the acquired land be used as a site for the circus retirement home. In other words, he pissed on Denton's parade."

"And he made you head of the foundation to build the home."

"Correct."

"Who will run the discretionary trust now that Conrad's gone?"

"His successor will be elected by the board. Most likely it will be his wife. She's closely involved and highly capable."

"So the circus home will go forward regardless of Conrad's death."

"I don't see how Denton can stop it. He's furious about it, but the way his father set the whole operation up is set in stone. My guess is he's busy as a cat covering shit before the trusteeship looks too closely at the way he finagled the land deal."

I took a deep breath. "I never dreamed that circus clowns made so much money."

"Angelo was a shrewd investor. He had an uncanny knack for selecting winning companies and becoming a major stockholder. He screened out ones he thought were bad for the environment or for people's health, and it paid off. All told, the trusts he set up pay out something like fifty million a year in grants."

"Do you know a man named Brossi?"

"Leo Brossi? Yeah."

"He went to Conrad with a story about how his father was Angelo's brother. He said his father had originated the Flutter-By act back in Italy when he and Angelo were boys, and he wanted some of the money Angelo had left."

He shook his head. "Leo Brossi's a con artist always one step ahead of a posse, but I can't see him murdering anybody."

"You have any idea who did?"

"Believe me, Dixie, if I did, I'd be the first one to tell the police. I liked Conrad a lot."

I noticed he had switched to calling me Dixie instead of Ms. Hemingway. I stood up and held out my hand.

"Thanks for talking to me, Ethan."

"Did it help?"

"Not really, but it was informative."

"Maybe we could get together sometime and talk about something besides murder or trust funds."

I turned so fast that I almost tripped over my own feet.

This time he couldn't help but hear my heels clacking on the stairs. I sounded like a drummer beating a fast retreat. Ethan Crane probably thought I found him repulsive. He probably thought I was a rude, ungracious nut. If I hadn't been so embarrassed, I would have gone back upstairs and explained that I was . . . what? An untouchable? A cloistered pseudo-nun made virginal again by widowhood? Or maybe truly an ungracious nut.

As I reached toward the downstairs door to push it open, somebody else pulled it from the other side. Guidry stood in the gaping doorway, one linen-sleeved arm holding the door to the side, his eyes taking in my short skirt and high heels, his face registering about a dozen different emotions.

"Dixie." Flat-voiced, not letting any surprise slip through.

"Guidry."

Still holding the door open, he stepped aside so I could go through on my stilty heels.

He said, "I think we'd better talk."

He nodded toward an open-air café across the street. It wasn't exactly an order he'd given me, but it wasn't a social invitation either. Wordlessly, we waited for a break in traffic, and then walked over the steaming pavement to a sweaty, dispirited place where plastic tables crouched under a thatched roof and a scattering of wilted patrons were sucking cold drinks through clear straws. Ceiling fans whirred overhead to circulate hot air and scare away flies, and a few black seagulls strutted about picking up microscopic crumbs from the paved floor.

A mustached man's head appeared in the window where orders were dispensed, and Guidry called, "We'd like a couple of iced teas."

The head disappeared, and Guidry tapped his slim fingers on the plastic tabletop.

"You mind telling me why you were at Ethan Crane's office?"

"I wanted to ask him some things."

"I guess you have a key to his house, and he discusses all his cases with you while you take care of his furry friend."

"Wrong on both counts, Guidry. I've never even met Ethan Crane's furry friend."

The mustached man came out carrying two tall paper cups with plastic lids. He plunked them on the table and pulled out two straws and a stack of paper napkins from his apron pocket.

"Anything else?"

Guidry put down a five-dollar bill and shook his head. "That's all, thanks."

I peeled the paper off my straw and jammed it in the X-spot on the plastic lid.

I said, "Conrad Ferrelli named Ethan Crane to head the foundation that's going to build a home for retired circus professionals. The circus people I've talked to are afraid it won't happen now that Conrad's dead. They think Denton Ferrelli will put a stop to it. I wanted to know if he could, so I went to see Ethan Crane to find out."

Guidry's gray eyes looked at me over the top of his paper cup. He didn't look natural with a plastic straw stuck in his lips. I doubted that he'd sucked through a lot of straws. Probably had a butler do that for him.

He said, "Aside from the fact that a murder investigation is going on and you're not part of it, I suppose there's nothing wrong with that."

"I don't have to get your permission to talk to people, Guidry."

"So what did you find out? Can Denton Ferrelli stop the retirement home from being built?"

I wondered if that was the question Guidry had planned to ask Ethan Crane himself. Maybe he had a point. Maybe I had interfered in a murder investigation. The possibility that I had made my voice a bit defensive.

"It doesn't sound like he can. Angelo Ferrelli set up

some trust funds that are all under the control of a company that serves as trustee. Conrad was CEO of the trustee company. Denton heads a trust that improves communities, and he brokered a deal that bought a big piece of real estate. The plan was to dock a casino boat there, but Conrad squashed the deal. He took the property for a circus retirement home, and when it's built all the various trusts will funnel some of their funds into it. Denton is pissed about it, but there's not much he can do to stop it."

"So he doesn't stand to gain from Conrad's death?"

"Evidently not."

"You sound disappointed."

I shrugged. "Everybody who knows Denton Ferrelli says he's a thoroughly hateful person. He resented Conrad. He hated the way he dressed. He hated his involvement with the circus."

"Hatred's a pretty strong motivation for murder."

"But he's hated him all his life. Why kill him now, if he's not going to benefit from it?"

Guidry's straw made a rude sound at the bottom of his paper cup, and he put the cup down with an annoyed frown.

"You didn't have any reason except curiosity for wanting to find out about Denton Ferrelli?"

The memory of the voice on my answering machine coiled in my head. I didn't want to sound like a damsel in distress, but playing tight-lipped martyr could get me knocked off by some psychotic killer.

"A man left a message on my answering machine this afternoon. Just two words: *You're next.*"

"You thought it was Denton Ferrelli?"

"I don't know who it was."

He tilted his head toward the slim leather handbag I'd laid on the edge of the table.

"You carrying?"

"Yes."

"Got a CCW?"

I rolled my eyes and gave him an *are-you-kidding?* look. Up north, especially in landlocked states, it's illegal to carry a concealed handgun. In swamp-ridden Florida, it's damn near mandatory. The state's official stance is, Hey, man, we're sticking out down here like the country's hind tit, surrounded by oceans and alligators and Commie Cubans, threatened by hurricanes and tidal waves and foreign tourists, and we by God need to be able to shoot something. Over eight million of us consequently have a permit to carry a concealed weapon, otherwise known as a CCW. That's why so many retired geezers in Florida wear belly packs over their shorts and knit shirts— they're carrying semiautomatics. It's a miracle more of them don't blow their nuts off.

Guidry sat for a moment twisting his tall paper cup on the table, his face pensive as if trying to make a decision. He snapped the cup down on the table and looked up at me, his eyes clear and direct.

"Dixie, this is strictly confidential, but I want you to be careful. This murder has psychopath written all over it."

I swallowed a sudden lump in my throat and stared at him. There's a fine distinction between a sociopath and a psychopath, and homicide detectives are careful about it. Sociopaths kill for the hell of it, just because they can. Murder is a cool clinical activity for them. Because they don't see their victims as fellow human beings, there's nothing personal about it. But when a psychopath kills, it's personal. Psychopaths kill with a passionate hatred born of irrational fury over real or imagined injustices. Like a venomous brain cancer that consumes reason, psychopathic hatred gains intensity once it's unleashed, spilling over to include anybody in the way. When they've killed once, psychopaths not only feel personally vindicated, they want to kill again.

I said, "Why do you think that? The lipsticked grin?"

"When we removed Conrad Ferrelli's body, we found a dead kitten under him. The coroner thinks it suffocated under Conrad. But before Conrad fell on it, the kitten's legs had been broken."

My stomach quivered. "I don't understand."

"My guess is that somebody broke the kitten's legs and left it in the bushes for Conrad to hear crying. Conrad is on the street, hears the kitten, goes in to see what it is, and the killer gets him while he's bending over looking at it. If I'm right, it wasn't the murder that gave the killer satisfaction, it was seeing Conrad's pain when he found that poor damned kitten."

I felt swimmy-headed. The thought of somebody doing something so cruel to a kitten was almost more than I could take.

Guidry said, "Most killers get rid of somebody they think needs to die, and that's the end of it. Psychopaths aren't like that. They get their jollies from the *way* their victims die, not because they're dead. Whoever killed Conrad Ferrelli wanted that hurt kitten to be the last thing he saw."

"Conrad always drove Reggie to the beach to run, so I don't know why the killer thought he would be on the street. Or why he *was* on the street, for that matter. And how could the killer be sure Conrad would hear the kitten and come looking for it?"

"I don't know. That's the hole in my theory. I'm just saying it was somebody with a particularly twisted mind who killed Conrad Ferrelli, so I want you to be especially careful."

My pulse was pounding at the base of my throat. I thought of the feeling I'd had when I came home that afternoon that somebody had been in my apartment. But it had probably been my imagination. It had probably been fear making me paranoid. No sense mentioning it to Guidry and having him think I was a hysterical nut case.

He said, "Don't go out and try to solve this. It's too dangerous. Lay low, keep your protection handy, and let me handle it."

The conversation was over. We both stood up, and he gave my legs in the tall sandals another sweeping glance.

"I'll see you, Dixie."

He left me under the thatched roof and walked across the street to disappear inside Ethan Crane's building. I hoped Ethan wouldn't be asleep when Guidry got there.

9

Stray rain clouds had moved in while Guidry and I talked, and on the drive home a few sprinkles plopped on the Bronco's windshield. In the carport, I took the .38 out of my purse and scanned the locks on the storage closets. I wanted to make sure nobody had opened one and was in there ready to pop out at me. I was tense as a lizard under a cat's paw. Passing clouds gave the air a curious transparency, so that everything seemed covered by yellow Saran Wrap.

Upstairs, I kicked off my high heels, climbed into shorts and a T, and scooted out to make my afternoon runs. Nobody tried to kill me, and nobody jumped out at me in any of the houses.

At Mame's I found her in Judge Powell's study, lying on the Persian rug rung in front of a red leather sofa. She had an expression in her eyes that made me uneasy. Animals always know when their lives are drawing to an end, and when they do their eyes get a curiously sad and patient look.

I sat cross-legged on the floor and pulled her into my lap. She sighed and curled herself between my legs with her head on my knee. I thought she probably missed the Powells, so I made my voice as low as possible, hoping I sounded like the Judge.

I sang, "You can put the blame on Mame, boys, put the blame on Mame."

In a few minutes she crawled out of my lap and trotted to the kitchen to eat some kibble. We made a hasty run into the yard to let her go to the bathroom, but streaks of lightning were flaring across the sky, and we didn't stay out long. When I left her, she went to the door with me and wagged her tail good-bye.

The same cars that had been in Stevie's driveway the night before were there again. There was a tasteful wreath on the door now, with a dull gray velvet ribbon topped by a clown's mask. The mask was stark white, with red lips and a few black marks on the face, remarkably like the photograph of Madam Flutter-By.

When Stevie opened the door, she looked as weary as I felt. Dark circles were under both eyes, and new grooves bracketed her lips. Her face lit when she saw it was me, and she practically reached out and jerked me inside. She put a hand on my back as if she were afraid I would bolt if she didn't, and steered me down the hall to the living room. The same crowd was drinking and smoking. Denton Ferrelli was standing at the side of the room, his stained face poker stiff.

Stevie said, "I'm afraid I'm going to have to ask you all to leave me alone with Dixie now. We have some things to take care of."

Everybody looked at me standing there in my rumpled cargo shorts, and I could almost hear their sneers.

Marian, Denton's bitch wife, said, "What kind of things?"

I could feel Stevie's hand trembling on my back, and I felt like drop-kicking the highball glass out of Marian's hand.

Stevie took a deep breath and said, "Marian, that's really none of your business."

Marian opened her mouth in a snarl, but Denton walked to her side and took her glass. He set it down on the table with a sharp click.

"Some people care more about animals than people, Marian. Let's leave Stevie and her dog-sitter to their interests."

He made it sound as if Stevie and I had something dirty going on with Reggie. We stood silently while everybody gathered themselves and straggled out. Denton was the last one out, and he turned to give me a long hostile look before he slammed the door shut.

Stevie seemed to sag, as if she'd used up all her starch in speaking up to them. She waved vaguely toward the kitchen. "I need to talk to you."

In the kitchen, Reggie's used food bowl sat on the floor, and the water in his other bowl was cloudy. Stevie sat at the bar and watched while I washed the bowls and put fresh water out for Reggie. I filled the teakettle and put it on the stove to boil and got down two teacups.

I said, "What about food?"

"What about it?"

"Have you had any?"

She considered. "I had some crackers."

"When?"

She shrugged. "I don't remember."

"Stevie, you have to eat." I sounded like Michael.

I rummaged in her freezer and found a box of vegetable lasagna that I popped in the microwave. While it heated I tore romaine leaves into a salad bowl and drizzled them with olive oil. Michael would have clutched his chest at my cavalier way with it, but it was food. The microwave dinged and I slid the lasagna onto a plate and poured a glass of wine. While Stevie ate, I dropped teabags in a yellow teapot on the counter and covered them with boiling water.

Stevie seemed to have forgotten that she'd wanted to talk to me. She polished off the lasagna and salad and drank the wine in one gulp.

I poured her a cup of tea and one for myself and sat down beside her.

She said, "I do all right for a while, and then I feel like I can't go on."

"But you will. You'll do whatever you have to do."

"Was it like this for you?"

I nodded. I didn't want to tell her that I couldn't remember what the first few days had been like after Todd and Christy were killed. I'd been deaf and blind and numb. I had no memory of anything.

I said, "It will get easier."

"When?"

"When it does."

She nodded as if that made sense.

I said, "Josephine Metzger was hoping Conrad would be buried in the coat she made for him."

Stevie looked surprised. "She said that?"

"She said he was one of them."

"That's true, he was. But Denton and Marian would have a cow if he wore that coat in his coffin."

"Would you like me to bring it back?"

She blinked back tears and grinned. "Would you? Conrad will love it."

"I'll stop there in the morning before I come here."

I washed up her dinner dishes and left her drinking tea and staring into space. Whatever she'd wanted to talk to me about had drifted away into some mournful void.

A heavy rain shower hit me on the way home and stayed with me all the way. All the blue had left the sky and left it yellow gray, not unlike my mood. Michael was still at the firehouse on his twenty-four-hour shift, and Paco would be leaving soon for his secret job at the telemarketing firm where he wore a transmitter taped under his shirt. I hadn't had anything to eat since breakfast, and my stomach was pleading for something cheesy, salty, or fried. Preferably all three. In my refrigerator were some jars of mustard and mayonnaise and jelly. In my cupboard were a couple of cans of chopped tomatoes bought in a rash moment when I thought I might make spaghetti sauce sometime, along with a box of Cheerios gone soft with age and humidity.

At my driveway, I kept going, dejectedly making my way through depressing rain to the only possible solution. In the drive-through lane at Taco Bell, I ordered four taco supremes with extra everything. I pulled into a parking space in the front lot and ate them while I watched normal people pass by in twos and threes. I told myself there were lots of other people sitting alone in their cars eating in the rain.

Millions, maybe, or at least a few thousand. One or two, probably.

I knew it wasn't true. Of the six billion or so people in the world, including the ones in China, I was probably the only one doing that. It was damned depressing.

It was still raining when I got home, and Paco's car was gone. It was dark under the carport, and I held my gun in one hand while I got out of the Bronco and ran upstairs. My fingers actually trembled while I unlocked the French doors, and I kept my gun out after I got inside. I stood inside the door and tested the air, sniffing to see if I got the same feeling of a recent intruder that I'd got earlier. Everything felt normal, but I still did a search before I went back and lowered the hurricane shutters. If anybody was in there, I didn't want to trap myself inside with them.

I stood a long time in a warm shower and then crawled into bed with the .38 on the table beside me. I felt like I'd been up for a month or two, and tomorrow probably wouldn't be much better. It wasn't supposed to be this way. I was a pet-sitter, damn it, not a deputy sheriff. I shouldn't have to be concerned about anything except my pets. Like Mame, who was alone across town while rain beat on her roof. Mame, who was old and deserved better than having her people go off and leave her for such a long time. With Mame on my mind, I fell asleep. Feeling sorry for Mame didn't make me any happier, but it was at least better than feeling sorry for myself.

10

The rain had stopped when my alarm went off at 4 A.M. I groped my way to the bathroom and went through my morning routine: splash face, brush teeth, pull hair into ponytail, step into shorts, wiggle into a T, tie clean white Keds, sling on backpack, pick up gun. I raised the storm shutters and opened the French doors, scanning the dark porch corners for any lurking killers as I stepped out. The air was sauna-damp, but an early sea breeze kept it from being stifling. The sky was gun-metal gray but clear, and along the rim of the horizon was a pale pink foretelling of dawn. Wavelets broke on the beach with the fizzing sighs of Alka-Seltzer plopping in water, and a few early birds were comparing tales of what they'd done during last night's rain.

Downstairs in the carport, my Bronco was still the only one at home. Michael's shift at the firehouse would end at 8 A.M., and nobody knew what Paco's schedule was. A couple of egrets on the Bronco's hood sullenly watched me get in the car and then took off with a great fluttering of white wings. On the twisting lane to Midnight Pass Road, heavy oaks were still dripping rain, and flocks of parakeets alarmed by my passing caused more drops to scatter when they flew away.

At Tom Hale's condo, I parked in a visitor's spot by the front door and went inside the deserted lobby to the elevator. Billy Elliot was waiting inside the door, snuffing and dancing on the tiled foyer. I hugged him hello and snapped his leash on, whispering so as not to wake Tom, and then we both trotted down the hall to the elevator and across the lobby to the front door.

As soon as he sniffed fresh air, Billy Elliot stretched his long body out ready to race. I heard a motor running and looked to the side of the lot. It was the same pickup on those ridiculous big tires, idling with its lights off. Maybe this lot was being used for a drug drop or something. I pulled Billy Elliot back until we got to the big open space and then let the leash play out.

Billy Elliot took off like a comet, and so did the truck. The difference was that Billy Elliot was running away from me and the truck was driving straight toward me. I swung my head to look toward the sound at the same moment he turned on his high beams, catching me in their glare like an unsporting hunter.

In seconds, the truck was on me, so close I could feel its heat, so close I could feel the vibration of its speed under my feet. Paralyzing fear shot through me like sick electricity, sheer animal panic like I'd never felt before. I had been afraid before, afraid of drunks with guns, afraid of wrecking when tires slewed on wet-slick streets, afraid of snakebite when I saw a rattler at my feet, but this went beyond fear. The death that is always there, always hovering, always ready to slam its foot on anything that moves, had arrived. Somebody in that truck intended me to die, and there wasn't anything I could do about it.

There was nowhere to go: no ditch to fall into, no wall to climb over, no time to run away. Throwing the leash handle clear, I spun around to face my death. The giant tires were so close I could see the deep grooves in their tread. The noise was deafening, like a banshee's scream.

Suddenly a man's calm voice high on the right side of my head said, *Hit the dirt, Dixie.*

I dove for the pavement, sliding flat out between the tires, face turned to the side, mashing ribs and cheekbone and pelvis into the asphalt. Hot exhaust fumes swept over me, so close they ruffled my hair, and then a rush of cool air signaled that the truck had passed over. I couldn't see it, but I heard it roar out of the parking lot onto Midnight Pass Road.

Mewling and gasping for breath, I clawed my way to my feet and crab-ran toward the side of the lot. I stumbled between two parked cars and dropped to the curb when my rubbery knees refused to hold me up anymore. Choking on bile and grit, I put a shaky hand to feel the wetness on my burning face, but it was tears, not blood. My nose was running and my blubbering mouth leaked saliva down my chin. Adrenaline poured through my veins in an overwhelming rush, shaking me so hard my teeth rattled. I hugged my thighs and rested my chin on my scraped knees, gulping air like an asthmatic, trying to quit crying, trying to quiet my galloping heart.

A scraping sound brought me to my feet, my hand digging into my pocket for the .38. I'd forgotten about it until now, but even if I'd remembered, it wouldn't have been any good to me against that towering truck. But I could sure as hell use it now. I used both hands to hold it stiffly at arm's length. The peculiar sound was coming closer. If that truck driver had left a friend to finish me off, I was going to blow the blue-eyed shit out of him. Whoever was coming, he was dragging something on the asphalt, something metallic, like a chain. Jesus, somebody planned to beat me with a chain. I whipped a look to both sides behind me to see if there was more than one of them. I didn't see anybody, but the sound was coming closer.

Through the spaces between the cars, Billy Elliot streaked into view, oblivious to everything except the joy of running, still happily following his simulated race track, dragging his leash behind him and not missing me at all. I stuck the gun in the waistband of my shorts and walked unsteadily to the the end of the cars that hid me.

"Billy! Come!"

There must have been something in my quavering voice that told him this was no time to fool around, because he slowed to a trot, made a wide turn, and came at a gentle jog to sit in front of me. His tongue lolled out of his grinning mouth, and he seemed more satisfied than I'd ever seen him.

I got his leash and shakily reeled it to the handle.

"Don't think running without me is going to be a regular thing."

Billy Elliot fell in behind me, stoically enduring the shortened leash and my plodding steps back into the building. As we went into the lobby, we met a couple of plump middle-aged men and their plump middle-aged dogs. The men gave me startled looks and pulled their dogs close to their sides. Billy Elliot snorted, as if to say that I might not be much to look at, but he was still sleek and svelte.

In the elevator, I reacted like the men downstairs when I saw my reflection in the mirrored wall. My shorts and T were smeared with black road grease, and my right cheek looked like somebody had rubbed it with sandpaper. My nose was still streaming and my knees were oozing blood. I wiped my nose with a quivering hand, and realized my palms were scraped. So were my arms.

By the time we were off the elevator and at Billy Elliot's floor, my heart had calmed, at least enough that it didn't seem to be trying to leap out of my chest with every beat. But I was still shaky, and my legs still felt like silly putty. I had to use both hands to get the key in Tom's door. When I got it open, the lights were on and I smelled coffee.

From the kitchen, Tom yelled, "Morning, Dixie! Want some coffee?"

After a couple of inaudible bleats, I managed to yell back that I didn't have time, but thanks, and we both yelled good-byes and I left. If he had known what shape I was in, Tom would have ministered to me like a mother hen. But I didn't want him to see me begrimed and shaking and snot-smeared. I felt ashamed, as if almost being run down by a maniac in a big truck was like getting caught with my hands in my own pants. Like a hurt animal, I wanted to crawl off in the bushes and lick my wounds.

I slunk down the hall to the elevator. On the way down I leaned against the wall, my body thrumming with pain. The lobby was clear, and I bolted through the doors and slammed into the Bronco. Like a homing pigeon, I turned south on Midnight Pass Road and drove to my apartment.

When I pulled under the carport, sunrise was just beginning to pink the milky horizon, and wavelets were gently sucking at the beach. I was glad Michael and Paco were still gone. I didn't want them to see me bruised and scraped. I took the stairs two at a time, unlocked the French doors, and hurled down the hall to the bathroom, peeling off clothes as I went.

I stood in the shower and sobbed while water lifted asphalt grit from my pores. It wasn't so much physical pain that made me cry, it was the shock of knowing somebody hated me enough to squash me like a cockroach. I hadn't felt hated since my fourth-grade teacher had struck daily misery into my heart with her sighs and baleful looks. I had finally announced at the supper table that I wasn't going to school ever again, and my grandmother called the teacher and asked her what I was doing that made her dislike me so much. The teacher was a little taken aback, but she admitted it was just plain annoying how I wasn't Working Up to My Potential. My grandmother told her my dad had died over the summer, my mother had run off to start a new life, and I had plenty of time to Work Up to My Potential after I got my life in order. The teacher promised to be nicer to me and I went back to school, but for the rest of the year her disappointment was like little hooks of gravity pulling me down. I felt the same way now. I hated being hated.

When I was all cried out and clean again, I patted dry and applied liquid Band-Aid to my scrapes. Then I looked hard at my reflection in the mirror and told myself that I had spent three years overcoming the sick weariness that goes along with being a victim, and I wasn't going back there. The person driving that truck would love to know I felt humiliated, and as long as I did, he might just as well

have killed me. That son-of-a-bitch had another think coming if he thought I was going to slink around in fear.

I put on fresh Keds and a clean bra and underpants, this
time not going for fancy lace or satin because I didn't give
a shit how my underwear looked when I shot the bastard
who had come after me. I was going to find him and I was
going to make him feel as much fear as he'd caused me.

11

I had two other dogs to walk before I went to Secret Cove, and they were both willing to let me poke along on my sore knees. The cats on my schedule didn't care one way or the other how fast I moved, but a couple of them wound themselves around my ankles to show sympathy. I carried my .38 shoved into the waistband of my shorts, more or less covered by my loose T. My bruised rib cage reminded me with every movement that it had slammed against hard pavement, and my right cheek had swollen so it looked like an overripe plum. Good thing animals aren't judgmental or nosy.

With every painful move, I muttered "Ouch! Ooh! Shit! Fuck!" and thought about the driver of the truck. Two big questions had to be answered: who was he and how did he know I would be running in the Sea Breeze parking lot that morning. There was no question about why he'd tried to kill me. I already knew that. He was the man who had killed Conrad Ferrelli, and he wanted to shut me up so I couldn't testify against him.

Before I went to Secret Cove, I swung by the Metzgers' to retrieve Conrad's coat. In the driveway, I dropped my gun into my pocket and put on a pair of dark shades to hide my red eyes. Priscilla opened the door to my ring, smiled shyly, and beckoned me down the hall to the workroom. As I followed her, the Metzgers' seal-mitted Russian Blues, Elsie and Serenity, trotted to meet me. Aerialists of the cat world, Russian Blues are fine-boned graceful cats with brilliant green eyes. I was flattered they remembered me, because Blues take awhile to warm up to strangers. I was too sore to kneel and stroke their silver-tipped fur, but they didn't seem to mind, just threaded themselves in and out of my legs for a moment before light-footing it back to the workroom. Maybe they had been showing sympathy too.

In the workroom, Priscilla's baby was asleep in her playpen, and Conrad's coat was on a tall white-haired man. Josephine was behind him, moving her hands across the shoulders.

She took one look at me and said, "My God, Dixie, what happened to you?"

I tried to shrug and pass it off but ended up grunting because shrugging hurt.

"I fell."

"You didn't get that banged up from falling, Dixie Hemingway. Now what happened?"

Everybody in the room was staring at me, including the man wearing Conrad's coat.

I said, "A truck tried to run me down this morning."

Suddenly I was crying again, and Josephine had gathered me into her arms and was patting me and making shushing noises like you make to a baby, and I was leaning into her and feeling a whole lot better. When I was finally cried out, Priscilla scurried out of the room and brought me tissues and thrust them at me, and the man in Conrad's coat smiled and nodded at me as if I had just accomplished something important. Maybe I had.

He said, "That truck, what kind was it?"

"It was a normal-sized pickup but up high on big huge tires."

For a split second, Josephine and Priscilla and the man all cut their eyes at one another. They quickly looked back at me, but now there was something apprehensive in their faces, something akin to guilt or fear.

Josephine said, "Did you see the driver?"

"No, it was too dark. I was running with a dog in a parking lot, and the truck just came blasting toward me. I was out in the open and there wasn't any place to go. I was terrified."

Josephine said, "Well, I guess so."

"I fell to the ground—dived, really—and it went over me. That's how I got bruised."

They all pulled themselves up stiffly as if they were living the moment with me. The baby made a shrill squeal that startled everybody and broke the tension. Priscilla rushed to her sewing machine and Josephine gestured to the man beside her.

"Dixie Hemingway, meet Pete Madeira."

His white grin knocked off about thirty years. "Are you related to Ernest Hemingway?"

"People always ask that, but I'm not."

He waggled woolly black eyebrows that looked like fat caterpillars inching above his pale blue eyes. "I'm not Madeira wine either, but I've been known to intoxicate."

Josephine slapped his arm. "Behave yourself, Pete."

Pinching fabric at the coat's shoulder, she said, "Pete wants Conrad's coat, but it doesn't fit, and I'm not altering it. The shoulder is the main thing. If the shoulders don't fit, the whole thing will look wrong."

It didn't take a tailor to see that the coat slid off his shoulders, pulling the lapels too far apart and giving the whole coat a sloppy look.

Pete turned his mouth down in mock despair. "Are you saying I don't have broad manly shoulders?"

"I'm saying the coat don't fit you, Pete."

She unbuttoned the plastic chrysanthemums and pulled it from him. He turned to me and spread his arms to the side.

"It's the story of my life. Women are always telling me I'm not big enough."

Josephine put the coat on a hanger and hooked it over the rack. "Don't let anybody kid you, Pete, size does matter."

The baby chortled as if she got the joke, which made us all grin.

I said, "Actually, Jo, I'm here to take the coat back to

Stevie Ferrelli. I told her what you said, and she thinks it's a great idea."

Josephine's face brightened. "Well now, that's the best news I've had in a long time." She turned to Pete and said, "I told her Conrad should be buried in the coat."

"Of course he should. I'm surprised you had to point that out."

Josephine said, "Give her a break. The woman's probably in shock."

She took the coat down and brought it to me, but Pete was right behind her, reaching for it.

He said, "I'll carry that out for you."

I bit back a reply that I was a big girl and didn't need a man to carry a coat for me, and handed it over. We said our good-byes to Josephine and Priscilla and went out together, Pete proudly leading the way with the coat laid over his forearms like a holy shroud.

At the Bronco, he carefully arranged it on the backseat and then straightened up with a deep sigh. "You know, it's the strangest thing. Ever since I heard about Conrad, I've felt like it was Angelo who'd died. It's like going through losing him all over again."

"You knew Angelo Ferrelli?"

"Close to sixty years. I don't think anything has ever hurt me as much as Angelo's death. I'm ashamed to admit it, but losing him was almost worse than losing my wife and daughter. Not that Angelo and I had anything fruity between us, but we started out in the circus together, like soldiers in foxholes in the thick of battle."

"You were a clown?"

"I *am* a clown, honey. Just 'cause I'm old don't mean I've hung up my clown shoes."

He gave me a lecherous wink and grinned. If he'd been fifty years younger, it would have been annoying, but there's something endearing about a flirtatious octogenarian.

He said, "I teach a clown class now. You ought to come visit us. There are a lot of clown alleys in Sarasota."

"Alleys?"

"An alley is a group of clowns that do the same kind of work. Comes from the time when the ringmaster would yell, 'Clowns, *allez*!' when it was time for the clowns to come on. *Allez* means *go* in French, but to Americans it sounded like *alley*, so that's what we call it now. I belong to a hospice alley. We go to hospices and entertain the patients, the caregivers, and the families. People don't hurt so much when they're laughing."

I felt ashamed that I'd lived in a circus town all my life but had always thought of clowns as people who entertained at children's birthday parties.

Wincing at a pain shooting through my ribs, I said, "Stevie Ferrelli told me that a man came to see Conrad about a year ago claiming to be the son of Angelo's brother. Do you know about a brother?"

He shook his head. "In sixty years, he never mentioned a brother."

"He said Angelo had stolen the Madam Flutter-By act from his father, and he wanted Conrad to give him money."

Pete stared at me. "Angelo never stole anything from anybody! I knew him when he was working up that act in 1944. I'm sure of the date because that's when the big fire happened. God, that was an awful night. Angelo came back for me and lifted a tent pole off me, otherwise I'd have burned to death. The band played 'Stars and Stripes Forever' to signal everybody to evacuate the tent. They played until everybody was out. They barely escaped themselves."

He seemed lost in memory for a moment, then brought himself back.

"Anyway, Angelo was fooling around with the Madam Flutter-By act then, you know, getting the makeup right, the costume right. It takes awhile to get a character down. But it was all his own idea, I know that for a fact."

"Conrad never mentioned anything to you? About the man claiming Angelo had stolen the act?"

"I never heard of it before just this minute, and it's a load of elephant shit, excuse my French. Who was that guy, anyway?"

"Stevie said his name was Brossi. She hasn't heard anything about him again, so maybe he dropped the whole thing. He told Conrad his father started the act when they were growing up in Italy."

He laughed. "Angelo wasn't from Italy! He always said he was, but that was part of his act. He was from Cleveland or someplace, a poor kid with big dreams who ran away to join the circus. Most of us were like that."

"Stevie thinks he was from Italy."

"Maybe Conrad thought the story about being from Italy was true. Hell, Angelo might have ended up believing it himself. Clowns, actors, writers, they all live in their imagination so much they get reality a little bit confused."

Before we parted he scrabbled in his pocket and pulled out a business card. "Any time you want to know anything about Angelo Ferrelli, you give me a call."

His pale blue eyes grew cloudy, the same wary, half-guilty look he'd had when he heard about the truck. "And you take care of yourself. You see a truck like that again, you call the police."

Even this early in the morning, my Bronco had become a kiln while I was inside. After I started the engine and had the AC blowing full blast, I gave Conrad's coat an anxious look to make sure it hadn't melted while I talked to Pete. Mame and Reggie were my last two calls of the morning, and I decided to take Conrad's coat home before I stopped at Mame's.

No cars were in Stevie's driveway, and she answered the door quickly. Conrad's coat was folded over my arm, but she barely glanced at it.

As I came in, she said, "What happened to your face?"

"I slipped on my stairs in the rain last night and hit it."

"God, your arms are bruised too."

"It's okay, I put some liquid stuff on it. I'm just sore."

She nodded, relieved to be allowed to ignore my bruises.

I said, "Where do you want me to put the coat?"

She looked down at it as if she'd never seen it before. "You can put it in Conrad's study."

She moved toward the kitchen, and I went down a side hall. I remembered caving like that after Todd and Christy were killed. One minute I would be alert and the next I would be in a deep dark hole where sound barely reached me.

In Conrad's study, I laid the coat over the back of his tall leather desk chair, spreading it so it wouldn't wrinkle. It looked almost natural there, as if Conrad were sitting in the chair wearing it, only he didn't take up any space.

On the way out, I paused to look at a bulletin board covered with photos of children's faces. Many of them were disfigured, some horribly so. Beside each disfigured face was another normal happily smiling face. It took a few seconds to realize the photographs were before-and-after shots of children whose facial deformities had been surgically repaired.

I went to the kitchen and found Stevie standing in front of the sink, staring blindly out the window.

I said, "I noticed photographs of children in Conrad's office."

She turned to me and smiled. "Aren't they wonderful? That project gave Conrad more pleasure than anything he's ever done. Me too."

"You pay for plastic surgery for them?"

"Sometimes we bring them to the United States, sometimes we send surgeons to them. Some surgeons donate their services, and we provide transportation and the patients. Some countries have good surgeons of their own, but they need supplies or proper facilities. We do whatever is needed."

"You'll continue to do that?"

She looked startled. "Why wouldn't I?"

I felt myself blush. "I don't know why I said that."

"Yes, you do. I'm a young widow, and so far as anybody knows, I've never done anything on my own, I've just been Conrad's shadow. But that's not true. We were a team, and everything we started will continue."

"What about Denton?"

"I'll take care of Denton. He may plan on taking over the Ferrelli Trust, but he won't."

I said, "Stevie, you're exhausted. Turn off the phones and take a nap."

She closed her eyes and leaned back against the sink, looking ten years older than she had when she opened the door to me and Guidry two days before. When she opened her eyes, they were swimming in tears.

"You'll come back this afternoon and walk Reggie?"

"You bet. I'll see you then."

She walked me to the door and gave me a quick hug good-bye. I've always wished I had hugged her back more tightly before I left.

12

When I pulled into Mame's driveway, I saw her behind the glass watching for me. She was almost her old frisky self. I couldn't say the same for myself. Before I brushed her, I clipped her leash on her collar and limped with her into the backyard and let her squat in the bahia grass and amble around on the pea-gravel path. Lifting her to the table to brush her made me groan. Good thing she only weighed eleven pounds. Another ounce would have killed my ribs.

I gave her fresh water and a half cup of senior kibble and left feeling optimistic about her. She was a tough little dog. She was going to be fine.

I was so hungry I was ready to eat the upholstery in my car, but this was Wednesday, the day I skipped breakfast at the Village Diner and drove over the bridge to the Bayfront Village to take Cora Mathers to her weekly hairdresser's appointment. Cora was the grandmother of a former client who'd got herself murdered on my watch, and I felt responsible for her. Also, I liked her. Cora had survived more tragedies than most people even see on TV, and she still got up every day with a childlike hope that it was going to be good.

Bayfront Village is an upscale assisted-living condominium. Designed by architects who couldn't decide between neoclassical, art deco, or Mediterranean, it has the befuddled look of a staid matron cast as an ingenue in a musical comedy. I pulled under the portico, put my gun in the glove box, and told the valet I was going in to get Cora.

He grinned. "Bet she's in that senior sex class."

"Excuse me?"

"Some lady is teaching about senior sex this morning. I'll bet Miz Mathers is in there with the rest of them."

I ignored his leer and went through the glass doors to the lobby. Inside, the air wasn't much cooler, but a lot of elders sitting in the hyper-decorated conversational area wore sweaters. I didn't see Cora, but there was an easel outside a meeting room with a hand-lettered sign announcing TANTRIC SEX FOR SENIORS.

I ducked around the easel and stuck my head in the door. A hefty woman in a loose caftan stood beside a table holding a headless and armless sculpture of a woman cut off at mid-thigh. The woman had pendulous breasts and a bulging pudenda as big as a manatee's head. The sculpture, not the teacher. Maybe the teacher too. Who could tell with that loose thing she was wearing?

About a dozen white-haired women and three men sat in folding chairs in front of her. Two of the men were asleep with their chins sagging on their chests, and the other one had taken his hearing aid out and was fiddling with it. The women all sat on the edge of their seats in rapt attention.

The teacher said, "In Eastern cultures, she is worshiped as the Great Mother, the Eternal Feminine. She has many names, and she lives inside every woman."

She stroked a finger down the cleft of the statue's vulva. "This is called the *yoni*. In the temples, worshipers stroke the Great Mother's *yoni* in reverence for the life it represents. This is a sacred spot on your bodies, ladies. Whether he knows it or not, when a man touches a woman's *yoni*, he is worshiping the Great Mother."

Pink blushes rose to white hairlines as women remembered times their *yonis* had been worshiped. To tell the truth, I felt a little pink myself.

The class ended, the teacher wrapped the sculpture in a sheet, and everybody straggled out.

As they passed me, the man with the malfunctioning hearing aid shouted to his wife, "Did I miss anything?"

She yelled, "I'm a Great Mother."

He smiled. "Of course you are, dear."

Cora saw me and waved. Cora would have to stand on tiptoe to reach five feet, and soaking wet she wouldn't have weighed eighty pounds. She wore a bright bird-printed shirt made for a much larger woman, over red pleated shorts that stopped an inch above her little freckled knees.

She said, "They're teaching us about sex. I thought I already knew all about it, but I guess I didn't."

I steered her outside to the Bronco and helped her into the passenger side. The valet grinned and nodded in a rather slimy way, pleased that Cora had been where he said I would find her. I ignored him and ran around to the driver's side and eased the Bronco down the brick drive, careful not to ram anybody pushing their walkers to the front door.

She said, "I guess it's never too late."

I looked at my watch. "Giorgio will wait for you."

"I meant for sex. Been a long time since I had sex, but I'm thinking maybe I'll give it another try."

It had been a long time since I'd had sex too, and I didn't want to talk about it.

She said, "I'm gonna have Georgie do my hair different."

Her hairdresser's name was Giorgio, and her hair stuck out around her face in wisps that seemed God-ordained to me, but if Cora wanted a new look, she ought to get one.

An hour later, Cora's white wisps had been converted to lavender wisps, and my nails had smooth cuticles and were buffed so they shone like abalone shells. To celebrate, we went to the Oasis on Siesta Drive for lunch. The waitress didn't seem put off by my bruises or the cat hairs clinging to my khaki shorts, and since it was off-season we had our choice of tables.

We both ordered the daily special, and while we waited Cora leaned over to peer at my face.

"Who hit you?"

"Nobody, I fell."

"That's what I always told people too. I'd say I fell or ran into a cabinet door."

"I really did fall, Cora. This morning."

"You shouldn't let a man hit you. I always told Marilee that, but I guess she didn't listen."

There were so many misconceptions in that sentence I didn't know how to begin to answer it. Marilee had been her granddaughter who was murdered, but it hadn't been by a man who hit her, and no man had ever hit me. I was saved by the waitress bringing our food. Another good thing about summer, chefs all over town are waiting with poised food for the natives. Not like during season, when they can let money go to their heads and forget who really loves them.

The luncheon special was a crab cake atop a black bean cake atop an artichoke heart, the whole business wrapped in crispy thin phyllo and sitting on a bed of watercress and chopped tomato, all of it drizzled with silky gorgonzola cream. I took a greedy bite and decided that if I ever decided to have an affair, or just an afternoon quickie, it would be with the Oasis chef.

Cora looked doubtfully at her plate and patted her neon hair.

She said, "You think this makes me look younger?"

It really made her look like a lavender Easter chick, but I nodded vigorously. "Takes twenty years off."

"Is that all? I'd like to take off thirty or forty, but I guess looking sixty-eight ain't bad."

I said, "What would you do if you were thirty or forty years younger?"

She pursed her lips and studied my bruised cheek again. "You mean your age? Well, being young ain't all it's cracked up to be, is it?"

She inched forward in her chair so her chin was closer to her plate, her lavender frizz catching the overhead light and casting rainbows on the white tablecloth.

"You take me, for example. I have a lot more fun now than I did when I was young. 'Course I have a lot easier time of it now. Marilee saw to that, God rest her sweet soul. I guess if I was poor now like I was when I was young, I wouldn't like being old any better than I liked being young."

She took a bite of crab cake and chewed thoughtfully. "Now if I had me a man," she said, "that would make it even better. I never had money and a man at the same time."

I said, "There are plenty of widowed men at Bayfront Village. Why don't you snag one of them?"

"They're all too old to do it. I don't see any reason to get a man that can't do it, do you? Hilda Johnson took up with one of them old men, and he took some of that stuff that makes a man's tallywhacker hard. His never got soft again, at least not for several days. Hilda was pretty excited about it at first, but then he commenced complaining that it hurt and she finally let him call an ambulance. I don't know how the doctors got his thing soft again, but he's kept it to himself ever since. We don't know if he's embarrassed or just afraid of Hilda."

I took a big swallow of water to hide my grin, and Cora leaned forward and lowered her voice.

"Some of the women at Bayfront are getting them little vibrating things. Gladys Majors has a whole catalog full of them. One of them is so little it fits on the end of your finger. Uses a little battery like for a hearing aid. You know, you could sit right there in your living room and blow your brains out with that thing and nobody would ever know."

I swallowed wrong and had a coughing fit so bad the waitress came to see if I wanted her to thump my back. I waved her away, croaking that I was just fine, because a thump on the back would have probably caused me to faint from pain.

To change the subject, I said, "Cora, have you ever known any circus people?"

"Sure, lots of them. Ringling used to be a good place to work. We had a neighbor in Bradenton had something to do with the elephants. Dyer. His name was Dyer. Had a sneaky boy named Quenton that was sweet on Marilee, but she never had anything to do with him."

As I remembered, every male in Florida had been sweet on Marilee.

Cora said, "Why're you interested in circus people?"

"Oh, I met a man whose father was a clown, and that got me thinking about it."

"That fellow Dyer had to shoot an elephant one time. It went crazy or something, and he shot it with a gun that had drugs in it. He said it ran a few steps and then just keeled over dead. He felt bad about it, but you can't have a crazy elephant running around trampling people."

We were both subdued after that, thinking about what it would be like to shoot an elephant with enough drugs to kill it.

As we were leaving, I held the door open while Cora inched her way over the threshold. Noontime traffic zipped past on the street beyond the parking lot. A dark blue pickup raised up on tall tires drove past, and I jerked to attention. It sped south, toward the curve and the north bridge to Siesta Key.

Cora stood on tiptoe to see what I was looking at. She said, "How do they get in those things? Do they have to use a ladder? Silly things, you ask me. Look like they'd be dangerous."

As I stepped off the curb to help Cora down, pain from my bruised ribs shot through my torso. "They're damn dangerous."

After I took Cora back to Bayfront Village, I wanted more than anything to go home and take a nap, but I stopped at the market to pick up staples: fruit and yogurt and cheese and Cherry Garcia ice cream. In the ten-items-or-less line, I read the headlines on idiot magazines while I waited behind a man who had at least twenty items. When it was my turn, the checker rolled everything over her scanner and stuffed it in a plastic bag.

When I handed her money, she said, "If I eat ice cream,

it just runs right through me. Takes about fifteen minutes, and out it goes."

Not knowing how to respond to that fascinating information, I said, "No kidding?"

She counted out my change. "Yep, I have a problem with fat. It's in one end and out the other, whoosh!"

She demonstrated, shoving both hands down her sides. The man in line behind me suddenly wheeled his cart backward and went to another checker.

She gave me a friendly smile. "Have a nice day."

The automatic doors sighed me through, and I crossed the parking lot carrying my fatty ice cream and watching for speeding blind people or pickups on monster tires. Life is treacherous.

13

When I made the last turn on the twisty drive leading to my place from Midnight Pass Road, I saw that neither Michael nor Paco was home. I also saw a dark Blazer parked at the side of the carport. Guidry was in it, sitting like a meditating Buddha with the windows rolled down.

I said, "Shit."

I pulled into my slot, took the gun from the glove box and jammed it in my pocket, got out of the car, and opened the back to loop plastic grocery bags over my wrists. Guidry ambled around the corner like a tourist coming to watch the pagans do their worship rites to heathen gods. He had on a linen jacket the color of white asparagus, pale olive pants, and a darker olive knit shirt. He looked cool and unhurried. His bare toes in his expensive leather sandals looked clean and manicured. His gray eyes were calm and alert. I hated his guts.

He said, "Can I help you with those?"

I said, "I've got them." I didn't sound very gracious, but then I didn't feel very gracious.

He followed me up my stairs and waited while I unlocked the French doors. I didn't invite him in, but he came in anyway and took the one stool at my so-called breakfast bar, casting a speculative eye at my bare white walls. I tossed ice cream in the freezer and dumped fruit in a basket and finally looked directly at him.

He said, "Want to tell me how you got those bruises?"

"I fell."

"Uh-hunh. Would that have been around four-thirty this morning? In the Sea Breeze parking lot?"

My face went hot and I felt my lower lip creep forward like a four-year-old's.

He said, "We got a nine-one-one call this morning from a woman in the Sea Breeze who said she got up to go to the bathroom and saw a truck try to run a woman down in the parking lot. She said it looked like it rolled right over her. She watched the woman get up, and then she went back to bed and waited until daylight to report it. She said the truck was already gone and she didn't want to bother anybody so early, but she thought we ought to know. She said the woman had a greyhound with her. If memory serves, you go running with a greyhound at the Sea Breeze every morning."

I got a bottle of water from the refrigerator and opened it. Then I relented and got another one out and handed it to Guidry. While he unscrewed the cap on his, I stood on my side of the bar and took a long pull at mine. After he had chugged down half a bottle—he must have been hotter than he looked—I gave him a surly glare.

"Okay, somebody tried to run me down in the Sea Breeze parking lot this morning. They drove a pickup jacked up on huge tires, and the only reason I'm not dead is that I threw myself under it before it hit me."

"You get plates? See the driver?"

"It was too dark. I didn't have time. He went out on Midnight Pass Road toward the bridge."

"Why didn't you report it?"

"What for, Guidry? I didn't know who it was, I didn't have any proof, and it was probably halfway to Myakka City by the time I quit shaking."

"You shook?"

"Damn right I shook."

"First time I ever heard you admit you could be scared."

"The point is, Guidry, the point is that Conrad Ferrelli's

killer thinks I can identify him, and somebody tried to kill me this morning."

"Could be coincidence."

"Yeah, like the moon and tides."

"You have any idea who it could be?"

"I think it's Denton Ferrelli. He's a slimy guy. Everybody says he's a jerk."

"You want me to arrest Denton Ferrelli because he's a jerk?"

"I just think you should look into him very carefully."

Guidry got up from the stool and ambled into the living room area, looking around as if he were at an art gallery. "I expected you to live with a menagerie, but you don't even have a goldfish."

"My life works better without anybody depending on me."

"Any*body*?"

"Like a pet, I mean."

"You don't have any pictures on your walls either. No plants, not even a pot of ivy. You don't seem the type to live like an ascetic."

"What the hell does my apartment have to do with somebody trying to kill me?"

He shrugged. "I'm just trying to figure you out."

"Somebody's trying to kill me, Guidry. Figure that out."

He turned and gave me a long look, his gray eyes momentarily softening before they grew analytical again.

"You know what I think?"

"No, Guidry, what do you think?"

"Don't get me wrong, Dixie, I respect what you've been through, and I respect your feelings. But I think the time comes when grief becomes protective coloration to keep people away."

Fury rose in my throat. "What do you know about it, Guidry? What do you know about losing somebody?"

"I don't know about it, Dixie. I probably never will, because I don't think I have it in me to care so much about somebody that I would feel the kind of loss you feel. But you do. You know what it's like to love that much. You've done it, so you know you can do it again. But as long as you hide behind grief, you'll never have to. You can stay safely outside it, live in a sterile cave, wrap yourself in pain every night instead of a man's arms."

My eyelids stung, and I wanted to leave him speechless while I made an indignant exit. But it's hard to leave in high dudgeon when it's your own apartment. Besides, I had a sneaking suspicion he was right.

Guidry said, "Relax. I've said all I'm going to say about it. It's just something I've been wanting to tell you."

Once again, Guidry had left me feeling out of control. I hate that. Not that I want to be the one always in control. I just hate it when I'm not.

I said, "You've never said how Conrad died."

"Correct."

"I need to know. If the same person wants me dead, I need to know how he killed Conrad."

"What makes you so sure it was a man?"

"Come on, Guidry."

He walked back to the breakfast bar and leaned his elbows on it. For the first time since I'd known him, a river of emotions flowed over his face.

"He died of a massive injection of succinylcholine chloride shot into his right buttock. It's a neuromuscular paralysant. It paralyzes the lungs, so lung surgeons use it while they have a patient on a ventilator."

The words trickled through my brain like ice water. "And without a ventilator?"

"Suffocation. Heart failure. Death."

I said, "How long?" and was surprised to hear that I was whispering.

He swallowed. "The drug gets to the diaphragm within seconds of injection. Death is within five minutes, give or take."

I thought of Conrad, lying on the ground unable to breathe.

"Was he unconscious?"

"He was fully conscious until he died. It's a particularly sadistic way to kill a person."

"Why didn't you tell me sooner?"

"It took the ME awhile to be sure. They had to run tissue spectrographs. They found enough of the drug in his tissues to kill an elephant, and I mean that literally. Until it was declared too inhumane, it's what they used in Africa to cull elephant herds. They flew over in helicopters and shot the elephants with dart guns."

"Did the ME give you a time of death?"

"She can't be sure, Dixie, you know that. But judging from lividity and rigor, she thinks Ferrelli hadn't been dead more than a couple of hours when you found him. That puts his murder no earlier than four-thirty. That fits with what Stevie Ferrelli says, that Conrad usually left about six to run with the dog on the beach."

"Where was Denton Ferrelli then?"

"He and his wife both say he left their home on Longboat Key about six o'clock. He drove to the Longboat Key Moorings where he docks his speedboat. He took the boat out for a spin around the bay, something he does every morning, and docked at about six forty-five. He walked over to the harborside golf course at the Longboat Key Golf Club, where he met three other men. They waited for the greenskeepers to finish up and teed off shortly after seven o'clock."

I slitted my eyes like a hound on a fresh scent. "Who are these three other men?"

"Leo Brossi was one."

"Aha!"

"Yeah, maybe. But the other two are okay, at least so far as we know. State Senator Wayne Black and a banker named Quenton Dyer."

I had a feeling I'd heard that name before, but I couldn't remember where.

I said, "They could be lying."

"Over a dozen people saw them."

"Denton could be lying about when he left home. He

could have got up early, driven to Siesta Key and killed Conrad, and still been on time for his golf game. It wouldn't have taken long to cover the body with that loose mulch. And Denton's that cold, he could do it and not break a sweat."

"You saw Conrad Ferrelli's car a little after six. Even if Denton and his wife are lying about the time he left home, Denton Ferrelli couldn't have been driving the car you saw."

"What about Brossi?"

He shook his head. "Brossi would kill his own grand-mother for a buck, but Ferrelli's murder was driven by an overwhelming rage. The lipstick on the mouth, the dead kit-ten. That's motivated by hatred and revenge, not money."

I suddenly heard Cora's voice: *That fellow Dyer had to shoot an elephant one time. It went crazy or something, and he shot it with a gun that had drugs in it.*

"You said the drug was shot into Conrad? Shot how?"

"The ME found a needle puncture."

"Guidry, that man, Quenton Dyer, the one who played golf with Denton, the one you said was a lawyer—"

Guidry was nodding like one of those duck things that bob over a glass of water.

"Yes?"

"His father was with the Ringling Circus. He worked with elephants, and one time he had to kill one with a big shot of drugs. He did it with a gun."

I leaned back and looked triumphantly at him.

"How the hell do you know that?"

"Cora Mathers told me. You remember Cora? Marilee Doerring's grandmother? When she lived in Bradenton, one of her neighbors was a man named Dyer. He worked for Ringling, doing something with the elephants, feeding them or training them, I don't know what. He had a son named Quenton. It has to be the same man."

"You think—"

"That must be how he and Denton Ferrelli met. They were both circus kids. And if Dyer's father knew how to use drugs to kill elephants. . . ."

Guidry appeared to be chewing on the inside of his cheek, the first sign of uncertainty I'd ever seen in him.

"Quenton Dyer is an investment banker. He sits on the boards of half a dozen important businesses."

"So?"

He sighed. "Okay. It does seem like more than coincidence. But the fact remains that both men were seen at the Longboat Key Golf Club at seven o'clock that morning, not too long after you saw Conrad's car driving away."

I slumped over the bar. If Denton Ferrelli wasn't the killer, I didn't know where else to look. And if I didn't know who to be afraid of, the killer had a better chance at me.

Guidry reached out and ran the back of his fingers over my bruised cheek with a surprisingly gentle touch.

"Are you going to be here alone tonight?"

My heart did a little blip, a girlie kind of jump like women get when they've had a welcome proposition. I felt like slapping my own chest. I nodded, but I frowned too so he wouldn't think I'd reacted the way I'd reacted.

He got up and headed for the front door. Then he turned and gave me a hesitant look.

"Look, I don't want to be an alarmist, but I don't want you to take this lightly either. It's not a good idea for you to be here by yourself if a psychopathic killer has taken an interest in you."

"I have a thirty-eight in my pocket. I have metal hurricane shutters that cover the French doors."

He nodded toward the window over the kitchen sink. "Somebody could come through that window. You also have a bathroom window. I checked while I waited for you."

"It would take a two-story ladder to get in those windows."

"Or a one-story ladder set in a pickup raised on giant tires. A pickup is a convenient place to carry a ladder."

"Guidry, I can't Jive scared. I'll keep my gun ready. I'll keep the windows locked. I'll be careful."

"When will your brother be home?"

"He should be home any time now. He was on a twenty-four-hour shift that ended this morning at eight o'clock."

"What about Paco?"

I let his slip of the tongue pass without saying "Ha!" Guidry and Paco kept up a pretense of not knowing each other, but I'd known all along they did. Guidry was homicide and Paco was undercover, but those guys all know one another.

I said, "I don't know when Paco will be home." I wasn't going to divulge any information about Paco's schedule, not even to another cop. If Guidry wanted to know when Paco would be home, he could ask Paco.

His gray eyes studied me for a moment, and then he nodded as if he'd answered his own unspoken question.

He said, "Okay. Call me if you learn anything." He left without looking back.

I went to the French doors and locked them and lowered the hurricane shutters, leaving their accordion edges pointed outward so light could enter through the slits on the folds. It made my apartment seem like a treehouse with sunlight filtering through leafy branches. In the bedroom, an air-conditioning unit occupied a cut-out space high on the wall. Next to the ceiling were two horizontal panes of glass, four feet wide and four inches tall. They were for light, not ventilation. Nobody bigger than a lizard could squeeze through them.

I went in the bathroom and studied the jalousied glass window. To come through it, a person would have to remove the strips of glass from the frame one by one. If I was home, I was pretty sure I would hear that. I went back to the kitchen and ate a banana and looked at the window over the sink. Guidry was right. Somebody with a ladder could come through that window, and they wouldn't make a lot of noise doing it. I needed an alarm in that window.

Grabbing the keys to Michael's house, I went back to the French doors, opened them, and raised the hurricane shutters. With one hand in my pocket gripping the stock of my .38 and the other hand gripping Michael's door key, I scurried across the cypress deck to his back door. I felt like one of the little anole lizards that race around in the hot sun. I wouldn't have been surprised if *my* throat had turned red and ballooned out. I let myself in the kitchen door and locked it behind me, then hurried for the stairway that led to the attic. There were zillions of our grandparents' things stored in Michael's attic. I was bound to find something I could use as an alarm.

Half an hour later, I was cobwebby and sweaty, but I'd found the perfect alarm to hang in my window, a rusty heart-shaped iron thing with two dozen little bells on it. It had once hung outside the kitchen door to let my grandmother know when somebody came or went. Just a touch caused all the bells to clatter with a racket loud enough to wake manatees a mile offshore.

I had also found an old trunk filled with clothes my mother had left behind. I opened the trunk and inhaled that odor peculiar to clothing that has lain dormant for a long time—a miasma of faint decay and near mold that seems to grow in the absence of a wearer. Everything inside was neatly folded. My mother hadn't been the type to fold things haphazardly, even when she knew she'd never see them again. I pulled out a soft cotton cardigan, taupe with a thin horizontal stripe. It had been twenty-three years since she left, but I remembered that cardigan. Mother wore it with a linen skirt printed with gold sunflowers. Yes, there was the skirt, along with a linen dress in a similar print but with deeper tones. I'd never realized before how often my mother chose those colors, gold and rust and deep yellow. There was another cardigan in a pale beige, a loosely knit thing I didn't remember.

I stacked everything on the floor and tried to remember the last time I'd seen my mother dressed in any of these clothes. Before she left us, she had started living in shapeless muumuus and terry scuffs. She would slide her feet across our sand-gritty floor, a cigarette dangling from one corner of her mouth, her blond hair unkempt and straggly. Not at all the pretty woman she'd been, but a woman dissolved by grief and anger over my father's death. I felt a flash of recognition. I had been almost the same after Todd and Christy died, and for the same reason. Not just that they'd died, but the *way* they'd died. For the first time, I understood why my mother had left us. Loving people is too dangerous.

I put everything back in the trunk and closed it. Some day Michael and I would have to get rid of all the memories in the attic, but not today. Today I had to put up an alarm so a psychopathic killer couldn't crawl in my kitchen window and murder me before I shot him. With the bell thing clattering with each painful step, I went back downstairs, out the back door, and across the deck to the stairs to my apartment. I detoured into the storage closet under the carport for some screw-in hooks that Michael or Paco had neatly stored in a glass jar on a shelf.

By the time I got upstairs and let myself in the French doors, my scraped knees were screaming. Groaning and cursing, I climbed on my kitchen counter and crouched in the sink to screw the hooks to the trim above the window. Then I hung the rusted bell thing on the hooks and climbed back down. It looked like shit, but nobody could come through that window without hitting the thing and setting off a noise like a herd of belled cows on the run.

Now that I had an alarm, I took a long warm shower because standing under hot water was the only time I didn't hurt. I was afraid to nap outside in the hammock now, so I turned on the air conditioner in my bedroom and fell naked onto my bed. I woke so chilled and achy from the AC that I took another warm shower. At this rate, I might dissolve soon, like drowned soap.

I pulled on a terry-cloth robe and padded to the kitchen to make a cup of tea. While the water boiled, I tapped the iron bell thing over the sink and grimly listened to the wild clanking sound. Yep, that would wake me, no question about it. When the teakettle whistled, I poured boiling water over a drab tea bag. I drank it while I looked through the makeshift alarm at the treetops outside the window.

I thought about what Guidry had said, that I was using grief to keep the world away. I thought about my mother running away after my father died. I'd always thought she deserted Michael and me because she was too shallow to do the hard thing and raise us alone. I'd always thought I had more courage, more character, more depth. But maybe I didn't. Maybe my prolonged mourning was really a revolving fear, a hamster wheel I ran on because I didn't have the courage to move forward. My mother had run away physically. Maybe I had run away emotionally. The question was, What could I do about it? The answer was, I didn't have the foggiest idea.

With that decided, I went down the hall to the closet and got dressed for my afternoon pet visits.

I carried my .38 by my side as I went downstairs to the Bronco. I could see a few rain-blue clouds out in the Gulf headed toward shore, but the sun was fiercely hot. A pelican dozed in the carport's shade, along with a couple of great blue herons and an entire chorus of egrets. They all turned their heads to look at me with eyes dulled by afternoon heat, too listless even to flap a feather of alarm when I started the engine.

Michael and Paco were still gone.

My Bronco still had bird shit on it.

Somebody still wanted to kill me.

14

At the Sea Breeze, Tom Hale opened his door before I knocked, his round black eyes peering up anxiously through wire-rimmed glasses. Billy Elliot stood beside Tom's wheelchair looking a little subdued, probably because Tom was so grim. Tom spun his wheelchair out of the way and motioned me inside.

"Tell me what happened this morning, Dixie."

I tried giving him a blank look, but he wasn't having it.

"Everybody in the building knows somebody tried to run you down in the parking lot. Who was it?"

"If I knew, he'd be behind bars by now. It was somebody in one of those pickups with huge tires. Not anybody who lives in the Sea Breeze."

"He drove straight at you?"

Suddenly cold, I crossed my arms over my chest. "I threw Billy Elliot's leash aside, Tom. He wasn't close to me."

"Good God, Dixie, I wasn't worried about that!"

We both looked quickly at Billy Elliot to make sure he hadn't taken offense, but he was smiling with his tongue lolling out the side of his mouth.

I said, "I guess you heard about Conrad Ferrelli getting murdered."

"Yeah, it's all over the news."

"I was there. I was walking a dog, and I saw Conrad's car drive away real fast. At the time I thought it was Conrad, but now I know it was his killer."

"You saw him?"

"No, but he probably thinks I did."

Tom raised an eyebrow.

"I waved at him, Tom. I even yelled Hey."

"Shit, Dixie."

"That's what I mean."

"You think the guy in the truck was the one who killed Ferrelli?"

"Who else? Somebody wants me dead, Tom."

We stared at each other for a minute while the words bounced off the walls. They sounded melodramatic, but they were true.

Tom said, "Look, I can take Billy Elliot for a walk myself. I don't want you taking that risk again."

"No way, Tom. I'm not letting that son-of-a-bitch make me change anything. I'll run with Billy Elliot, and I'll walk every other dog in my care. I'll go on about my business same as always. I'll just do it a lot more carefully."

"You carrying?"

I patted the gun in my shorts pocket. "You bet, and I'm a damn good shot. I got a first-place marksmanship award at the Police Academy."

"Yeah, you're tough."

"Damn right."

I grabbed Billy Elliot's leash, snapped it on his collar, and quick-stepped to the elevator, wishing I felt as tough as I talked. Billy Elliot and I both stopped and looked both ways before we stepped into the parking lot. I wondered if Tom had given Billy Elliot a lecture about how to behave when in the company of a woman who might get herself run over.

Except for my scraped knees complaining, our run was no different than usual. When I took Billy Elliot back upstairs, Tom was in the kitchen busy with his accounting work and merely shouted good-bye. We were both doing a good job of pretending everything was normal.

After Billy Elliot, I only had three other dogs on my list. I walked two of them and then took care of the cats and birds and rabbits before I headed north on Midnight Pass

Road for Secret Cove. My mind kept going back to the driver of that truck. At the turn into Secret Cove, my car took over and kept going straight to the dogleg at Higel Avenue. City planners like to keep people on their toes by having streets change identity, so Higel makes a sharp right and becomes Siesta Drive, which goes over the north bridge to the mainland, where it becomes Bay before it crosses Tamiami Trail and becomes Bee Ridge.

I passed Video Renaissance and the tae kwon do studio on Bee Ridge, and turned left on a street of old frame houses where rusted sedans and dented pickups sat in driveways. I parked in front of a big garage with an open bay door and got out, shading my eyes to look inside the darker recess of the garage. Several collectors' cars sat in half-finished states, and I could hear the whining sound of something grinding on metal at the back of the shop.

Birdlegs Stephenson came out, wiping his hands on a rag and grinning ear to ear. I hadn't seen Birdlegs in several years, but he was still as skinny as ever, brown hair pulled back in a ducktail, long legs in faded holey jeans, his thin torso covered by a stained Bucs sweatshirt with the neck and sleeves cut out.

In high school, Birdlegs sat in front of me in algebra and fed me answers to stupid test questions like how long will it take a train to travel to Chicago if its smoke is blowing back at thirty miles per hour. Like there are still trains with smoke. That's how I learned to read papers on somebody else's desk without appearing to move my eyes. The trick is to tilt your chin upward and let your eyelids droop to half mast. That makes you look as if you're deep in thought, but in reality you're staring ahead and down, and if somebody just happens to casually move his test paper to the side of his desk, you can see what he did to solve that idiotic question. If Birdlegs hadn't let me cheat off his papers, I would have written *Who* cares? and never would have graduated high school.

He said, "Hey, Dixie, long time no see!"

"How're you doing, Birdlegs?"

"Can't complain, how about yourself?"

"Somebody in a hyped-up pickup on huge tires tried to run me down, and I want to find out who it was."

He raised his eyebrows and lowered his eyelids to look down at me, much the same way I used to look down at his test papers.

"What do you mean, they tried to run you down?"

"I mean I was running in a parking lot and they tried to hit me."

"Some of those guys put those things up so high they can't see the ground. Maybe they didn't know you were there."

"Trust me, Birdlegs, they knew I was there."

"Jesus, what'd you do?"

"Hit the ground and let it roll over me."

"Good God."

"That's how I felt about it."

"Did you see what make the truck was?"

"It was too dark to see anything."

"What size tires did it have?"

I held my hand flat beside my waist. "About this high."

He measured the distance to the ground with squinted eyes. "Probably forty-twos, maybe more. Tires that big aren't safe."

"Is that what they call a Monster?"

He laughed. "No, Monsters are up on about sixty-six-inch tires. You won't see any Monsters in a parking lot, just at fairs jumping over cars. What about the rack and pinion?"

"I don't know anything about racks or pinions, Birdlegs."

"Probably moved it," he mused. "Tires that big, they'd have to. Bet they used a chassis and a lift kit both. Boy, that's dangerous. Center of gravity that high and no good coil-over suspension system, that thing'd turn over if it hit a piece of gravel."

"Tough titty if it turns over, Birdlegs. It's the danger to me I'm worried about."

"I haven't heard anybody say tough titty in fifteen years, Dixie. Not since high school."

"I haven't matured much."

"I like that in a person."

"So do you know anybody who drives a rig like that?"

"Do I look like a redneck to you? Most of those guys are young, feeling their oats, makes them feel big to sit up high looking down on people. Then they get wives and babies and have to come down to earth. Take off the big tires and be like everybody else."

"This one tried to kill me, Birdlegs. You'll forgive me if I don't get misty-eyed over his lost dreams."

He laughed. "Sorry. I guess I was talking more about myself. Remembering what it was like to do things that dumb. Most of those old boys are okay, though. Just because they drive those dumb high-risers doesn't make them killers. Tell you what. I'll ask around, see if anybody I know has any idea who it might have been."

"I'd appreciate it, Birdlegs."

"What're you going to do if you find him? I mean, if you don't have any proof, you can't arrest him, can you?"

"I couldn't arrest him even if I had proof, Birdlegs. I'm not a deputy anymore."

He reddened, suddenly remembering. "Oh, hell, Dixie, I forgot what happened. I'm sorry, I wouldn't have mentioned it—"

"It's okay. Tell me about that car over there."

Relieved, he looked at the dreamy convertible I was pointing at. It had a glossy red body, black leather interior, lots of shiny chrome, and a sleek silver hood ornament.

"Ain't that a beauty? That's a Honda S-six hundred, 1964. Only a few hundred of them still around. Sweetest little car you ever saw. First car Honda mass-marketed. Fifty-seven horsepower engine and a top speed of ninety miles per hour."

"You did all the work on it?"

"It was a rusted mess. Guy imported it from some place in South America. I'm gonna hate to see it go."

"What does something like that sell for?"

"Restored like this, about twenty, twenty-five thousand."

"Is that all? I'd think it would be a lot more."

"Nah, they're not in the big leagues, they're just sweet little cars."

"Who owns it?"

"Guy named Brossi. Leo Brossi. He collects vintage cars. Buys them and sells them."

Carefully, I said, "Is he somebody I should have heard of?"

"Nah, he's not anybody. Just rich. Owns a call center over on Fruitville."

"Must be a successful call center."

"Must be. I guess the no-call business hasn't hurt those places much. They still call me anyway, and I'm on the no-call list. Who has time to report every one of them? They probably get away with it a lot."

"Is Brossi going to pick the car up soon?"

"Yeah, it's done."

"Birdlegs, do you know a state senator named Wayne Black?"

"Sure, Dixie, I hang out with senators and governors and A-rab potentates all the time."

"How about Quenton Dyer? He's a banker."

"Him neither."

He was beginning to look toward the work he'd left, so I thanked him for his time and started to leave.

"Call me if you find out who might drive that raised truck, okay?"

"Sure thing, Dixie."

I was tempted to tell him to call me when Leo Brossi came in to pick up his restored Honda S600. I was beginning to be very curious about Leo Brossi.

Mame wasn't waiting by the door when I got to her house. I found her in the kitchen sitting in front of her food bowl. I knelt beside her and stroked her head.

"Hey, Mame, sorry I'm late. I had to go see somebody about a car."

She licked the inside of my arm and gave me a forgiving look.

All the kibble was gone, which was a good sign. At least she'd been eating. I washed her bowl and got out the big bag of senior kibble and put about a tablespoon in it in case she got hungry during the night. Then I picked her up and carried her to the lanai for a little play time. She didn't seem inclined to play, though, so I sat down in a padded glider and held her in my lap, stroking her and gently rocking.

Lanais on Siesta Key are enclosed by screened cages shaped by black or white aluminum ribbing. The Powells' cage had black ribs and soared two stories high, coming to a gazebolike point above the roof of the house. The swimming pool occupied the far side, and the inner side was protected from the elements by a wide overhang to which the cage was attached. Sitting under the sheltered roof and looking through the screen at the sky and trees and flowers was like being in a luxurious birdcage with a really big water dish.

Songbirds were calling to one another, and young red-shouldered hawks were wheeling above the palms. A line of enormous sunflowers stood at the back of the lot, their fuzzy green stalks twisted hopefully toward the declining sun. A squirrel suddenly raced up the lanai screen holding a sunflower big as a dinner plate. He held the stem in his teeth, with the flower head facing the lanai, so it looked as if the sunflower was zipping up the screen by itself. Mame and I went still and breathless until the moving sunflower disappeared over the roof, and then we looked at each other with wide-eyed amazement.

I said, "My gosh, did you see that?"

Mame didn't answer, but her eyes were still bright with excitement when I told her good-bye. That racing sunflower had been a once-in-a-lifetime event for both of us.

My feet were dragging when I got out of the Bronco and went to Stevie's front door. When she opened it, she looked as weary as I felt.

She said, "Thanks for coming by, Dixie." But she didn't move out of the doorway, and her voice was flat.

"Do you need me?"

She gave me an apologetic half smile. "Not really. I walked Reggie earlier, and I'm going to turn in early."

I started to go, and she put out a hand. "Don't think I don't appreciate your stopping by. It's just that everything is so . . ."

She leaned her head against the edge of the door and closed her eyes, clearly overcome by fatigue and stress.

"Stevie, I understand. You need to rest. I'll stop by in the morning in case you need anything."

She gave me a grateful smile and closed her door. Every cell in my body ached as my heavy legs carried me back to the Bronco. With each step, I whispered "Ouch, ouch, shit, fuck, ouch." I felt as if I had gained about a hundred pounds since my alarm went off at 4 A.M. I hoped Michael and Paco would be there when I got home. Maybe they would have dinner with me and give me some advice. Or at least some pity.

I drove south down Midnight Pass Road, past the village and the fire station where Michael works, past the vacation condos and apartment complexes and waterside restaurants, and finally eased the Bronco down my twisty tree-lined lane. Paco's car was in the carport, and so was his Harley, but Michael's car was still gone. I parked next to Paco's car and gave the storage closets a fast scan to make sure they were still padlocked from the outside. I pulled my .38 from my pocket, holding it out of sight as I pushed the door open. Even with Paco home, I wasn't taking any chances.

The air under the carport felt like steam rising from a wet dog, but when I stepped into the clear, a whisper of sea breeze moved across my skin. I stopped a moment and looked toward the descending sun, then put my gun back in my pocket. In the presence of such beauty, a weapon of death is an obscenity. The back door opened and Paco strolled out to watch the sunset with me. We didn't speak, just stood side by side watching an enormous garnet orb touch the sea, hover for a quivering minute, then give itself to the water in a velvet slide that turned sea and sky ruby red.

After a few minutes, I took a deep breath of salty air.

Paco squeezed the back of my neck with gentle fingers that knew how to find the point that could stun or kill.

I said, "Where's Michael?"

"He's covering for another fireman whose wife had a premature baby. Four-pound boy. It's little, but they think it'll be fine."

"Awwww."

"You wanta go for sushi?"

My heart lifted. Michael calls sushi expensive bait and won't touch it, but Paco and I slip off and indulge sometimes when Michael's gone.

I said, "Ten minutes."

Paco said, "Make it fifteen, and wear something hot. I'm tired of seeing you in that grunge getup."

My heart lifted higher. I needed to feel sexy. Sexy feels powerful. And nobody in the world can make a woman feel as sexy as a gay man.

15

I hustled upstairs to shower and smooth my aching self with a sweet coconut scrub that left me smelling faintly of piña colada. When I patted dry, I was tender with my purple rib cage and pelvis bones. Since I was going for sexy, I did a little creative work with makeup to disguise the bruise on my cheek. To cover my scraped knees, I put on a long white knit skirt slit nearly up to my crotch in the back. Then I pawed around in the stacks of knit tops on my closet shelves and found a hip-hugging black halter with a low V neckline. I put on strappy sandals with tall heels, screwed my hair on the top of my head with some errant strands falling down as if by chance, and stuck my .38 in a slim black straw purse.

Before I went out the French doors, I fished my client codebook and key ring out of my backpack. I put the codebook in my purse and stowed the key ring in the floor safe in the corner of my closet. Ordinarily, I feel they're safe in my apartment when I'm gone, but that night I didn't feel like anything was safe in my apartment, including me.

Paco was waiting for me downstairs on the wooden deck, and we both made exaggerated sounds of appreciation at each other's knockout beauty. Except I wasn't exaggerating. When Paco's in full prowl, he's like a healthy young panther, sleek and gorgeous. His shiny black hair was rumpled just enough to look suggestive but not messy, and he wore black slacks made of some mystery fabric that fell without clinging to his legs but molded to one of the best butts in the universe. His shirt was clingy black silk that hugged his broad shoulders and slim torso like hot resin oozing from a cedar plank. I had no doubt that he wore an ankle holster under his black slacks, and possibly some other hidden weapons in his armpit or waistband.

I said, "Aren't you working tonight?"

"Nope, called in sick. Let's roll."

The best sushi in Sarasota is at the Pacific Rim on Hillview. As we followed the young sari-clad hostess to a spot in the center of the room, female jaws fell open all over the room at the sight of Paco, and some women at the sushi counter nearly toppled off their stools. Jealous eyes sent me viperous looks that hoped I'd eat bad blow-fish and die. If they had known that Paco's heart beat fast only for my brother, their ovaries would have lain down and wept.

A waiter skimmed over the floor with twin baskets of cold damp towels and cups of tea. We wiped our hands on the towels and told the waiter we didn't need to see a menu, we knew what we wanted: Thai beer, sashimi, the chef's selection of sushi, spiced noodles, and cucumber salads.

When the beers came, Paco held his glass up in a toast. "To the woman who stood down a monster truck and won."

I grimaced and clicked his glass with mine. "You heard about that?"

"Honey, every cop in Sarasota County has heard about that. Nobody can remember anybody else doing what you did. That took some fast thinking."

"Todd told me to hit the dirt, Paco. I heard his voice in my head clear as day."

I tapped the right side of my head to show him where I'd heard it, but I could tell he wasn't sure he believed me.

Our waiter brought the sashimi, fresh, delicate, thin-sliced, and served with raw vegetables and citrus-flavored ponzu sauce. I added a lot of wasabi to my ponzu, and Paco shuddered.

I said, "I like things hot."

"That's because you don't have any sex. It's compensation."

It was a familiar refrain. For the last year, Michael and Paco had been on a dedicated campaign to get me to find a man. They had loved Todd like a brother, but they both thought it was time for me to live like a normal woman. They didn't seem to understand that I didn't have a button I could push that would make me stop imagining Todd by my side.

I pointed a chopstick at him. "Never antagonize a woman with a sharp pointy thing in her hand."

Paco grinned and popped a slice of amberjack in his mouth, then followed it with a dab of shredded daikon, tossing it back as deftly as an Egyptian eating a rice ball without letting it touch his lips. Paco uses chopsticks the way he does everything else, gracefully and surely. When I eat with chopsticks, I'm slow and careful because I'm mortally afraid I'll accidentally miss my mouth and poke myself in the eye. I'd get a lot more eaten if I used a fork. I personally believe that's why Asian women are so dainty and petite. They're malnourished, poor things, because women's hands aren't made for handling chopsticks. If Asian women ate with forks, they'd be as big and gawky as Caucasian women.

The waiter brought our sushi, and I put my chopsticks down and ate a cucumber roll with my fingers.

I said, "The guy in the truck is still out there."

Paco used his chopsticks to pinch a tuna roll and dip it in soy sauce.

He said, "People are looking for him. There aren't that many jacked-up trucks around here. They'll find him."

"Paco, I can't identify anybody. I can't identify the driver of the car I saw after Conrad Ferrelli was killed, and I can't identify the driver of that truck."

He grunted and concentrated on the sashimi and sushi.

After the noodles arrived, he said, "You think they were the same people?"

"Who?"

"The car and the truck, doofus."

"Oh. Yes. I don't know. Maybe."

"As long as you're sure."

He leaned back to let the waiter put down chilled vine-gared cucumber in thin green strips.

I said, "Paco, Guidry said that Denton Ferrelli was playing golf with Leo Brossi and two other guys at the time Conrad was killed. A state senator named Wayne Black and a banker named Quenton Dyer. You ever hear of Brossi or the other men?"

Paco's jaw tightened and he leaned across the table and looked fiercely at me.

"Dixie, I want you to listen to me very clearly: Keep. Out. Of. This. There are things about this killing that are a lot bigger than just a murder. A *lot* bigger. If you go around asking questions, you will be hurt. I don't mean you *might* be hurt, I mean you *will* be hurt. Let the cops handle it. You understand?"

He looked so vicious that I shrank back in my chair. This was a side of Paco I rarely saw, the undercover cop side that knew things and went places and did things I couldn't even imagine.

I said, "I'm not going around asking questions."

"Did you or did you not go to see Virgil Stephenson today asking questions about the truck?"

Birdlegs is Virgil?

"How do you know about that?"

He sighed. "Once again, Dixie. This is a lot bigger than a murder. Please, please, please listen to me. Keep your mouth shut, don't talk to anybody, don't ask any questions. Got it?"

Sloppily, I used my chopsticks to pluck up some sweet-tart cucumber salad. I felt like a mother bird gathering worms to feed her nestlings. The salad was cool, delicious, creamy. When I put my chopsticks down, my hand was trembling.

Paco reached across the table and covered my hand. "Dixie, I love you. I don't want to see you hurt. Okay?"

I blinked a couple of times to get rid of stupid tears before I raised my head and looked at him. His dark eyes were intent and determined and kind. I looked away toward the sushi counter, where several women thought Paco and I were having a lovers' quarrel. They were watching us with hope on their faces, each one poised to grab Paco if he dumped me. Paco realized what they thought at the same moment, and we both burst out laughing.

When we got home, I said good night and started up the stairs to my apartment, but Paco followed me.

I said, "What're you doing?"

"I'm spending the night with you."

I turned and looked down at him, for a hysterical second thinking maybe I'd accomplished every woman's fantasy and converted a gay guy.

"Guidry told you to stay with me, didn't he?"

"Who?"

I slammed my hand on the railing. "Damn it, Paco, I don't need a babysitter!"

He passed me, leaving me glaring at his beautiful buns as he continued to climb the stairs.

"Didn't say you did, babe. Like I told you, this is bigger than a murder, so I'm spending the night here. Anyway, Michael would crunch my balls with a lug wrench if I let anything happen to his little sister."

I looked around, at the silver sea and pale shore behind me and the towering dark trees on either side. I didn't have anything to fear from the sea, but the trees could shelter more than birds and squirrels. For the second time that day, I heard Todd's voice. *This isn't about you, Dixie.*

Okay, maybe it wasn't Todd's voice. Maybe it was the memory of his voice and my grandfather's voice and Michael's voice and Sergeant Owens's voice and every other male voice that had caught me up when I was beginning to think the world revolved around my concerns and reminded me that it didn't. Paco knew things I didn't know. Guidry knew things I didn't know. Conrad Ferrelli's murder was somehow involved in something even darker and more sinister than murder. I just happened to be a tiny little grain of grit in a large dirt ball.

I followed Paco up the stairs and got the door keys from under the gun in my purse.

I said, "Do you want me to unfold the sofa bed?"

"Nah, just give me a pillow."

I went to find him a pillow and sheet, and when I came back he was in the kitchen looking at the iron bell thing hanging in front of my window.

He said, "Bitchin' alarm, babe."

"You're not going to take off your clothes and walk around my apartment naked, are you?"

"Wouldn't think of it."

"Damn."

"When we catch the guy, maybe you can see him naked."

I wondered if he had said "when *we* catch him" on purpose, or if I wasn't supposed to guess that the SIB was involved in a murder investigation. In either case, I intended to play dumb. Not that I would have to pretend very hard, but I wasn't quite as dumb as I seemed.

I also wasn't as obedient as I seemed. While I appreciated that law-enforcement officers were the only ones who could or should be doing the investigating, they weren't the ones who had faced a homicidal truck bearing down on them like a nightmare from hell. Furthermore, they weren't the ones who had only recently clawed their way from victimized weakness to a semblance of self-respect. If I slunk away in meek silence, all the gains I'd made in the last year would be lost, and I would once again be at the mercy of forces larger and more powerful than myself.

I would be careful. I would not tread on the law's toes. But I would not wait for the sheriff's department to find the person who had killed Conrad and wanted to kill me.

16

I slept hard until four o'clock, when the alarm went off, and woke knowing I'd felt safer with Paco in the living room. I hit the alarm and stumbled down the hall to the bathroom, trying to be quiet so Paco could sleep. But when I had brushed teeth and hair, pulled on clean shorts and a T, and laced up fresh white Keds, Paco was up and at the door waiting for me.

He said, "You have your gun?"

"Sure. Oh, wait, I forgot my keys."

I did a U-turn back to the closet to retrieve the client keys from the floor safe. I knelt in the corner of my closet and pulled up the loose floor tile. I opened the top of the floor safe and then leaped backward, screaming. I collided with Paco in the closet door, and for a second we did a crazed dance while I tried to get past him and he tried to come in.

Then he looked over my shoulder and yelled, "Holy shit!"

A pygmy rattler had slithered out of the floor safe and was streaking toward us like lightning.

Paco began running, pulling me with him. I didn't need any help, I was moving fast.

Pygmy rattlers are aggressive and mean, especially when they've been confined in a tiny space like my floor safe. Their venom can be lethal, or it can cause you to lose a foot or a hand. The snake was dark gray, about twenty-five inches long, with a thick body, distinctive triangular head, and dark blotches along a reddish brown stripe running down the center of its back. It was pissed, its rattles sounded like a bumblebee.

Paco and I raced for the living room sofa and climbed on it. We watched the floor for the snake, which didn't appear. My heart was lurching crazily, and I kept remembering the folk myth that snakes always travel in pairs. But this snake hadn't traveled on its own, it had been placed in my floor safe while Paco and I were eating sushi.

After a while, I sat down on the arm of the couch. "I don't hear it, do you?"

He sat down on the other arm and listened. "No. What does that mean?"

"I don't know. I guess it means it's not shaking its tail."

"But it could be lying in wait."

"Yeah. What're you going to do?"

"What do you mean, what am I going to do? I'm not a snake handler!"

"Maybe you could just run in the closet and get my keys so I can go take care of my pets. Then you could call somebody to come get it."

He gave me a round white-eyed glare.

"If it comes in here, I'll shoot the son-of-a-bitch, but I'm not going in that closet."

Paco spent his life infiltrating mobs and gangs ruled by vicious killers. He went into situations that would make the Terminator pee himself, but he seemed about as freaked by the snake as I was.

"Sissy."

"Shit, Dixie."

"Michael would get it."

"Michael's a fucking fireman. Snakes don't bother him."

We sat morosely for a couple of minutes, and then Paco stood up and gave me a desperate look.

"I'm going in there and get your keys, Dixie. But I swear if that snake bites me—"

I gave him a tremulous smile and a perky thumbs-up.

He took long strides, setting his feet down as quietly as he could, and disappeared from view. In a few seconds I heard a metallic jingle and Paco came sprinting back, carrying my key ring.

He climbed back on the couch and said, "You owe me big-time, Dixie."

"I do."

He dropped the keys in my open palm. I tried not to think about snake spit on them.

Paco said, "Okay, go walk your dogs. I'll call somebody to come get the damned snake."

I stood up on the sofa and gave him a cautious hug, both of us nervously watching the floor. I took my gun out of my pocket, slid off the end of the sofa, and scurried to the French doors, anxiously waiting while the hurricane shutters folded upward.

As I opened the doors, Paco said, "Dixie? You understand what this means, don't you?"

"I understand, Paco."

"Okay. I love you, kid."

I smiled at him. "Me too."

The sky was taking on the pearly sheen of false dawn, and a sleepy sea was halfheartedly lapping at the shoreline. A few mourning doves were beginning to check their voices to see if they still worked, and some early-waking cranes were stalking along the beach looking for breakfast. I said a silent good morning to the day and clattered down the stairs to my Bronco.

When I got to the end of the long curvy drive and turned north onto Midnight Pass Road, an unmarked car that had been parked on the shoulder pulled behind me. I would have been scared if it hadn't been such a nondescript car. No self-respecting murderer would drive a car like that. Guidry must have assigned a deputy to follow me. He wasn't making any effort to be invisible either, so the department wanted me to know I was being guarded. I gave a sentimental gulp until I realized that it wasn't just for my safety that Guidry wanted me tailed. I was like a little fish around a killer whale. Conrad Ferrelli's killer was after me. If the cops followed little me, they had a better chance of catching big dangerous him.

At the Sea Breeze, the tail pulled into a space at the far corner of the lot and waited while I ran with Billy Elliot. When I left the Sea Breeze, it left too, staying about half a block behind. It was with me for the rest of the morning, dropping farther back as traffic began to move on Midnight Pass Road, always parking well away from the site I went to. After a while I sort of forgot about it. I followed my usual routine, zigzagging back and forth between the Gulf side and the bay side of Midnight Pass Road, either to a condo on the main thoroughfare or down a short tree-lined lane to a private home.

I was on a lanai pulling my slicker brush through an American shorthair's gray coat when I realized the full significance of the snake in my safe. The safe had originally been installed to hold valuables like jewelry or money, but since I didn't have any valuables, I used it as a kind of unlocked fireproof holder of important papers. The person who put the snake in the safe had wanted to let me know he was familiar with my apartment and its secrets.

I finished grooming the cat and set him on the floor; then I pulled out my cell phone and called Paco. The phone rang several times before he answered, and his voice sounded breathless.

He said, "They're here now—the snake guys. They've got him."

I said, "Paco, before they leave, have them pull my bed out from the wall. There's a drawer on that side of the bed. Ask them to open the drawer, but tell them to do it carefully."

There was a pregnant silence on the other end of the line. Then I heard Paco's muffled voice as he held the phone to his chest and called to the men in my apartment. I waited. In a minute or two the line became clear, and I heard thundering footsteps and shouts in the background.

A man yelled, "Use the hook! Use the hook! Goddamn it, use the hook!"

Somebody else laughed, and another man yelled, "Wa-hoo!"

Paco said, "Sweet Jesus."

I said, "I slept on top of rattlesnakes last night, didn't I?"

"Just one."

"Are you standing on the couch?"

"You bet your sweet ass."

"Are the guns still in the compartment?"

He held the phone to his chest again and yelled a question, then came back to me.

"They say there are three guns in Styrofoam niches. A nine-millimeter Glock, a Colt three-fifty-seven, and a Smith and Wesson thirty-two."

A cold shiver ran up my spine. The gun drawer hadn't exactly been a secret, but I hadn't told anybody about it, not even Michael or Paco.

He said, "Those were Todd's personals, weren't they?"

"The Glock and the Colt were. The thirty-two is mine."

Paco's voice was grim. "I'll have them check every inch of the place, Dixie."

I said, "More than likely they won't find anything. Somebody just wanted me to know I don't have any secrets."

There was more shouting in the background, and Paco began speaking in a rush.

"Michael just got home, Dixie. He's a little bit—uh, rabid. I'll call you later."

He clicked off, and I grimaced in sympathy for him. Every man gets in a bad mood when he feels that he's failed to protect his loved ones. When Michael gets in a bad mood, he's like Godzilla on steroids. I was glad I wasn't there to hear it.

I pressed the hang-up button on my phone. Now the phone showed only two batteries on its screen. As if I didn't have enough stress, my stupid phone was nagging me to charge it. You'd think some electronic wizard could design a battery-free phone so our lives wouldn't be controlled by little passive-aggressive boxes and their blinking demands.

I told the cat good-bye, gathered up my grooming equipment, locked the front door behind me, and went out to the Bronco. I felt numb, too scared even to work up a decent case of the shakes. I started the motor and let the AC run while I called Guidry. Surprisingly, he answered on the first ring.

I said, "Thanks for the tail."

"Don't mention it."

"Do you know about the snake in my apartment?"

"Sorry about that. I thought you'd be okay last night with Paco. We didn't watch your place while you were gone."

"I was just on the phone with Paco. There was another one in a drawer under my bed where I keep my guns. I slept on it last night."

My voice went up an octave, and I recognized, with a kind of clinical detachment, the sound of rising hysteria.

Guidry must have recognized it too, because he said, "We're not going to let anything happen to you."

I clicked off and laid my head on the steering wheel. I felt the way a lobster must feel when it's been out of salt water too long, like I was shrinking inside my own skin. Every instinct told me Denton Ferrelli was responsible for his brother's death and for those rattlesnakes in my apartment. Every instinct told me he was responsible for the truck that had tried to run me down. If he hadn't done it himself, he had hired somebody to do it.

This is war, I thought, and then almost laughed at myself for thinking it. How many times had I heard our grandfather say that? Probably half a million at least. If the county sent a tax bill he thought was outrageous, if the fishing commission declared a quota on red snapper, or if an invasion of no-see-ums sent him running for cover, he would bellow, "This is war!" Well, okay, so I'm my grandfather's progeny. I don't take injustice.

I got out my nagging phone and called Information to

get Denton Ferrelli's office phone number. When I called it, a woman with a voice all in her nose obliged with the address. With the tail following me like exhaust smoke, I headed for one of the glass-fronted mainland high-rises facing the marina. I took a glass elevator to the penthouse and stepped into a lobby the size of my entire apartment. A sleek young woman wearing a red power suit sat in front of a telephone at an antique library table. She gave my hairy shorts a sneering glance and smiled frostily. If she'd known I had a .38 in my pocket and venom in my heart, she might not have looked so friggin' smug.

I said, "Tell Denton Ferrelli that Dixie Hemingway is here to see him."

She gave me a bunched-mouth little smile and said, "I'm sorry, Mr. Ferrelli isn't in."

This was definitely a woman who had let a career of answering a phone go to her head.

I wheeled away toward the row of closed doors. "Never mind, I'll find him."

She scrambled under the edge of her desk for an alarm bell, and I hotfooted it to the widest, most impressive-looking door and turned the knob. Denton Ferrelli and another man were sitting opposite each other in deep black leather chairs. Behind them, a glass wall overlooked the sun-sparkled blue marina and its rows of boats. It was a view that must have given relief to eyes strained from studying multimillion-dollar deals.

The woman in the red suit ran up behind me and screeched, "I told her you couldn't see her, Mr. Ferrelli!"

Denton Ferrelli smiled lazily, those cobra-lidded eyes fixed in place. "Never mind, honey, I'll take care of it."

I said, "The rattlesnakes were cute, Mr. Ferrelli."

He gave me a blank look that was either a terrific act or genuinely ignorant.

He said, "I don't know what you're talking about, but I assume it has something to do with your fetish for animals." He tilted his head toward the man with him. "Leo Brossi, this is Conrad's dog-sitter. She's a big animal lover."

Brossi was a lot smaller than Denton, probably not taller than me, and slim as a knife blade. He had a deep leathery tan and hair the brassy pink of a copper pan that's had tomato juice spilled on it. He looked up at me with a smirk.

"Does that mean you like being fucked by big dogs?"

I don't remember what happened next because I sort of blacked out for a minute. When I came to I was punching Leo Brossi's head with both fists and he was cowering in the chair and cursing. Denton had risen to stand next to Brossi, and he was leering at me. It was the leer that stopped me. Denton was getting a hard-on from watching me beat the crap out of Leo Brossi.

I jerked my hands away and stepped back, breathing hard and thinking how nice it would be to see Denton Ferrelli sail through the glass wall into the marina.

Behind me, red suit whinnied, "Do you want me to call the police, Mr. Ferrelli?"

Denton Ferrelli shook his head. "That won't be necessary. The dog-sitter just got a little carried away."

Leo Brossi's nose was streaming blood down his shirtfront, and it looked like one of his eyes was on the way to swelling shut. He was glaring from me to Denton like an agitated tennis fan.

I said, "My name is Dixie Hemingway. I suggest you remember it."

I spun around and went through the door, feeling their eyes on me as I marched across the lobby to the elevator. I felt good. I felt damn good. I'd done a stupid, irresponsible thing, and I was glad.

But on the ride down in the elevator, I remembered the blank expression Denton had given me when I mentioned the rattlesnakes. I didn't want to believe it, but it was possible that he hadn't had anything to do with the snakes in my apartment. And if he hadn't, who had?

In the parking lot, the tail was on his cell phone with a worried frown on his face. He looked relieved when he saw me come out, and hurriedly hung up. My own cell phone was ringing by the time I got in the Bronco. I didn't need to look at the ID readout to know it was Guidry. I didn't answer it. I wanted to savor this delicious feeling of victory for a while longer before I had to face the fact that I hadn't won anything at all, and there was a good chance I had put myself in even more danger than I'd been in before.

A little voice in my head said, *Now see, that's the reason why you can't be a deputy anymore.*

The little voice was right, but I still wasn't sorry. Hitting Leo Brossi had felt better than anything I'd done in a long time.

17

I took Tamiami Trail along the marina's curve to Osprey Avenue, then turned on Siesta Drive to go over the north bridge and back to Siesta Key. I wanted to explore the odd look that had passed between Josephine and Pete and Priscilla when I told them about the truck trying to run me down. Too many people knew things I didn't know. I don't like being ignorant, especially when my life is on the line.

At the Metzgers' house, Priscilla opened the door and silently beckoned me inside. She was wearing a knit top about the size of a cocktail napkin, and her thin upper arms bore large purple thumb bruises. I followed her down the hall and looked anxiously at the baby in the playpen. She was unmarked and standing, smiling happily at her mother. When I looked at Josephine, she was watching me with a veiled woman-to-woman acknowledgment in her eyes.

Josephine said, "Your bruises are looking better, Dixie."

She stressed *your*, and Priscilla reddened.

I said, "Remember the truck that chased me? Can't be too many of them around. I'd like to know if either of you knows somebody with a truck like that."

Josephine's mouth tightened and her eyes flicked toward Priscilla, but she shook her head.

"If I knew somebody was trying to kill you, Dixie, I sure wouldn't keep quiet about it."

Priscilla blushed again, but she kept her head bent over her sewing machine. The baby squealed and pumped her chubby knees while she held the top rail of the playpen with both hands. I went over to the baby and picked her up. I couldn't help myself. She gave me a beatific smile and drooled on my hand.

Priscilla said, "Ooooh, gross!" and leaped up to dry my fingers with a tissue. "She's teething," she said. "I hope it won't last much longer."

She spoke in a child's breathless rush. I supposed she'd never spoken in my presence before because she hadn't had anything to say.

Josephine looked up from her sewing machine and Priscilla hurried back to her own place. She was stitching something that looked like a monster tutu. I remembered when Christy had drooled like that when her teeth were coming in, but I didn't remember being grossed out about it the way Priscilla was. The difference probably was that I had been twenty-six when she was born and I doubted that Priscilla was even eighteen.

As I put the baby back in her playpen and helped her find her chew toy, Josephine said, "Dixie have you heard from Pete? He remembered something he wanted to tell you. Something about Denton Ferrelli and a man named Brossi."

Priscilla's head bobbed up from behind her sewing machine, then she bent back to the tutu thing.

The baby squealed at me, and I leaned over and smoothed the fine hair on her head.

I said, "She'll be walking soon."

Priscilla looked up and smiled proudly. "I walk her around a lot to give her practice."

I smiled. "I did that too, with my little girl."

"You have a little girl?"

"I did. She was killed when she was three."

I was shocked to hear myself say that. I'd never before spoken of Christy so easily, never before put her into a normal conversation like that. Somehow it felt right to do it, as if she were still with me, living in my words about her.

The room was silent, both sewing machines brought to a halt, a tiny moment of recognition of Christy.

I said, "I have a dog waiting for me. I'd better be on my way."

Neither of them said good-bye, just gave me silent waves. Nobody seemed to want to intrude on the moment that had just passed.

As I was getting into the Bronco, Priscilla ran out and put her hand on my arm.

In her sweet little-girl voice, she said, "What you said . . . about somebody chasing you in a truck?"

"Uh-hunh?"

"Well, the thing is, I may know somebody who has a truck like that—one of those trucks up on big tires. . . ."

Her voice faded more with each word until it was almost nonexistent, as if she were losing all the air in her lungs as she talked. I waited a moment to give her a chance to go on, but she seemed unable to say more.

"Priscilla, do you think you might know who tried to kill me?"

"Oh, I don't think he would really kill you. He probably just wanted to scare you. I mean, he's not like that."

It has been my experience that women who say about violent men, *he's not like that* are missing the obvious. I mean, if he does it, that's what he is.

I opened my mouth to set her straight and then thought better of it.

"This person you know, can you tell me who it is?"

"Well, if I did, would it get him in trouble?"

It was such a dumb question that I couldn't think how to answer it. What did she think, that I planned to send him a Hallmark card? When all else fails, go with the truth.

"Priscilla, the person driving that truck is mixed up in something a lot bigger than trying to run me down."

"And that would get him in trouble?"

I suddenly realized there was a note of hope in her voice. She wasn't worried about getting the guy in trouble, she *wanted* to get him in trouble.

"It would get him in *big* trouble."

"Okay, I'll think about it. Bye."

She whirled away and ran inside. I stared after her and gritted my teeth. Damn! Trying to coax Priscilla to tell me what she knew would be like training a cat to use a commode. Possible, but only with an incredible amount of patience, a trait I was fresh out of right then.

I looked at my watch and groaned. It was after ten, and I still hadn't made it to Mame's house. With Mame's old bladder, she shouldn't be left so long without going outside. Guiltily, I jerked the Bronco into reverse out of the driveway and sped off so fast the tail parked at the curb fishtailed when he started after me.

At the entrance to Secret Cove, I slowed to the ten-mile-an-hour limit on the narrow brick-paved street. In that green tunnel of leafy oaks, everything seemed serene and safe. Mame was waiting at the glass insert by her front door, and she did a little happy bounce at my feet when I came in. After I took her out back to pee in the bahia grass, she trotted with me to the kitchen and watched me put out fresh water and food for her. Then we ambled out to the lanai for her morning brushing. The sky was a smooth sweep of robin's-egg blue, yellow butterflies were flitting around an overgrown bush of lemon oregano outside the lanai door, and a woodpecker was rhythmically drumming on a mossy oak in the backyard. If I hadn't known better, I would have been lulled into believing the world was pure and innocent.

After her brushing, Mame and I played chase-the-tennis-ball until we were both winded, and then I nuzzled her good-bye and left her watching me through the glass by the door. The temperature was climbing toward 90 degrees now, and the air was beginning to suck the energy out of anything living. The tail had parked behind me in the driveway. His head was tilted back on his headrest and his eyes were closed. He was older than I had thought, his jaws soft and slack, with the look of somebody more accustomed to a desk job than following a woman around in the heat.

When I slammed the Bronco door, I watched him in the

rearview mirror. He jerked upright, quickly started his engine, and whipped into the street so I could back out of the driveway. Only problem was that he pulled out in the short direction leading to the Ferrelli house. The street was too narrow for me to pass him, and it seemed churlish to make him come back in and back out the other way, so I headed in the only direction he'd left me.

All I had to do was turn right at the looped end of the street and drive the extra distance past the summer-closed waterside properties to Stevie's house. But in the short stretch to the turn, I thought about what Priscilla had said about the truck. She obviously knew something, and my guess was that Josephine and Pete did too. Josephine had evidently decided to wait and let Priscilla tell me in her own time, but Pete might be persuaded to talk.

I slowed to a stop and pulled out the card Pete had given me with his clown class address. On the back, he had scribbled the days and hours he taught. Class was going on right now, so with the deputy tail close behind me, I headed north, back over the bridge toward Lockwood Ridge Road.

Sarasota has been a circus town since the late twenties, when John Ringling made it the winter quarters for the Ringling Brothers and Barnum & Bailey Circus. My parents grew up seeing famous performers like Lou Jacobs, Emmett Kelly, and the Flying Wallendas on the street. They watched the filming of *The Greatest Show on Earth*, and during the world premiere went to the big circus parade down Main Street. Sarasota High School kids still perform high-wire and trapeze acts at Sailor Circus, and a second generation of the original Sarasota circus people have established Circus Sarasota, a European-style one-ring circus. Circus is so much a part of Sarasota that I'd always taken it for granted, like the manatees and dolphins.

Pete's clown class was in a one-story white stucco building with circus murals painted on the outside walls. A huge black-topped parking lot surrounded it, but there were only about two dozen cars. I parked the Bronco and went into a deserted lounge with a long bar running along one side and a scattering of round cocktail tables in the middle. I threaded my way through the tables, following the sound of laughter, and found another room that had the look of a restaurant's main dining area, with all the tables rearranged so people could see the speaker. Pete stood at the front of the room, and everybody else was intently watching him.

He grinned when he saw me, and I waggled my fingers at him and took a seat at a table by the door. I had expected the class to be young people, but they were mostly middle-aged or older, with a sprinkling of teenagers. All of them had friendly open faces and bright inquisitive eyes.

Pete took up his lecture where he'd left off. "You've learned wardrobe, juggling, and makeup. From now on we'll be concentrating on skits. Before this course ends, we'll go to some hospitals and perform skits. In the circus, skits are called gags. There are some standard gags like the Firehouse Gag that every clown knows, but you'll be creating your own gags too. You have to do it the same way a movie director plans a scene—seeing it the way the audience will see it. A gag has three parts: the beginning, the middle, and the blowup. You set the situation in the beginning, lead the audience to believe a certain outcome in the middle, and surprise them with a different outcome in the end. My old friend Angelo Ferrelli—known to you as Madam Flutter-By—was a master at creating clever skits."

One of the teenagers said, "Was he an Auguste?"

Pete looked pained. "No, he was a Whiteface. For those of you who don't remember, Auguste makeup is in natural tones. In traditional skits, the Whiteface clown has the dominant, more dignified role, while the character or tramp clown is the one who gets kicked in the pants or hit with a pie. Tramp makeup is scruffy and unshaven like Emmett Kelly. Regardless of type, a clown is called a *joey*, and when a joey dies, we say he's done his last walkabout."

Pete disappeared behind a screen and, in what seemed like only a couple of seconds, reappeared transformed by a wild red wig, a round red nose, and baggy plaid pants. He and a woman named Loretta then demonstrated a skit that hung on her explaining how to fold a bandanna, while Pete followed instructions using a banana. It was silly and childish and made me laugh so hard I forgot about murder and fear and venomous snakes.

The skit ended with Pete looking foolishly at his plastic-lined pockets, where he had put his folded banana. Behind him, Loretta was surreptitiously squirting shaving cream onto a paper plate.

She balanced the filled plate on her fingertips and said, "Hey, Pete!" When Pete raised his head, she hit him square in the face with the pie, which for some reason caused us all to howl uproariously. Loretta tenderly brushed away the foam with a soft whisk while students furiously scribbled notes.

Pete said, "We don't use whipping cream for pies because it makes such a mess."

He turned to the audience. "Speaking of making a mess, anybody know why we don't throw confetti in the circus anymore?"

He waited a beat and answered himself. "Because it sticks to hot dogs and falls in people's drinks, and when the circus moves on somebody has to clean it up. We use popcorn now. Nobody minds getting hit with popcorn, and when the tent comes down the birds eat it."

Pete ducked behind the screen again, and it suddenly hit me that the pain-forgetting laughter that had filled the room was the whole point of clowning. That's why clowns are called holy fools. The Albert Schweitzers and Mother Teresas of the world are revered for their work with the sick and dying, but clowns do it anonymously. They put on funny faces and crazy costumes and do rib-tickling skits for no reason other than to make people forget their troubles for a few minutes.

The egomaniacs who kill and rob and destroy think themselves powerful, but any idiot can create destruction. The truly powerful are the men and women who use imagination and hard work to create moments of innocent laughter. For the first time, I understood why Conrad Ferrelli had wanted to give clowns and other circus professionals their own retirement home. They deserve it.

In a few seconds, Pete came out looking like himself again.

To the class, he said, "I want you to watch a video now of some famous clown skits. Watch closely. Take notes. This is something I'm going to want you to do for the rest of the course. The skits look easy. They look unrehearsed and spontaneous, but every move is carefully choreographed. Every skit has been rehearsed hundreds of times. You have to know all these gags and be able to perform them smoothly before you graduate. When the video ends, take a break and meet back here at one o'clock."

I looked at my watch. It was eleven-fifteen. With luck, I could pick Pete's brain until one o'clock.

He headed toward me with an enormous grin. "What a nice surprise."

"Pete, would you have breakfast with me?"

"Honey, I had breakfast five hours ago, but I'll have lunch with you. And I was just kidding about women saying I'm too small."

"I'm sure you're a titan among men, Pete, but that's not why I want to have lunch with you."

"You want to ask me questions about Conrad Ferrelli, don't you?"

"Do you mind?"

"Hell, no, I'll tell you whatever you want to know. But I'll bet people looking at us will think I'm your hot honey."

I laughed. "If I'm lucky, Pete, that's what they'll think."

"Come on, I'll take you to a place that has the best hot Cubans in town."

In Florida a hot Cuban is a sandwich made of thin-sliced ham, spicy pork, baby Swiss cheese, and sliced dill pickles. It's called a Cuban because it's stacked in a split Cuban roll, which gets its crispy crust from being baked in palmetto leaves. The whole thing is smashed flat in a hot buttered *plancha*—sort of like a waffle iron—and grilled until the cheese melts and the pickle juice steams into the meat. I only eat about one a year, because one gauge of how much time you have left before your arteries clog up is the number of Cubans you've eaten in your lifetime.

I followed Pete to a hole-in-the-wall café, and the deputy followed me. I wasn't sure what the etiquette was for having lunch while being tailed, but when I got out of the Bronco, I gave him a wave and pointed inside. He must have been given orders not to talk to me, because he pretended not to see my hand signals.

Pete gallantly held the door open for me, and we gave our Cuban orders to a fat man in a white apron, then moved down the counter to pick up our drinks from an open cooler. Pete got a beer and I pulled out unsweetened iced tea. We carried them to a dark plastic booth and slid in to wait.

18

Up close, Pete's face was a lot more reflective than he had seemed. Deep laugh lines fanned at the corners of his eyes, but the eyes were intelligent and watchful.

I said, "Josephine said you had something to tell me about Denton Ferrelli and Leo Brossi."

"Yeah, the name rang a bell, so I made some calls. Brossi owned a fleet of casino ships that operated under the name Moon Surfer. Had about fifteen of them going out of different ports. Another company owned by a guy named Samson started sending casino ships into the same ports Brossi was using. Samson was gunned down on his way home one night. Papers called it a gangland-style killing, but nobody was ever arrested."

"What's Brossi's connection to Denton Ferrelli?"

"Well, that's what's interesting. Turns out Brossi got the money to buy his casino ships from the trust that Denton Ferrelli manages. It was supposedly a way to stimulate the economies where Brossi's boats operated."

I said, "The property where Conrad planned to build the circus retirement home was originally bought to dock a casino ship. Denton bought it, and Conrad took it away from him."

Pete's eyebrows rose, and the cook in the apron hollered, "Cubans up!"

Pete jumped to his feet, hurried to the counter, and carried back plastic baskets holding Cubans and french fries, with little tubs of mustard and ketchup on the side. We busied ourselves for a minute pulling napkins from a stainless-steel holder and turning our baskets until they faced us to our satisfaction.

Floridians take their hot Cubans seriously. Fights sometimes break out over whether it's okay to add mayonnaise or tomatoes to them. When I dipped mine in the tub of hot mustard, Pete winced.

I said, "Pete, somebody is trying to kill me, and it has to do with Conrad's death. I can't prove it, but I think it's Denton Ferrelli."

He said, "Denton's always been twisted. When they were growing up, Conrad was a sensitive kid, maybe too sensitive, and Denton was a bully. Angelo gave Denton hell if he caught him tormenting Conrad, but Denton made the boy's life miserable."

He gazed over my head for a moment, looking into past memories.

"To be fair, there were people who made Denton's life miserable too. Nearly every town we went to, some fool would say something about his birthmark, call it the mark of the devil or ask him if he was one of the circus freaks."

He shook his head like a dog shaking off water.

"One of the clowns had a monkey act. This little spider monkey would play like he was exposing all the tricks, you know, running around and seeming like he was screwing everything up for the guy doing the gag. It was all rehearsed, of course, but the audience loved it."

He gave me a stern glare.

"The monkey loved it too. All that propaganda those PETA people put out about how circus animals are mistreated is a bunch of crap. We probably took better care of our animals than they take care of their kids. That monkey lived in the train car with the clown, sat in his lap at the table, rode on his shoulder half the time. Anyway, Conrad made friends with the monkey, and Denton teased him about it a lot, called the monkey Conrad's girlfriend, things like that."

A pained expression crossed his face, and he took a long

swallow of beer. When he looked at me, his eyes were suspiciously shiny.

"Denton sneaked in one day and broke the monkey's legs. Snapped them like twigs. It broke Conrad's heart. The kid was never the same after that. He went quiet and stayed to himself."

My throat closed, and I laid my Cuban down. I can't stand to hear about kids or animals being hurt, especially when it's on purpose.

Pete said, "It wasn't the first time Denton hurt an animal, but everybody had felt sorry for him with that mark on his face and they'd cut him a lot of slack. But when he hurt the monkey, that was it. It nearly killed Angelo. I mean, how could you live with something like that, knowing you had a kid that vicious?"

I shook my head. I couldn't imagine how anybody could live with that. I couldn't even breathe, thinking about it.

Pete said, "You know what the worst thing was about Denton hurting that monkey? He took it home to Angelo's train car and laid it on the doorstep. Then he yelled to Conrad to come out. Acted real friendly, like he wanted to do something with him like a big brother. He was about ten, and Conrad was around five. Conrad fell for it and opened the door. There was the little monkey crying in pain, and Denton doubled over laughing."

I thought of the kitten with broken legs, the last thing Conrad had seen before somebody shot him with a drug that paralyzed his lungs. Perhaps the last thing he saw before his heart stopped beating had been Denton laughing.

Watching me closely, Pete said, "I've thought Denton was a killer ever since his mother died. She worked with the horses, rode standing up on a white stallion, God, it was beautiful. She had a kind of psychic communication with those horses. I've seen her stand on one side of the ring and them on another, and I swear they read her mind. They would all move in unison, like a dance troupe."

He took a swallow of beer and set the bottle on the table with a sharp thud.

"That's how she died, with the horses. They were in a ring around her, standing on their hind legs, and somebody shot a dart into one of them. He stumbled and they all fell on top of her, kicking and hitting one another. She was trampled to death."

I shuddered. "What an awful way to die."

"Awful to watch too. The horses were screaming, the audience was screaming, little children were shrieking. The horses had to be put down. She would have hated that."

"You think Denton—"

"He was there that night, watching, but I never saw the kid shed a tear. Conrad was hysterical, poor kid, but not Denton. I don't think it even touched him."

He snapped his mouth shut as if he didn't want to let out what he was thinking and then said it anyway.

"They never did find out who shot the dart into the horse."

I thought about what Guidry had said, about elephants being shot with dart guns from helicopters. But those darts had been filled with deadly drugs.

Pete fixed me with a keen blue stare. "Denton was there when Angelo died too. They were alone on Denton's boat, and Angelo supposedly fell overboard and drowned. Angelo never even liked boats. That makes two deaths when Denton was present. Three, counting Conrad."

"Denton wasn't actually around when Conrad died."

"You know that for a fact?"

I shook my head. "I don't know anything for a fact, Pete."

"Well, that's good, honey. People who know things for a fact are among the stupidest people on the face of the earth. You keep not knowing, and you'll be a lot smarter."

Maybe it was because the hot mustard had gone to my head, but I understood what he meant.

Pete looked at my face. "I shouldn't have told you that. It's enough to make anybody sick. Let's talk about something else. Like how you probably need an older man in your life."

My mouth was so dry I had to take a long drink of iced tea before I could speak.

I said, "Pete, did Denton ever have anything to do with snakes?"

"Snakes? Not that I know of."

I rotated my iced tea on the tabletop.

I said, "When I was at Josephine's this morning, Priscilla said she knew somebody who drives a truck like the one that chased me. She wouldn't tell me who it was, but you know, don't you?"

He wiped his mouth with his napkin and leaned back in the booth. "Priscilla's a good girl, Dixie. She was on the street for a while, bad family, abuse, the whole nine yards. But she's trying really hard, you know? She's not but sixteen and she's got that baby, and she's a good little mother. I've helped her all I can, gave her a room over my garage, sent her to Josephine for a job, I don't want to rock her boat."

"Somebody put a rattlesnake in my apartment last night. Two of them, in fact. One was under my mattress. I slept on it."

He flinched as if I'd stuck a knife in him. "Good God."

"I'm sorry to put you in the middle, Pete, but there's a deputy outside tailing me because my life is in danger. There are law-enforcement people at my apartment right now, going through it inch by inch, looking for other snakes or poisonous spiders or whatever. Somebody tried to run me down with a truck, and if Priscilla knows who it is, she'd damn well better tell me or she's going to have to talk to the sheriff's department."

"Did you tell Priscilla about the snakes?"

"Just the truck."

"I'll talk to her, Dixie. I think she probably doesn't understand how important it is. But any information needs to come from her, not from me."

"I'll wait a few hours, Pete, but that's all."

His mouth tightened into a grim line. "I'd like to make sure Priscilla is safe before she tells you anything. Your life may not be the only one in danger."

I wadded my napkin and tossed it on top of my partially eaten sandwich.

"I have to go. Thanks for the Cuban."

I leaned down and kissed his forehead before I left, causing his woolly eyebrows to waggle. Pete Madeira was a sweet man. Sexy too. I wondered if he would like to meet an older woman with lavender hair.

On the way out, I stopped and bought a Coke and a cold Cuban wrapped to go, and took it out to the guy tailing me. He was parked in the shade of a pin oak, but his car was a furnace and his face was red and covered with beads of sweat.

He tore off the wrapping and crammed half of it in his mouth. "Thanksh," he said. "I was shtarving."

I said, "You didn't have to cook out here, you could have come inside. It's not like I don't know you're following me."

He swallowed, a visible lump going down his throat like a boa constrictor's.

"Lieutenant Guidry would have my balls for lunch if I did that."

"I'm going back to Secret Cove and the Ferrellis' house. Just so you know."

His mouth was full, so he waved his Cuban at me and nodded.

While I waited for the AC to cool the steering wheel enough to touch, I called Guidry.

This time he answered by snapping out a curt "Guidry here."

I said, "I just talked to the clown I told you about. Pete Madeira."

"You've been talking to a lot of people."

"Pete said Denton broke a monkey's legs, when he was ten and Conrad was five, and then showed it to Conrad. He said Conrad was never the same afterward."

A beat went by, and Guidry's voice suddenly became very military.

"Repeat, please."

"Conrad had made friends with a spider monkey a clown used in his act. Denton broke its legs and laid it on the doorstep of the Ferrellis' train car for Conrad to find. Then he laughed. Pete even thinks Denton may have had something to do with both his parents' deaths. His mother died when somebody shot a dart into a horse she was working with, and all the horses went berserk and stomped her to death."

"A dart?"

"He broke a monkey's legs, Guidry, just like the kitten's legs were broken. It's connected. I know it's connected."

"Okay. Thanks."

He clicked off as if he had someplace important to go. I wished it was to arrest Denton Ferrelli, but I knew he had to have something more concrete than the story of a child's sadistic act.

I backed the Bronco out of the parking space and headed back toward Secret Cove. The Cuban sat heavy in my stomach, the pain in my ribs was worse, my scraped knees stung, my head was sweaty, and my right eyeball was scratchy. I needed a shower and a nap. I needed to charge my phone. But I was afraid if I went home I'd imagine snakes leaping out at me from every corner. I wasn't even sure I could sleep there again. I told myself that Stevie might need me, but the truth was that I wasn't ready to be alone with myself yet.

There were no cars at Stevie's house and no signs of activity. When I got out of the Bronco, I heard Reggie's muffled barking from somewhere inside. I rang the doorbell and waited. The barking continued, rapid and agitated. Not from the other side of the front door but from somewhere farther back. From the muffled sound, I thought he must be in a closed room.

I rang again and rapped on the door. "Stevie? It's Dixie Hemingway."

I waited some more. The barking became even more agitated. Reggie could apparently hear the doorbell and was responding to it.

I looked over my shoulder at the deputy in the driveway.
The Cuban must have got to him, because he had slumped
down in his seat, head resting on the headrest, chin tilted
up and eyes closed. I left the front door and walked briskly
around to the side of the house where a jalousied breezeway connected house and open carport. Conrad's silver
BMW had been impounded for forensics, but his Jeep
Cherokee was inside, and so was Stevie's Mercedes. From
the sound of Reggie's barking, I was pretty sure he was
locked up in the laundry room between breezeway and
kitchen.

I trudged back to the front door, looking toward the
deputy as I went. His mouth had fallen open, and I could
hear his snores. If Guidry caught him sleeping on the job
like that, he'd cover him in honey and roll him in an ant
bed, but I was sort of glad he was asleep. He wouldn't see
me use my door key to open the Ferrellis' door.

Stevie hadn't exactly hired me to take care of Reggie,
but she had asked me to come by. Well, she hadn't exactly
asked me, but she'd said she appreciated it when I did. She
was a woman stunned by grief. She wasn't thinking
clearly. She must have left the house with somebody and
unintentionally left Reggie closed up in the laundry room.
If I could call and ask her, I was certain she would tell me
to go inside and rescue Reggie. She would tell me to make
sure he'd been fed and that he had water and to take him
for a walk if he needed to go to the bathroom.

I gave one last look at the deputy and got my key ring
and code book from my backpack. I looked up the security
code, selected the Ferrelli key, and unlocked the door. Inside, I started to punch in the security code on the keypad,
but it wasn't activated, so I hurried toward the source of
Reggie's barking. Through the living room and dining
room, through the kitchen to the closed door to the laundry
room. On the other side of the door, Reggie was having
hysterics and clawing at the door.

Doberman pinschers are among the most graceful dogs
in the world. Strong muscular dogs with wide chests, a

running Doberman is a picture of fluid movement that is pure joy to watch. But a Doberman leaping to attack you is awesome and terrifying.

Reggie and I had both been traumatized. It had sent me into attack mode, and I figured Reggie might be ready to attack somebody too.

Before I opened the door, I talked to him a little bit. "Hey, Reggie, it's your friend Dixie. I heard you barking and I thought I'd come see what was up. Okay? Stop barking now, and I'll open the door and let you out. Okay?"

He stopped barking, but continued to whine and scratch at the door.

I said, "That's a good boy. Good boy, Reggie. You're a good boy."

I sent him pictures while I talked, pictures of the door opening and him trotting into the kitchen and wagging his docked tail. Pictures of me giving him a big bowl of fresh cool water. Pictures of me stroking his neck while he stood calmly grinning at me.

I put my hand on the doorknob. I said, "Okay, now, I'm opening the door. That's a good boy, Reggie."

The door opened inward, so I had to push it against him until he got the idea and slipped aside and through the opening. He wasn't wagging his tail or grinning. Instead, he galloped through the kitchen and disappeared, his toe-nails clicking on the tile floor as he ran toward the back of the house. There was a desperate urgency in the way he ran that made the hairs on the back of my neck stand up.

19

Suddenly frightened, I ran after Reggie. He made straight for the master bedroom, shoved a partially closed door open with his shoulders, and stopped short with his head turned toward the bed. An icy premonition made me come to a skidding halt behind him. He made a shrill sound so pathetic that my skin crawled, a whimper almost human in its sadness.

Horror was sending slithery tendrils up my spine. I argued with it. Maybe Stevie was asleep. Maybe she was such a sound sleeper that she hadn't heard the bell. Maybe she couldn't hear me in the hall.

I called, "Stevie, it's Dixie Hemingway. Are you in there?"

Reggie looked over his shoulder and made that sound again, and I yelled louder.

"Stevie? Stevie, it's Dixie!"

I waited another second, then began a slow walk toward something I didn't want to find. As I neared the bedroom door I could see the side of a king-sized bed with a floral bedspread pulled neatly under a matching pillow sham. That could mean Stevie had got up early, made the bed, and left the house with Reggie in the laundry room. That's what my brain said, but my pounding heart told me it wasn't true.

The odor hit me, and I stopped. Violent death has a unique odor impossible to describe. The combined scent of terror and decomposing flesh. Of expelled body wastes and shock. Once you've smelled it, you recognize it immediately.

I leaned forward, craning my head to try for an entire view of the room. Stevie lay on the bed with her legs dangling off the end. She was naked, her hands folded over a black-and-white photograph laid on her pubic area like a woman caught nude and modestly covering herself. Her skin was blue-gray, and her engorged tongue protruded dark blue like her swollen lips.

Backing away, I made a guttural whimper low in my throat, then turned and ran down the hall and out the front door. In the driveway, I pulled my cell phone out of my pocket and dialed 911.

When the dispatcher answered, my voice was surprisingly calm. I gave her the address and said, "The woman in the house is dead. It looks like a murder."

"How do you know she's dead, ma'am?"

"I'm an ex-deputy. I know a dead body when I see one."

"Somebody will be right there, ma'am—"

Before she had a chance to say anything else, I clicked her off. A sudden burst of fury made me slam my hand against the hood of the car. Adrenaline hit me, and I stiffened my legs and pushed my back against the side of the Bronco and shook. Violent death is so obscene, so ugly, so outside the way a life should end that it seems to disarrange the natural order of the entire universe. Every human being is diminished by one violent death, no matter how far away it happens. Even distant planets probably feel the hurtful energy coming from a brutal murder and wobble in their courses.

When I could move, I walked to the deputy's open window and shook his shoulder. He snapped his mouth shut and jerked upright, sweaty and embarrassed.

I said, "The woman inside is dead. I've called nine-one-one, and somebody will be here in a minute."

He gaped at me like a hooked fish. I felt sorry for him. He had just blown any hope of a bright career with the sheriff's department.

I went to my Bronco and sat sideways on the passenger seat and called Guidry's private line. When I told him I'd

found Stevie dead, he barked, "Where's the deputy following you?"

"He's here. He's waiting."

"Son-of-a-bitch!"

He clicked off, and a green-and-white patrol car pulled
into the driveway behind the tail. The deputy who got out
was a woman. Somehow I was glad it wouldn't be a man
who first saw Stevie sprawled naked on her bed.

I said, "She's in the bedroom at the end of the hall, but her
Doberman pinscher is in there with her. I'd better get him before you go in. He's so upset he might attack a stranger."

The deputy stood aside while I got a cotton loop leash
from the back of my Bronco. I went back inside Stevie's
house, walking down the hall toward the bedroom again.
Reggie had lain down on the bedroom floor, and when he
heard my footsteps he raised his head and looked hopefully at me.

Without looking at Stevie, I knelt beside him and
stroked his satiny neck.

"I'm sorry, Reggie, there's nothing I can do. We have to
go now and let other people come in."

I slipped the leash over his neck and put my arm under
his forequarters to lift him to his feet. Docile now, he let
me lead him through the house to the breezeway. I slipped
the leash off, gave him fresh water and petted him some
more, and left him there with a promise to come back later.

When I went out the front door, Guidry had arrived and
was slicing, dicing, and mincing the deputy assigned to follow me. The other deputy was standing off looking at the
sky and pretending not to hear.

I said, "The dog's in the breezeway; you can go in. Turn
left at the first hall and go straight back."

Guidry and the second deputy walked through the open
front door together. As they disappeared inside the house, I
imagined them making that same walk down the hall as I'd
made and seeing Stevie splayed on the bed as I'd seen her.

They were back in two or three minutes, Guidry talking
on his phone as he came. His face was unreadable as he

hooked the phone on his belt and stood in front of me. A muscle worked at his jaw, but otherwise he looked calm. I don't know how I looked, but every cell in my body was going off like popcorn.

I raised my hand to push back hair that had come loose from my ponytail, and was surprised to see that my hand wasn't shaking. A year ago, finding a baby bird fallen from its nest had been enough to make me come totally undone. Maybe the pendulum had swung too far the other way and now I'd lost the ability to feel.

Guidry said, "Okay, tell me."

"I heard Reggie barking and knew something was wrong."

His eyebrow went up, and I felt rising anger.

"Don't give me that look, Guidry. I knew something was wrong because of the way he was barking. I checked the carport and saw that Stevie's car was here. I thought she must have left with somebody else and unintentionally left Reggie shut up, so I used my key and went in to let him out and give him water. He was shut up in the laundry room. When I opened the door, he ran to the bedroom and I followed him and found Stevie."

"You used the security code?"

"It wasn't activated, but I have the security code."

"She had hired you to take care of the dog?"

"I've been here every day since Conrad was killed. Pets get forgotten when there's a death in the family."

Okay, so I was stretching it a little. I just didn't want to open the issue of whether I'd had the right to go in. Guidry gave me a searching look and sighed. Evidently he didn't want to open the issue either, especially since the only witness had been a deputy asleep on the job.

More cars began arriving, all the professionals who deal in violent death and its aftermath. Yellow crime-scene tape was stretched across the front door, a contamination sheet was posted for anybody entering or leaving the house to sign, and forensic technicians streamed past to measure and photograph and analyze. Media vans weren't here yet, but it wouldn't be long before they came.

I said, "Can I go home now?"

The muscle worked in Guidry's jaw again. "Anybody there?"

"Michael and Paco were both there the last time I checked."

"Check again and make sure."

I pulled out my cell phone and called Paco. I wasn't up to talking to Michael yet. My phone still needed charging. As soon as I got time, when I wasn't running from murderers or snakes, I would plug it in.

When Paco answered, I said, "Is it okay if I come home?"

"Why wouldn't it be?"

"Just making sure somebody's there."

"We're both here."

"Okay."

I put the phone back in my pocket and surveyed the cars parked behind me.

Guidry said, "I'll get them to move."

I'd never see him so cooperative. In no time, all the cars blocking the driveway had been pulled into the street, where they idled while I backed out. I didn't wave goodbye to anybody, just hauled ass out of there. I didn't start crying until I was on Midnight Pass Road. By the time I got home, I was cried out.

Three panel trucks were parked next to the carport, all with logos having to do with security or crime-scene cleaning. Paco was leaning against the back wall in the carport with his arms crossed over his chest, obviously waiting for me. He didn't say anything, just walked with me to the stairs leading to my apartment. Michael was up on the porch with two men who were doing something to my metal hurricane shutters.

I said, "What's going on?"

"Michael's having them install a remote so you can control the shutters from the outside. It'll work like a garage door remote."

"Cool."

"They wanted to put bars on your kitchen window, but

Michael doesn't like the idea. He wants you to be able to get out quickly in case of a fire."

My mind veered crazily away from a scene of a fire-bomb lobbed through my kitchen window.

Paco said, "What's wrong?"

I tilted my head on his chest, and he patted my shoulder. "Dixie?"

"Stevie Ferrelli has been murdered. I found her body."

"Oh, shit."

"Yeah."

"We're going to get through this, you and me and Michael. It'll be okay, Dixie."

"I know. I'm just a little shaken up."

Paco steered me to the deck and lowered me to a cushioned chaise in the shade of a giant oak. He said, "I think they're about through upstairs. I'll get rid of them, and then we can all talk."

Suddenly overcome with great weariness, I closed my eyes. In seconds, I was asleep, the sound of men's voices and seagulls' squawks and birdsong and the sighing surf all forming a blessed current to sweep me away from everything that had happened.

When I woke up, I lay with my eyes closed for a while and took stock of myself. So far as I could tell, I was sane. I wasn't running amok or anything, and I wasn't in a fetal position with my thumb in my mouth. Considering that three years ago I'd been more or less in a fugue state, and considering that in the last three days I'd found two murdered people, been chased by a killer truck, and had poisonous snakes put in my apartment, I thought my present sanity was a huge step forward.

Except for squawking gulls and the swishing slap of the surf, everything was quiet. I opened my eyes partway and looked up at my porch. Nobody was there, and my storm shutters were firmly closed. With my eyes partially open like this, I could see heat waves rising from the baked ground between my apartment and the deck. I turned my head and opened my eyes all the way to look around the shaded deck. Michael was floating in the pool beyond the deck, laid out like a walrus on an inflated raft. His eyes were closed, but every now and then he flapped his hands in the water, so I knew he was awake.

I got up and jumped feet first into the pool, sinking like a rock into the cool water. I frog-kicked under Michael's raft and popped my streaming head up next to his. We looked somberly at one another for a moment, assessing each other as only two people who've been together for a lifetime can.

I said, "Hey."

"Hey yourself. You okay?"

"I think I am, actually."

"Your apartment is clean as an operating room. The crime-scene cleanup guys went over every inch: drains, cracks, pipes, the works. Paco and I took everything out of your drawers and cupboards. We put in new shelf liners. We went through your closet and washed everything washable. You need new underwear."

I said, "Thanks, hon." But I knew him too well. There was something he wasn't telling me.

He tried to sit up on the raft and turned the thing over, churning up a tidal wave getting himself erect.

Cautiously, as if he were afraid he might push me over the edge, he said, "About that floor safe—"

"I know what you're going to say. I'll get a safe-deposit box."

"Did you have a newspaper clipping in the safe?"

The water seemed suddenly cold, and I shivered. "Just Gram's ring and my will."

"You remember the—ah, incident at the funeral? With that freak reporter? I don't know if you ever saw it, but the picture of your reaction made some newspapers."

"Oh, my God."

Terror curled in my stomach as I realized what Michael was talking about. It had happened as I left Todd and Christy's funeral. A mob had been outside, some to show sympathy, some to wave placards demanding the death penalty for the old man responsible for the accident, some to get a story. Still stunned by the enormity of loss, I'd let Michael and Paco push a path through the throng. A TV reporter had suddenly jumped in front of me and shoved a microphone in my face.

With a vapid red smile, she chirped, "What's it like to lose your husband and child at the same time?"

That's when I'd lost it. That's when all the rage I'd been holding came out. Pure and simple, I'd wanted to kill the stupid bitch. I let out a howl of pure hatred and lunged for her throat. Every camera present caught the moment. The scene played on TV news shows all over the country. Every newspaper in Florida had it on their front page. It even made *The New York Times*. I hadn't kept a copy, but the photograph was indelibly printed in my memory: my face contorted in primitive fury, my hands reaching for the frightened woman's jugular, while Michael and Paco grabbed for my arms, their faces registering shock and pain and compassion.

Somebody had known enough about me to leave a photograph that would recall an excruciatingly painful moment in my life.

Michael was watching me closely, probably remembering the moment outside the funeral with as much pain as it caused me.

He said, "Paco called Guidry, and he came and got it."

"Guidry was here?"

"Yeah. We didn't want to wake you."

Well, that was just too fucking great. Impeccable Guidry had been there while I slept. While I'd been laid out all scraped and sweaty and cat-hairy, he'd stood in his sophisticated linen and watched me drool while I slept. And he had the picture showing me going bonkers in front of the entire world.

I pulled myself through the water and climbed out of the pool. "You say my shower is clean?"

"Spotless. They poured stuff down the drain that would kill anything. The new remote for your storm door is on the table."

I squished across the deck, water pouring off my clothes and sloshing out of my Keds, and got the remote. As I crossed to the stairs to my apartment, I could feel Michael watching me from the pool, no doubt wondering if I was going to crack up in the shower.

20

The remote control sent my storm shutters folding into a slim line that disappeared in the cornice above the French doors. I wondered why I'd never had them set up so I could close them from the outside before. Inside, my apartment was so clean and shiny it amazed the eyes. It also had the peculiar ozone odor left by crime-scene cleanup.

I went into my fumigated and sterilized bathroom and took a long shower, then padded wearily down the hall wrapped in a towel. In my office-closet, where my shorts and Ts had all been washed, dried, folded, and stacked on the shelves with military precision, the message light was blinking on the answering machine.

One call was from clients who had planned to return tomorrow but had changed their plans and were staying over the weekend. I took their number to call and confirm. One was a hard-voiced man wanting to know my rates and grinching that I didn't have a Web site with my rates posted. I didn't take his number. I don't want a Web site. I don't even want a computer. I can't type worth shit, and I'm so technologically retarded that I forget to charge my cell phone. I sure as heck wouldn't be able to handle a Web site.

The third was Birdlegs Stephenson. "Dixie, I asked around about that truck and I have a name for you to check out. But you didn't hear it from me, okay? Two different people said look into a guy named Gabe Marks. Has a little place in the country near the Myakka River. From what they said, he's one mean sumbitch, not somebody you should tangle with by yourself. Like I said, if you talk to the cops about him, you didn't get his name from me."

I sat with my pen poised over my notepad staring at the machine. I'd never heard of anybody named Gabe Marks. Whoever he was, Gabe Marks had no reason to want me dead. Unless somebody had hired him to kill me.

Feeling heavy and sad, I called the people who were extending their vacation and talked to their voice mail; nobody talks directly anymore, we communicate through machines. I said I'd got their message and not to worry about their Airedale. I made my voice strong and cheerful, because that's part of my job, seeming on top of things. It's like being a parent, even when you don't know what the heck you're doing, your job is to act like you do so the people depending on you won't freak out.

I stood up and unwound the towel and pulled on clean underwear. Michael was right. I did need new underwear. As I was stepping into clean shorts, the phone rang again. I let the answering machine click on while I pulled on a sleeveless T.

A thin voice spoke. "Um—uh, Dixie? This is Priscilla."

I leaped to snag the phone and answered so loudly it scared her.

She said, "Oooh! I didn't think you were there."

"Priscilla, do you have something to tell me?"

"Well—um, Pete talked to me, and Josephine too. And they think I should—"

Her voice cracked, and I realized she was crying.

"Are you at Josephine's?"

"I'm at home."

"Tell me where you live."

She gave me an address about a mile from Josephine's, and I told her I'd be there in ten minutes. I laced up clean white Keds, dropped the gun in my pocket, and grabbed the door remote and my backpack. Outside the French doors, I lowered the shutters and looked over at the house. Michael had left the pool and was probably upstairs in the shower. Paco was probably asleep, resting up for his under-cover night job. With my storm shutters closed, they might think I was still inside my apartment. I could nip over to Priscilla's and be back before they even knew I was gone, thus sparing them the concern they might feel about me leaving.

What a load of horse manure.

The truth was that if I told them I was leaving to get the name of the person who had tried to kill me with a truck and a rattlesnake, they would hog-tie me and call Guidry. But I had promised Pete I would let Priscilla tell me personally. He had kept his promise and persuaded her to talk to me, and I would keep my promise and keep the police out of it.

I didn't exactly sneak away, but I went down the stairs as quickly and quietly as possible, and eased the Bronco out of the carport. It wasn't yet time for my afternoon rounds, so nobody was at the end of the drive to tail me.

Pete's house turned out to be a moss-green stucco bungalow almost hidden by old trees and hibiscus. Built before central air-conditioning, the house had a couple of window units humming and dripping on the side by the detached one-car garage. The apartment above the garage looked as if it had been built at the same time as the house, not added on later. A wide picture window overlooked the driveway, the glass covered by white pleated drapes. As I parked in the driveway, the drapes separated just enough for some-body to peek out and then fell back in place. I got out of the Bronco and walked around the corner of the garage, noting neatly trimmed flower beds running along the perimeter of the house. Somebody had spent time encouraging shrimp plants and green and white caladium to flourish. I won-dered if gardening was another of Pete's skills.

The stairway to Priscilla's apartment was steep and nar-row, with a wooden railing on the outside that seemed to have been recently stabilized and freshly painted. In the outside corner of the covered landing, an enormous staghorn fern in a moss-filled wire container hung from the ceiling. Priscilla opened the door before I knocked. She wore frayed cutoff jeans and a tiny ribbed T molded to her bony rib cage. Her pink hair was sleep-flattened on one side, and the bruises on her arms had turned a sickish blue. Her face was so ashen that her diamond nose stud and the gold rings rimming her ears seemed cruel impalings. She seemed agitated and flapped her hands to hurry me inside. As soon as she could, she slammed the door closed, turned a dead bolt, and slid a night latch closed.

Her apartment was one big room, with a tiny kitchenette by the front window and two doors at the back that I assumed led to a closet and a bathroom. The baby was asleep in a wooden crib in the corner, her knees tucked under her tummy and her rump raised in the air. A single bed against the wall had firm bolsters on its long side to make it double as a sofa. In front of it, a dented military trunk sat as a coffee table. The lid was open, and Priscilla hurried to it and started digging into it like a spaniel after a buried bone, pulling out articles of clothing and throwing them in a black plastic garbage bag next to the trunk.

She was obviously getting ready to run. Under any other circumstance I would have gone all mushy with regret and sympathy and concern. Now I just wanted the girl to get on with it and tell me what she knew.

I leaned against the wall. "What is it you have to tell me, Priscilla?"

In a strangled rush, she said, "I wasn't sure it was him . . . I didn't think he would do that . . . he's not like that, not really . . . he's good to the baby and lots of times he's real sweet . . . but when Pete told me about the snakes, I knew it was him . . . he'll kill me if he finds out I told!"

She gave me a look so fearful and young and lost that I was undone. This was a child raising a child, trying to make a nest for herself and her baby in an uncertain world. Life couldn't have treated her well or she wouldn't be here alone, living precariously on the charity of other people.

More gently, I said, "The person who drives that truck, is he your boyfriend?"

She nodded, big-eyed, and began to cry.

"The baby's father?"

More nods, more tears. She collapsed on the bed and buried her face in a tiny shirt—I supposed it was hers although it was almost small enough for the baby.

I went over and sat beside her. "Why the snakes? Why did that convince you?"

"That's what he does. He catches them and sells them. Alligators too. That's why he has those big tires, so he can drive in ditches and things. He grabs them with hooks and puts them in boxes in the back of his truck. Not the alligators. I think he has to shoot drugs in the alligators and then tie them up."

My heart did a little leap. "What kind of drugs?"

"Something to keep them from fighting so they don't get bruised or cut. If they're perfect, he gets about fifty dollars a foot for the skin. Not so much if they've got marks. He uses a dart gun to shoot them."

"They don't go to sleep?"

"Gabe said they watch him until he kills them, so I guess not."

"His name is Gabe?"

"Gabe Marks."

She raised her head and looked pleadingly at me, asking me for something I couldn't give: to erase whatever had led to this moment, or at least to reassure her that she and her baby would be okay.

The baby snuffled in her sleep, and Priscilla was instantly alert. I was beginning to see why Josephine and Pete were so protective. She was a combination of loopy child and sensitive, caring woman.

"How in God's name did you get mixed up with a man who traps venomous snakes and alligators for a living?"

Priscilla went back to stuffing clothes in the plastic bag. "I went to work at All-Call and Mr. Brossi introduced us. I wanted to be a clown, but I couldn't make any money at it."

"Gabe works at the call center too?"

"No, he does other work for Mr. Brossi, I'm not sure what. See, Gabe used to get the golf balls out of the water at the golf course. Nobody else would do it because of the snakes in there, but Gabe liked it, and that's where he met Mr. Brossi."

She held up a red knit sweater that I was almost sure was for the baby. "By the time it gets cold enough for her to wear this, it'll be too little for her. Don't you think?"

"Probably."

She laid it on the floor next to the garbage bag. "Then I'm not taking it."

"Where are you going?"

"Pete's taking us someplace. I don't know where, but I have to get away from Gabe."

Seemed like a good idea to me.

"Priscilla, about that call center—"

"Oh, that's an awful place, like a slave camp. They have these stupid rules about what you can wear, khaki pants or skirts with big ugly black knit shirts that are made for men but the women have to wear them too. Then they've got a blond bitch that sits on a tall stool and yells at you if you even speak to the person next to you. I hated that bitch so bad I used to have dreams about her. She had a basket by her stool for people to put presents in. If you gave her a present, you didn't get yelled at."

She might have trouble speaking until she felt comfortable with you, but Priscilla was really good at it once she got going. She had got so heated up over the blond bitch, she'd stopped getting clothes out of the trunk.

She said, "Mr. Ferrelli used to come there to see Mr. Brossi. Not the one that was killed, the one with the birthmark."

"Denton?"

"Uh-hunh. He was the only one besides Mr. Brossi that went in this private room where some special people worked. They were up to something in there. Mr. Brossi and Mr. Ferrelli would go in there and then come out looking like the cat that chewed the canary."

"Swallowed the canary."

"Whatever."

"Who else was in there?"

"I never knew their names, but there were five or six of them. They had keys to the door, and nobody knew who they were working for. The rest of us worked in groups, like everybody taking a company's orders or its customer service calls were all in one group. They had big signs hanging over us with the names of the companies we worked for. But that locked room didn't have any signs anywhere."

Priscilla replaced the rejected things in the trunk and closed the lid. "Everybody thought they were stealing IDs."

An electric jolt shot up my spine.

Priscilla said, "People call in to order something, they give you their name and address and phone number. Then they give you their credit card number. Lots of times, if you ask them for their social security number, they'll give that to you too. They don't have to, but they don't know that. Out on the regular floor, they watch you real close to make sure you don't keep notes when you're taking calls, but they record everything."

The transmitter Paco wore under his shirt was beginning to make sense. One call center processes thousands of calls a day. If crucial identifying information was being recorded and stored, a small group of protected thieves could use it to steal a staggering amount of money. And if Leo Brossi and Denton Ferrelli found out Paco was an undercover cop, they would kill him.

"How long ago was this, Priscilla?"

"I quit that place two months ago. That blond bitch yelled at me one time too many, and I left. That's when Pete got me the job with Josephine. She doesn't pay as much as All-Call, but she treats me like I'm a human being, not like a dog."

Most dogs get treated a lot better than most humans, but I let it pass.

A car door slammed downstairs, and heavy footsteps pounded up the staircase. Priscilla froze, and I did too, both of us looking toward the door as if it might blow open from the force of the anger in the steps. A fist hammered on the door, and a man's voice yelled, "I know you're in there, cunt!"

I didn't know which one of us he meant, but nobody calls me that and gets away with it. In her crib by the door, the baby raised her head and began to cry. Priscilla ran on tiptoe to pick her up. She stood swaying back and forth with the baby against her thin chest, looking at me over the baby's head with big frightened eyes.

A key scraped in the lock, and I shot Priscilla an astonished glare. *He has a key?* She looked embarrassed, as if it had just struck her that locking the door against somebody with a key wasn't a good way to keep him out. I sprang to my feet and pulled the gun from my pocket, holding it down and behind me. The doorknob turned and the door rammed forward, pulling the night latch from its mooring as if it were a hair.

The man who stomped through the doorway was a lot younger than I'd expected, maybe not even twenty, with a body big and hard as a refrigerator, a near-shaved head, and beady blue eyes lit with the fevered determination of a shallow mind. The floppy stuffed toy dangling from one hand was an incongruous touch, like a flower tucked behind a rhino's ear.

"What the fuck, Priscilla? What's this cunt doing here?"

This time I knew for sure he meant me.

Priscilla began to cry, curving over the baby like a turtle shell protecting its soft part.

He pivoted toward her with one arm raised, and she cowered like a whipped dog.

I yelled, "Don't you touch her!"

He whirled to glower at me. "Priscilla knows better than to argue with me. She's going to go get in the truck and wait. And then you and me are gonna have a little talk, and I'll show you what I do when cunts mess with my family."

Okay, that was two times I was certain he meant me.

I raised my gun and took a shooter's stance, feet spread, both arms straight out, the man's chest in my sights.

I said, "Priscilla isn't going anywhere with you, and you're leaving now. You're going out that door and you're getting in your big tall pickup and you're driving away."

"Yeah? Who's gonna make me?"

I moved the barrel of the gun a little bit, aimed at the staghorn fern in its mossy basket on the landing behind him, and fired a round that whizzed past his left ear. The plant exploded and bits of plant and moss struck the back of his neck.

I said, "That would be me."

21

The cocky grin left Gabe's face, and his little eyes darted right and left like a cornered rat.

"Listen, cunt—"

"Listen yourself, you muscle-bound Neanderthal. That's the last time you're calling me that."

I moved the gun to sight his head. Priscilla screamed, the baby screamed, and Gabe Marks threw the stuffed toy at Priscilla and ran down the stairs. As scream echoes bounced around the silent room, a car door slammed downstairs and an engine roared out of the driveway.

Priscilla sobbed softly against the baby's head. I backed up on wobbly legs and sat down on the bed. I laid the gun down beside me and put both hands on my thighs because there was a distinct possibility that I might fly apart, that my limbs might go shooting off like the thick fronds of the staghorn fern I'd shot. Adrenaline hit, and I began to shake.

A stern voice in my head said, *Would you really have killed him?*

The scary thing was that I didn't know the answer. By some quirk of genetics, a particular coordination of eye, hand, timing, and instinctive skill, I am an excellent shot. At the Police Academy, I always won the top marksmanship awards. In any exercise with paper targets at a shooting range, I always laid all my bullets in the spots where I intended them to go: the middle of the forehead or the center of the heart. Everyone who has ever shot with me has been awed and amused by my skill with a gun. Awed because they can't match it, and amused because I'm the least likely to ever actually kill anybody.

If there's anything I'm sure of, it's that we pay one way or another for everything we do, that every action brings a reaction. The way I see it, this means that killing somebody on purpose is bound to bring really bad things into your life. And yet I had almost blown a man away.

Not wholly because he was threatening Priscilla either, but because he'd called me a cunt.

It was another unpleasant discovery about myself.

Through the open door, we heard more footsteps coming up the stairs: light, quick steps. Pete appeared on the landing, taking in the demolished fern and the open door, his forehead creased with so much anxiety that his eyebrows were almost floating.

"I met Gabe's truck leaving. Are you okay?"

For answer, Priscilla kept crying and I kept shaking.

Pete said, "I had to go inside the bank, so it took longer." He looked around the room. "Where's your luggage?"

Priscilla sniffled and pointed to the black garbage sack. "I don't have a suitcase."

He stooped to pick it up, twirled it to make a neck, and tied it. "We'll pick up something on the way."

I said, "Where are you going?"

"I'm taking Priscilla and the baby to the airport, where they're taking a flight to see a lady I met several years ago at the Mooseberger Clown Camp. She's a hospice clown too, and she's got a spare room where Priscilla and the baby can stay for a while."

Priscilla said, "What about Josephine?"

He shook his head impatiently. "I'll explain to Josephine. If you've got pay coming, I'll send it to you. Now come on, let's get the hell out of here before Gabe comes back."

He seemed to notice the gun lying beside me for the first time. "Did you *shoot* at him?"

Priscilla and I exchanged a quick furtive glance. I didn't want Pete to know I'd fired a shot past Gabe's head. Only a nut would do something like that.

I grabbed the gun and shoved it in my pocket. "Pete, if I'd shot at him, he wouldn't have been able to drive away."

He let out a relieved breath and motioned me up. "Come on, come on, let's go!"

We began to straggle out, Pete with the black garbage bag over his shoulder like a cheap Santa Claus and Priscilla close behind with the damp baby clasped to her meager bosom. At the door, she turned to scuttle back and scoop up the stuffed toy Gabe had thrown, then hurried out with a quick guilty look at me. I pulled the door closed and clumped down the stairs to the driveway, where Pete practically shoved Priscilla into a black Ford Taurus. He waved good-bye before he got in and started the engine. I waited until he backed out and then pulled out behind him.

At the end of the street, where it connected to Midnight Pass Road, we turned in opposite directions, Pete toward the Sarasota airport, me toward home to explain to Michael and Paco where I'd disappeared and why.

Like a bad conscience, my cell phone rang while I was rehearsing what I'd say. Expecting it to be Michael, I gulped and answered it without looking at the caller ID.

Guidry said, "Dixie, I'm on my way to the ME's office to get the autopsy report on Stevie Ferrelli. I'd like you to go with me."

"Why?"

"Because you knew her and I didn't. Because you know things about the Ferrelli circus connection that I don't. Because the photograph on her body may have an importance that you understand. And because you may hear something that will fit with some cockamamie thing you've heard from one of your pet owners that will be just the key I need. You seem to have an uncanny way of collecting vital information, so I want you there."

"You want to say please?"

"Please. Ten minutes, Sarasota Memorial."

He clicked off without saying good-bye. While I dialed Michael's number, I muttered evil things about homicide detectives who use their authority to snag innocent civilians into helping them solve crimes, but to tell the truth I was flattered. Now my phone's screen showed only one little battery, and it was all but jumping up and down and screaming that it needed charging. I sent the demanding little critter a silent promise that I would plug it in as soon as I got home.

Michael answered on the second ring. "Where are you, Dixie?"

"I'm sorry, Michael. I thought I'd be home before now. I had to run an errand and it took longer than I expected, you know how that is, and then Guidry called and wants to see me in ten minutes. I'm on my way to meet him at the hospital. So I'm safe. Okay?"

I've seen anorexics move food around on their plate like that, doing it fast and stirring one thing into another thing to cover the fact that they're not really eating anything.

Michael made a little grunting sound that said he knew I was throwing words around to cover up what I had really been doing, but he couldn't argue with the idea that I would be safe with Guidry. I promised I'd call him after the meeting, and continued over the north bridge toward the hospital on Tamiami Trail. I parked in the visitor's lot and put the .38 in my glove box before I got out of the Bronco.

Guidry was waiting for me in the lobby, looking like an Italian tourist in a dark gray open-collared shirt, dark slacks, and an unstructured linen jacket the color of sea grass. Actually, he looked like an Italian gangster. A rich Italian gangster. For the millionth time, I wondered what his background was and why he was working as a homicide detective.

He nodded a greeting and touched the small of my back in a kind of unspoken take-charge gesture, man showing woman the way, man being the leader, woman trotting along as she is directed. I should have hated it, but I sort of liked the touch of his hand. Jesus, I was a mess.

In the Medical Examiner's office, we sat for a few minutes in a sterile waiting room. I looked around and thought about the number of people who had sat in these plastic chairs waiting to identify a loved one. At least I had been spared that when Todd and Christy were killed. Todd's lieutenant did it for me, and the ME's report to me had been mercifully brief. Massive head injuries had killed Christie. A crushed chest had killed Todd. Death becomes outrageously impersonal when it has come by accident. Reports take on an objective distance that is absent when death has been deliberately inflicted.

Guidry pulled a copy of a photograph from his pocket and handed it to me.

"Do you know who this is?"

It was a slim dark-haired young man, late teens or early twenties. He wore tennis whites and had a tennis racket slung over his shoulder and a shy smile on his face. I studied the features closely, thinking it might be somebody I'd known in high school.

"He looks vaguely familiar, but I can't place him. Who is it?"

"Nobody knows. That's the picture that was on Stevie Ferrelli's body."

I looked at the photo again. Stevie's killer must have shown it to her just before he killed her.

"He looks a little like Stevie. Maybe it was her brother."

"That's what I'm thinking. A brother who met with some tragedy that would hurt Stevie to remember."

"Did you show it to Denton?"

"He didn't know who it was. Or at least he claimed he didn't. His wife didn't know either."

"What about Stevie's relatives?"

"So far as we know, there aren't any. She seems to have no background, no history. Denton Ferrelli says Conrad married her in Europe, but he doesn't know where she came from."

"She told me they were at Yale together."

"She could still have come from Europe."

"She didn't have an accent."

A shadow crossed his eyes. "A lot of foreigners speak fluent English."

I couldn't believe Denton Ferrelli wouldn't know where his sister-in-law came from, but the Medical Examiner stepped to the door then and called us into her office, and Guidry put the photo back in his pocket. A tall Cuban-American woman, Dr. Corazon's almond eyes were shaded with fatigue as she motioned us to chairs in front of her desk. She ran a slim hand over cropped silver hair as we got ourselves seated.

Without any preamble, she said, "Stevie Ferrelli started life as a male."

Guidry leaned forward. "You mean she—"

"I mean she had sex-change surgery."

I said, "But she was so feminine."

Dr. Corazon gave me a look that dripped battery acid. "Probably why she didn't like having a penis."

Guidry shook his head slightly, like clearing his ears, and that seemed to annoy the doctor.

"Look, in the beginning there's no difference between boy babies and girl babies. They have the same mound of cells that will become sex organs. If the embryo gets a supply of androgen, those cells will form a penis and testicles. If it doesn't, the cells will form vagina and vulva. But it's all the same tissue. If nature has made a mistake and sent androgen to an embryo that grows up to be a woman in every other sense, it's a simple thing to rectify. Make an incision down the seam of the penis, take out the meatus, sew it back up and invert the empty casing into the peritoneal cavity to form a vagina. Attach the glans for a clitoris, snip out the testes, tuck the edges of the testicular sac under, and—voilà—you have vaginal lips. For all practical purposes, there's no difference between a surgically corrected woman and one born that way."

Guidry had tightly crossed his legs while she talked, and his forehead had a glassy sheen. His voice went up an octave too. "For all practical purposes?"

"For sexual intercourse, for sexual pleasure. Stevie Ferrelli couldn't have children, but in every other way she was a woman."

Guidry turned to me. "Did you know this?"

I shook my head. "I had no idea."

Dr. Corazon said, "In terms of a homicide investigation, it has no bearing whatsoever. Stevie Ferrelli was the wife of Conrad Ferrelli. She died early in the morning, probably between five and six A.M. She died of respiratory failure the same way her husband did. There was no indication of sexual assault. It took less time to pinpoint the cause because we were ready for it this time. Somebody gave her a massive shot of succinylcholine, also known as suxamethonium chloride. Trade name Scoline."

She turned to me and said, "You've probably heard of it as curare."

I didn't know why she thought I needed that explanation, but she was right. I'd heard of curare but not those other names.

She said, "We found the same needle puncture in her gluteus that her husband had. Spectrographic analysis found four hundred milligrams of the drug in her tissue. That's exactly the same amount found in Conrad Ferrelli. To give you an idea of how much that is, the amount of Scoline used to temporarily paralyze lungs during surgical procedures is one milligram for every kilogram of body weight, somewhere around fifty milligrams. The amount of succinylcholine in either of the Ferrellis' tissues would have paralyzed a thousand-pound animal."

I said, "Why do you say animal? I mean, why animal instead of person?"

She nodded at me as if I were a student who had asked a smart question. "Because the drug in large amounts like that is sometimes used to restrain animals during transfer or medical treatment."

"Like elephants?"

"Most veterinarians don't use succinylcholine with elephants anymore because it's so cruel. About the only time it's used with animals now is for restraining crocodiles and alligators during capture."

"Could it have been in a dart instead of a hypodermic needle?"

"Possibly. The puncture wound would be the same."

Guidry said, "Is the drug sold in darts already loaded with certain amounts?"

The ME shrugged. "You'd have to ask a veterinarian that question, but it certainly could be, and it would be safer for the person using it. Not that it's ever safe. Four hundred milligrams would temporarily paralyze a thousand-pound alligator, but if you accidentally stick yourself with that dart, you're dead."

Guidry spent a few more minutes getting forensic details of studies done, of liver inflammation as a sequela of the drug, but I didn't pay attention. My mind was on the fact that I had just met a man who made his living capturing snakes and alligators. A man who used a dart gun loaded with a drug to paralyze the alligators he caught. A man who was out to kill me.

I knew when the conversation ended only because Guidry stood up. I rose to my feet as well.

Dr. Corazon gave me a curious glance, probably wondering why Guidry had brought me, and gave Guidry a manila envelope containing her report. We said our good-byes and went out to the parking lot. Both of us were silent. I didn't know about Guidry, but the day's accumulation of shocks was making me punchy.

He said, "You want to get something to eat?"

Now that he mentioned it, I realized I was hollow as a barrel.

We walked across the street to a place where hospital personnel can get breakfast all day and slid into a booth against the wall. A waitress was at our table almost before we were settled, standing with her order pad ready.

I ordered a chef's salad; Guidry ordered an omelet with hash browns and bacon.

After we'd stipulated caffeinated coffee, not decaf, and

gone through the routine of choosing salad dressings and crispness of bacon—oh, my gosh, do I love bacon, but I have to draw the fat line somewhere—we sat without speaking until the waitress brought our coffee.

I was thinking how beautiful Stevie had been, and how she'd started life as a man. It put a different light on the project she and Conrad had financed to transform children born with disfiguring birth defects. Stevie had probably identified with the children and wanted them to have the same opportunities she'd had. I wondered how old she'd been when she had the surgery that allowed her to live as the person she truly was. It could not have been a decision her family supported, since she seemed to have cut all ties to them. Perhaps Conrad had been the one who made it possible for her. Of all the people in the world, Conrad would have understood how easily identities can be changed.

The waitress gave us coffee, and Guidry emptied two little containers of cream in his mug and leaned back and looked at me.

"With the Ferrelli house on the water like it is, anybody in a boat could have come down the Intracoastal Waterway and docked at one of the houses closed for the summer. It would be simple to slip through the trees to the Ferrelli house, kill Mrs. Ferrelli, and go back the way you came. With all the traffic on the water, nobody would notice another boat."

"Reggie would have attacked anybody who came in."

"My guess is that she got up and turned off the alarm, walked the dog, and then came home and got in the shower. There was no sign of struggle in the bathroom, no water splashed on the floor. The killer probably came in while she was in the shower and put the photo on the bed for her to see. We think she dried off, hung her towel up, and came out of the bathroom. She saw the photo and leaned over to see what it was, and he shot her with the drug."

I said, "If he came in the house while she was walking Reggie, Reggie would have sensed him when they came home and gone to find him."

"She wouldn't have put the dog in the laundry room while she took a shower?"

"Why would she? Reggie was always either in the house or in the breezeway. She wouldn't shut him up in the laundry room. Somebody else did that, and whoever it was knew the dog, or Reggie would have attacked him. Everything points to Denton Ferrelli again, Guidry."

"You're assuming that Denton Ferrelli is the only person in the world who knew their house and their dog. Did you know them well enough to make that assumption?"

I slumped back against the seat. He was right, of course. I had not been their close friend, I had just been their pet-sitter.

22

"The photograph was of Stevie, before her surgery," I said. "The person who killed her wanted to remind her of the unhappy young man she once was. Who else except Denton Ferrelli would know about the monkey's broken legs and also know about Stevie's past?"

Guidry said, "The fact that you and I don't *know* of somebody else doesn't mean there *isn't* somebody else."

I considered sticking my fork in his eye, but the waitress chose that moment to bring our food. My salad was nicely chilled, with plenty of gloppy Roquefort dressing. Guidry's bacon was stretched out like thin brown slats, a little black on the tips the way I like it, with no icky white bubbles.

He cut a bite of omelet, looked up, and caught me eyeing his bacon. He put his fork down and used his fingers to transfer half the bacon to my plate.

I said, "Oh, I never eat bacon."

"Menteuse."

I felt a little *gotcha!* smirk because I'd caught him being Italian, but I was distracted by the fried fat odor that makes all my little pleasure receptors fall on their backs and writhe in ecstasy.

"What did you just call me?"

"Liar. You eat bacon all the time, you just don't order it."

I nibbled at a slice of bacon while I considered that in

one day I'd been called a cunt and a liar. But on Guidry's lips the word hadn't come out as an assault the way Gabe's had. It had been more like a silky caress.

Nevertheless, that's what irritated me about Guidry—he kept saying things that were true. This was just the first time he'd done it in a foreign language.

"That's an Italian word, right?"

"French."

Aha! He was probably one of those Europeans he'd mentioned who speak English without an accent.

"Where did you come from, Guidry?"

He grinned as if he'd expected the question. "New Orleans. Born and bred."

"You're not Italian?"

"Actually, that's one of the few things I'm not."

"You have a first name?"

"I do, but most people call me Guidry."

"Hunh."

Before I could follow that line, he said, "I was with the New Orleans Police Department for several years. Decided I'd like a place with a little less excitement."

I ate some more bacon. "So has Siesta Key been less exciting?"

"It was until I met a cantankerous pet-sitter. It's been pretty exciting since then."

My heart did a stupid little leap, and a slice of tomato fell off my fork back onto my salad plate. I wouldn't have touched that sentence with a forty-foot pole.

I said, "I went to Mardi Gras once. I loved the jazz places."

"You like jazz?"

"Just old bluesy jazz. I have this fantasy where I'm in a crowded nightclub and a famous jazz band is onstage. The leader of the band steps to the microphone and says, 'Ladies and gentlemen, the best jazz singer in the world is in the audience tonight.' Then a big spotlight shines on me, and the audience gives me a standing ovation. I go up on the stage and sing like Billie Holiday or Peggy Lee, one of those. It just knocks everybody out."

He was grinning. "I didn't know you sang."

"Can't sing a lick. When Michael and I used to go to church with our grandparents, I'd throw the whole congregation off when we sang hymns."

He laughed. "It's a nice fantasy anyway."

"You have a fantasy, Guidry?"

"Yeah, I'd like to live on an island, just white sand and palm trees and tropical birds, plenty of fish to eat, a thatched hut with sea breezes wafting through, a beloved woman with me."

"Wafting?"

"You know, slowly blowing."

"Isn't that pretty much how you live?"

He took a bite of omelet and chewed it thoughtfully.

"My hut isn't thatched, and sometimes the breeze doesn't waft. Not to mention the lack of a woman."

My heart did that jiggle-dance thing again, and I changed the subject.

I said, "I think the killer used darts, and I think I know who he is."

"You've told me."

"I'm not talking about Denton Ferrelli. His name is Gabe Marks. He drives a pickup raised up on tall tires, and he makes a living capturing poisonous snakes and alligators. He paralyzes the alligators with a drug that he shoots into them with a dart gun."

"How do you know all this?"

"He's Priscilla's boyfriend. Priscilla works for Josephine Metzger making clown costumes. She lives in Pete Madeira's garage apartment. Pete's the—"

"The clown who told you about the monkey with the broken legs."

I was surprised he remembered.

"Pete also told me that Leo Brossi owned some casino boats, and that Denton Ferrelli's trust gave him the money to buy them. Pete thinks Brossi had a man killed who was giving his boats competition. That all ties in with what

Ethan Crane said about Denton getting the land here to use
for a casino boat dock. The land Conrad took for the circus
retirement home."

Guidry closed his eyes and took a deep breath. "I don't
know how you do it. People look up and see you coming,
and some reflex action makes them start spilling everything they know. Christ, they should use you for national
espionage."

It's true. I can be standing in line at the supermarket
or the bank or the post office and people will inevitably
start telling me the most intimate details of their lives.
It's as if they've been waiting for me to show up so they
can unload all their secrets. I don't know why that happens. I don't invite it. I don't even want to know other
people's secrets. It's just something I'm stuck with, like
skin that burns easily.

I said, "Gabe Marks does some kind of work for Leo
Brossi. That's where Priscilla met him, at the call center
Brossi owns."

"All-Call."

Once again, I was surprised.

Guidry saw it on my face and lowered his eyebrows.
"You're not the only one getting information, Dixie."

"They're all connected, Guidry—Denton Ferrelli, Leo
Brossi, Gabe Marks."

"Leo Brossi and Denton Ferrelli are an odd combination. Denton Ferrelli is a champagne criminal, smooth,
college-educated, well-connected. His contacts are lobbyists and politicians and mob bosses. He's kept his hands
clean, always had somebody else do his dirty work. Leo
Brossi came up through the streets, served time for pimp-
ing, drug dealing, extortion."

"He's the one who does Denton's dirty work?"

"More like Denton is the silent partner, so Leo takes the
hit. He's the one indicted, the one fined, the one with a
record. It adds to his gangster charisma, and Denton undoubtedly greases his palm liberally to keep him quiet.
With Denton's political connections, he's able to keep

Leo's fines and sentences to a minimum, so it's a good deal for both of them."

My fork was suddenly too heavy to hold. "I think it's pretty clear what happened. Conrad pulled the plug on Denton's casino boat, and he was getting ready to look deeper into Denton's other schemes, so Denton got Brossi's snake-catching boy Gabe to kill him. He used one of the darts he uses to capture alligators. Then they had to kill Stevie, because she was going to take Conrad's place heading the trusts. And Gabe's trying to kill me because he thinks I saw him driving Conrad's car."

I hadn't really known all that until I'd started saying it, and then it had all come together. What I didn't say was that Gabe now had another reason for wanting to kill me. I had humiliated him in front of Priscilla, and Gabe wasn't the kind of man to let humiliation go unpunished, especially humiliation from a woman. Inside my flesh, my bones suddenly felt thin and brittle. I reached for my coffee cup, but my hand was shaking so much that I changed my mind and put it in my lap.

Guidry's eyes were bleak. I knew what he was thinking. Denton Ferrelli had important business and political friends ready to vouch for his character and his whereabouts when Conrad and Stevie were killed. Furthermore, not a scintilla of evidence had come to light that put Denton Ferrelli or Gabe Marks at either murder scene. Everything that pointed to Denton as the one who had planned the murders, if not the one who had done the actual killing, was based on conjecture, not on actual evidence. The only person who could implicate him would be Gabe Marks, and there wasn't a chance in hell he would do that because it would put him in the electric chair. Without hard evidence, neither Denton Ferrelli nor Gabe Marks would ever be indicted.

Guidry said, "I know you're not going to like hearing this, but would you consider leaving town for a while?"

"I'm not running away, Guidry. Gabe may kill me, but he won't make me run away."

He didn't look surprised.

Now that I'd laid out the reasons why Gabe Marks was probably going to kill me, I went speechless. Guidry didn't say anything else either. He slipped a hand inside his jacket, pulled out a slim wallet, and laid bills on the table. I gathered myself to stand up, but he leaned across the table toward me.

"About the newspaper photograph in your floor safe."

The old sick feeling of shame and fury began to roil in my stomach.

Guidry said, "Forensics didn't get any prints from it."

"I didn't think they would."

"You know what your problem is, Dixie?"

"Plenty of people have told me what my problem is, Guidry. Spare me your opinion."

"You never got to finish the howl. You had a good one going, and they stopped it. They had to, seeing you probably would have done serious damage to that fool reporter if they hadn't grabbed you. But that stopped the howl coming up from your guts. It's still down there, and you need to finish it. You won't be well until you do."

Nobody had used the word *well* about me before, as if I weren't well now, as if I were sick. I looked up at Guidry and checked the expression in his eyes, looking for the slightest sign of ridicule. His gray eyes were clear and direct. Not pitying, not condescending, not even sympathetic. Maybe not even kind. Just direct. Guidry said what he thought, and he thought I needed to finish the howl that had been stopped three years ago.

I didn't answer him, and he didn't seem to expect me to. Wordlessly, we walked across the street to the hospital parking lot and got into our respective cars.

Afternoon rain clouds had rolled in while we were in the restaurant, putting everything into shadow and stirring up a breeze that fluttered palm fronds and bougainvillea branches. Thunder growled in the distance and thin traces of lightning flitted in outlying purple clouds. We were in for a storm for sure.

Before he drove away, Guidry gave me a wave that looked a bit like a soldier's salute. I started the engine and sat for a moment letting the AC cool the car. It was early for my afternoon rounds, but if I hurried I might get them over before the thunderstorm hit. Besides Mame, I had three other dogs on my list. I could get away with a short run with two of them, but the third was Billy Elliot, and Billy would be a quivering mass of nerves if he didn't get his usual long race. I pulled into a side street that would take me back to the key and Billy Elliot. Sometimes you have to put aside the possibility that somebody will kill you and just get on with life.

I called Michael while I was in the elevator in Tom Hale's building and explained where I was and what I was doing. I promised I'd cut all my visits short and get home early. He didn't lecture me, just promised he'd have dinner waiting. Grateful for not having to hear his worry, I didn't tell him I'd just eaten a late lunch.

Billy Elliot and I ran like banshees in the parking lot, both of us looking up now and then at the encroaching dark clouds. Back in his apartment, I handed him off to Tom and scooted out without taking time for chitchat. My two other dogs were nervous about the thunder and willing to make their runs just long enough to squat and do their business and then head back home. I didn't plan on walking Mame at all, so I made quick stops at the cats' and birds' houses. They were all slightly on edge with the instinctive knowledge that animals have when the earth is about to let rip with a quake or a big storm. I gave them fresh water and food and a little conversation and then went to Secret Cove.

I found Mame in Judge Powell's study, lying morosely with her nose on her front paws. I carried her outside to use the bathroom and invited her to play fetch on the lanai, but she wasn't interested. In the kitchen, most of the kibble I'd put out for her that morning was still in her bowl. I took a Jubilee Wafer into the study and held it in the palm of my hand so she could take it in her mouth. Mame loved

Jubilee Wafers the way I love bacon. She gave me a patient look and took it, but she didn't chew it, and I had the
distinct impression that she was waiting for me to leave so
she could spit it out.

Thunder cracked overhead, and I gave Mame a quick
kiss and left her. I told myself she was safe and dry. The
Powells had been adamant that I was not to have anybody
stay with her in their house, but I didn't feel good about
leaving her. I didn't feel good at all.

I felt even worse when I swung around the circle to
check on Reggie and a deputy on guard duty told me Denton Ferrelli had taken him away.

The wind was up by now, bending saplings and whipping palm fronds like flapping flags. Through the thick
trees and foliage, it sounded much worse than it was, like a
hurricane gale. Ominous thunder was rumbling all around
too, so that standing listening to the deputy I felt as if I
were in a dark cave with a bass drum's endless echoes
bouncing off the walls.

Angry, I said, "You let Denton Ferrelli take Reggie?"

"He's the next of kin, ma'am. Who are you?"

I didn't answer, just got back in the Bronco and headed
home. I was nobody. I had no right to Reggie, and Denton
Ferrelli did. But the truth was that Reggie going off with
Denton Ferrelli was almost surely Reggie going off to his
death. I didn't know how I could save him, but I knew I had
to try.

When I got home, a rain-colored car was parked beside
the carport, and a man in a white short-sleeved dress shirt
and dark polyester pants was standing beside it talking to
Paco. When I drove up they both looked around with almost stealthy expressions. Paco backed away with a dis-
missive wave, and the man opened his car door and got in.
His shoes were dull dark leather with thick rubber soles.
He wore white socks. Somebody should tell those federal
guys that white socks are a dead giveaway.

He made a sharp U-turn and headed down the lane
toward Midnight Pass Road, and I sprinted through quick-

ening rain to my stairs, pushing the remote to raise the shutters as I ran. Inside my dark apartment, I switched on lights and hurried to the bathroom to clean up before dinner. By the time I was out of the shower and dressed in threadbare old jeans and a stretchy T, the rain was coming down hard and fast.

My answering machine was blinking, so I stabbed the PLAY button and skipped through the messages. I stopped when I heard Pete's voice and let it play to the end.

"Dixie, Priscilla and I talked on the way to the airport, and I learned something . . . maybe it's . . . she said Gabe spent Sunday night with her, and he had a little kitten with him . . . she thought he'd brought it to her, but when he left Monday morning he took it with him . . . she said he left a little before five, but I saw him leaving in his truck about seven that morning . . . I don't know where he'd been between the time he left her and the time I saw him, but I thought it might be something you should know . . . may not be relevant."

I stood looking at the machine while pictures flashed like a montage in my head. The box of free kittens I'd seen Monday morning on Midnight Pass Road could have been put out Sunday evening. Maybe the box of kittens had activated Denton's need to inflict emotional pain. Gabe could have walked to Secret Cove from Priscilla's apartment, killed Conrad, and driven Reggie to Crescent Beach. From there, it would have been an easy walk back to Priscilla's for his truck. But Denton Ferrelli had to have been present when Conrad was killed. Denton had to have been the one who got Conrad to stop his car and step into the woods where the kitten lay.

I backed away from the answering machine as if it were a ticking bomb. I'd had about all I could take for the day. I couldn't absorb anything else. On the porch, I lowered the shutters and pulled a yellow slicker over my head before I ran down the steps and across the deck. A golden light glowed through the kitchen's bay window, and I could see Michael and Paco moving around inside. That was my beacon, my safe harbor.

23

I opened the back door and slipped into the kitchen, hurrying to shut the door behind me and trying to shed the slicker without making a puddle on the floor. The kitchen was steamy from an oversized stainless-steel soup pot on the stove. The pot sent out such a tantalizing aroma that my stomach forgot it had eaten in the last four hours. Let's face it—my stomach is like a female cat. Let a female cat be mounted by a horny tom and she automatically goes into heat. Let my nose get a whiff of spicy food, and my stomach automatically feels lust.

Two glasses of red wine were already at places set for Michael and me on the wide butcher-block island, and a glass of iced tea waited for Paco. Michael was at the stove stirring whatever was in the pot, and Paco was transferring leafy salad from a big wooden bowl to three small ones.

Michael waggled a long wooden spoon at me. "We've got gumbo."

"New Orleans gumbo?"

"You know any other kind?"

"Can I do something?"

"You can put rice in these bowls."

I spooned rice from a steamer into three wide bowls stacked by the stovetop. Michael ladled dark gumbo onto the rice and set the bowls on plates. Paco hauled out two crusty loaves of French bread from the wall oven, wrapped them in a clean towel, and tossed them on the butcher block. We all took our seats. By tacit agreement, we would enjoy dinner before we talked about anything that might spoil our pleasure.

The gumbo was in a roux so dark it was almost black, redolent with spice and shrimp and crab and oysters, flavors so exquisitely married that I had to be strict with myself not to make orgasmic whimpers. Nobody in the world can make gumbo like Michael. Well, maybe some New Orleans chef in a little café hidden in a narrow alley known only to the privileged cognoscenti does, but I don't know him. Guidry might know him, Guidry, who was from New Orleans . . . Guidry, who was not Italian but something else . . . Guidry, who was secretive about his first name . . . Guidry, who had called me a liar in French and told me I needed to finish the howl I'd started three years ago.

Paco cleared his throat and I jerked my mind away from Guidry. My bowl was empty and Michael and Paco were looking at me as if they'd been trying to get my attention for a good while.

Michael said, "I've been talking to some people with offshore racers, guys who know who's who on the water. They say Denton Ferrelli has a really sweet Donzi Thirty-eight ZR that can easily do ninety miles an hour. He docks it at the Longboat Key Moorings next to the Harborside Golf Club."

"I know. He takes it out for a run in the bay every morning."

"That's what I mean. Even watching out for manatees, he could kill his brother in Secret Cove and be back at the Moorings in under twenty minutes. Fifteen maybe."

I hadn't realized he could have moved so quickly. If what Michael said was true, Denton could have left Siesta Key as late as six-thirty and still have arrived at the Longboat Key Moorings before seven. From there, all he had to do was stroll next door to the first tee.

I said, "If he did, nobody saw him dock at Siesta Key. It probably wasn't Denton who actually killed Conrad. The killer used a dart gun filled with a drug used to capture big alligators. A thug named Gabe Marks makes his living capturing poisonous snakes and alligators, and he uses the same drug. He's the one who tried to run me down with his truck. I met him today, and I think he could kill somebody without batting an eye."

They were both looking at me with identical expressions of dread.

Michael said, "You don't think Ferrelli had anything to do with it?"

I thought of the red-lipstick smile slashed on Conrad's face. Of the mutilated kitten for Conrad to see just before he died. Of the photograph of herself as a man for Stevie to see. Only Denton would have got malicious satisfaction from those acts of psychological sadism.

"I think he was there, but I think it was Gabe who drove Conrad's car away."

Paco said, "Denton Ferrelli is a big player. The Feds have been trying to nail him for money laundering for years, but he always manages to wiggle loose."

I said, "Is that why the guy in the white socks was here?"

He shifted uneasily on his stool. "That was for something else."

I looked straight at Paco. "Denton Ferrelli and Leo Brossi are connected at the butt, and they're probably involved with the Mafia. I've been told that Brossi's call center may be a cover for an identity-theft operation."

Only somebody who knew him well would have noticed the way Paco's lips got firmer at the corners. Very carefully, he said, "Every investigation has to focus on one crime and one crime only, Dixie."

Michael stood up and began gathering the plates. "There's another baguette in the oven, and I have chocolate butter."

Paco and I went silent and big-eyed. Hell, offer me hot French bread with chocolate butter to smear on it, and I forget all about the possibility that I might be murdered. Michael tossed the hot loaf on the butcher block for us to pull apart with our fingers. He set out a bowl of soft butter mixed with dark melted chocolate. He poured cups of black coffee laced with cinnamon. A west wind howled through the old oaks outside, and rain drummed against the windows and on the roof. But we were inside, safe and dry, and we had bread and chocolate and coffee.

I rinsed our dishes and put them in the dishwasher while Michael transferred leftover gumbo to the freezer containers to take to the firehouse. Paco went upstairs and dressed in his All-Call khakis and dark shirt. He and I left at the same time, charging through the driving rain in two different directions. As I went inside my French doors and lowered the storm shutters, Paco's headlights swung out of the carport.

I hung my wet slicker over the showerhead to drip into the tub. Rain clattered on the roof and porch in an unrelenting din. I put on a Patsy Cline CD, but it was a tinny sound compared to the storm, and it didn't calm my twitchy nerves. I tried some mellow jazz, but that didn't work either. I went into my office-closet and entered my visits for the day in my record book. I wrote up a couple of invoices. I went to the kitchen window and looked through the heart-shaped iron thing at the tossing treetops.

I went in the bathroom and cleaned the sink and toilet and polished the water faucets until they were shiny. I spritzed the mirror over the bathroom sink with Windex and wiped away the mist. My face appeared in the arc made by my paper towel, my eyes looking back at me with a quizzical challenge. *Who are you trying to kid?*

I looked away and concentrated on cleaning the glass, but I finally had to look at myself again. I couldn't deny the truth any longer, not even to myself. I was attracted to Lieutenant Guidry. The shock of it was like a blast of arctic air. It was not only damn bad timing, what with a killer after me and all, but I hadn't expected to ever want another man after Todd. And certainly not another cop. But there it was, and I didn't know what to do about it.

Feeling trapped by the storm shutters, the driving rain, and my own thoughts, I wandered aimlessly through the apartment. I clicked the TV on and clicked it off. I picked up a book and read a few pages, then put it down.

I went in the bedroom where Christy's Tickle Me Elmo was propped against the pillow on my bed, the only toy of hers that I had kept. I sat on the side of the bed and stroked Elmo's red fur, hearing Christy's laughter bubbling, that sound of pure joy that made everybody within earshot smile. On my bedside table, Christy and Todd smiled at me from a photograph taken shortly before they were killed. Christy sat in Todd's lap, both his arms encircling her like a ring of safety. I picked the photo up and ran my fingertips over the glass.

Christy would be six years old now. She would be excited about starting first grade, and we would be shopping for number-two yellow pencils, crayons, scissors, and Elmer's glue. We would be debating which backpack to buy, whether it should have cartoon characters on it or be more plain and grown-up. We would be getting school clothes ready and making sure her vaccinations were current.

Todd would be thirty-five. Maybe he would have decided to work toward making lieutenant with the sheriff's department, maybe he would have been happy to stay a sergeant. I was now the age Todd was when he died. He will stay thirty-two while I grow older. He and Christy are like astronauts who stop aging when they leave earth's gravity. Perhaps death is actually a different kind of space travel, leaving behind one's body sleeve and moving into another space-time dimension in which there is no such thing as age or death. Or maybe they have moved into another dimension in which they continue to grow and have different lives. Who knows what happens after death? All I knew was that they weren't in my world any longer and never would be.

I put the photograph down and picked up Tickle Me Elmo. I hugged him tight to my chest and kissed the red fur on his head. I carried him down the hall and put him inside a clean pillowcase and laid him on the top shelf of my linen closet. Then I closed the door.

The air was charged, continuously vibrating with massive air quakes. The wind had picked up, moaning and shrieking with primeval urgency. It was the kind of storm that floods canals and swimming pools, topples ornamental trees, and spawns tornadoes. I raised the metal shutters and peered through the French doors. The sky was purple as a bad bruise. Down on the shore, rolls of dark bulimic swells were vomiting **strings** of seaweed.

I opened the doors and stepped outside. The wind was so strong that horizontal rain slammed under the porch over-hang and drenched me. I leaned over the railing and let the wind whip my hair around my face, let it offer my mind es-cape from its jail. After a while I went downstairs and slogged through wet sand and quivering thunder to the shore. Bracing against the howling wind, I faced the sea and raised my arms, spread-eagled to take the rain's hardest force.

Then I looked directly into the great maw of churning sea and raging wind and gave it back my own sound: my fury and hatred, my despair and hopelessness, the rage and heartbreak trapped inside since Todd and Christy died. Howled it from my toes and guts and lungs and heart. Howled like women have howled since the beginning of time and maybe before, sending a woman's demand to the ends of the universe to bring it into balance.

I don't know how long I stood raging into that dark storm, but long enough. When I was empty, I felt a door closing with a gentle click somewhere in my brain, while another door opened. Part of me wanted to put them back the way they'd been, another part of me knew that would be an act of cowardice. My husband and my child were dead, my capacity for love was not. Staying in the safe darkness of memory and yearning is easy. Going forward to the light of possibility takes courage.

As I trudged back through the downpour, I saw Michael's silhouette in his bedroom window and knew he had been keeping watch.

I left my sodden clothes in a heap on the porch floor and went inside and took a long warm shower. Then I crawled into bed and slept deeply and dreamlessly for the first time in three years.

24

The sky was pale and washed clear when I backed out of the carport next morning, and the air had a clean salty taste. A few early cranes were gathering goodies washed in on the tide, and songbirds were beginning to practice scales. If it hadn't been for the sure and certain knowledge that a killer was out to get me, I would have felt downright contented.

Billy Elliot was waiting for me in Tom's dark apartment, and he and I went downstairs and ran hard for thirty minutes around the parking lot. Nobody tried to run me down. Nobody jumped out and shot a poisoned dart at me.

So far, so good.

When we got upstairs, lights were on in Tom's apartment. I could smell coffee brewing and hear the TV. I knelt to unclip Billy Elliot's leash from his collar, and heard a newscaster's voice say Leo Brossi's name.

I yelled, "Tom? Okay if I come in?"

He rolled himself into the hall from the kitchen. "Of course. Want some coffee?"

"Did I just hear something about Leo Brossi?"

"Yeah, come watch."

He zipped back into the kitchen and I trotted after him in time to see a live scene of several handcuffed men being herded into a police van. The announcer's voice sounded young and excited, repeating several times that the men were charged with operating a massive racketeering, bribery, and money-laundering scheme headquartered at All-Call. He said the operation was far-reaching, involving more than the few men currently under arrest, and that it had been cracked through the combined efforts of federal and county law-enforcement officers. Leo Brossi's attorney had already issued a statement saying Brossi was completely innocent, and if any unlawful operation had been going on at his call center it had been without his knowledge.

I scanned the television screen for a glimpse of Paco, but he wasn't there. He had probably melted away the moment the arrests began.

I said, "Have they mentioned identity theft?"

"This is a lot bigger than identity theft. Sounds like they were laundering drug money. Moving it in and out of shell accounts."

The TV station broke for a commercial, and Tom muted the sound.

I said, "I don't understand how money laundering works. I mean, I know it starts out dirty and comes out clean, but I'm fuzzy about what happens in between."

"Okay, say you're a drug trafficker, and you've just sold some cocaine for a hundred thousand dollars. Drug sales are always in cash, and banks report cash deposits of more than ten thousand dollars, so you need to get the cash converted. There are several ways to do that. You can pay cash for things like antiques or gold or motorcycles or classic cars, and sell them to people who pay you with a cashier's check or a money order. You can go to your neighborhood Wal-Mart and pay cash for a bunch of TVs and VCRs and CD players and then sell them on eBay. A more fun way is to go to a casino, buy a hundred thousand dollars' worth of chips, gamble for an hour or two, and then cash in your chips. The casino will pay you with a cashier's check as if you were a big winner. Your drug money has now been laundered, and you can deposit it in a bank."

"But those guys at All-Call weren't buying and selling things."

"Say instead of a hundred thousand, your cocaine sold for a million, and say you get that much cash every week. You don't have time to go through all the rigmarole of the small-time dealer. So you find a friendly banker or savings-and-loan officer who will take your cash deposits without reporting them to the government. Pay the friendly banker a nice bribe, a million here, a million there, and your money becomes nice and clean."

I thought about the banker playing golf with Denton Ferrelli and Leo Brossi when Conrad was killed. Had he been getting bribes?

Tom said, "Now here's where the people at All-Call come in. Once you have the cash in a bank account, you can make wire transfers to accounts in offshore banks. With just a few strokes on a computer keyboard you can move currency around the world with complete anonymity. Move it often enough, and the tracks become so criss-crossed that nobody can trace them."

"Telemarketing firms have computers that can do that?"

"Are you kidding? For every ten people put in jail for money laundering, five of them are probably telemarketers."

"Hunh."

Tom's brow furrowed like a worried hound's. "Honest people think money laundering doesn't have anything to do with them, but drug sales finance terrorism. It affects all of us."

I said, "I wonder why they didn't arrest Brossi."

"Guess he wasn't there when they made the bust. But somebody infiltrated the operation and taped conversations. They've got weeks and weeks of proof. I don't think Brossi will be able to wiggle out of this one, not even with all his political connections."

I felt a tingle of pride. I knew who had infiltrated that ring and got the tapes. I wondered if Michael had known all along that last night was bust night, and if he had lain awake all night worrying about what might happen to Paco when the bust was made.

I left Tom and Billy Elliot in the kitchen and let myself out. Downstairs in the parking lot, more people had come out to exercise their dogs. The horizon was beginning to go blue around the edges, and steam was crawling off all the wet vegetation. Across town, Paco was probably doing high fives with the other officers who'd been in on the operation. I hoped he was feeling as much pride as he deserved.

To make up for the abbreviated time I'd given them yesterday, I spent a few extra minutes with each of the other dogs on my schedule. They all got fed and brushed and exercised. They all got smooched and petted and told how brilliant and beautiful they were. They all beamed and stretched and agreed with me. That's the great thing about animals. No false modesty with them. They don't puff themselves up with snooty grandiosity, but they don't turn down compliments either.

The morning sky was shading from coconut to apricot when I got to Mame's house. It was going to be a beautiful day. Mame wasn't watching for me at the glass by the front door, and when I went inside and called to her, she didn't come.

I found her in Judge Powell's study, her back legs splayed out in an awkward flattened way. A large oval on the rug beneath her was wet, and an acrid odor of urine filled the room. She raised her head and looked up at me with shamed eyes.

I knelt beside her and stroked her head. "What's wrong, Mame?"

She licked my hand and sighed. Her eyes said that I knew perfectly well what was wrong and not to play games. It was time, and we both knew it.

I got my client book from my backpack and looked up her vet's number. The difference between animal doctors and human doctors is that animal doctors assume you really need them when you call, so they talk to you.

I said, "I'm Dixie Hemingway. I'm taking care of Judge and Mrs. Powell's dog while they're in Europe, and—"

"I know. I've been expecting your call. Bring her to the office."

I scooped Mame into my arms and carried her to the padded cage in the back of my Bronco, wedging rolled towels around her so she wouldn't slide with the car's movement. She put her head down and closed her eyes. At the vet's office, there were only two other cars in the parking lot. Mame raised her head and smiled at me when I went to the back to pick her up, and I took a second to stroke her head and tell her what a beautiful girl she was.

The vet's assistant saw me coming and ran to hold the glass door open for me. She motioned to the door leading to the examining rooms. "You can take her on back. Dr. Layton is waiting for you."

The vet, a comfortably plump African-American woman with a mass of glossy black curls, got my immediate respect by ignoring me. When I put Mame on the examining table, the vet greeted her like an old friend.

"Hello, my lovely Mame. What a beautiful girl you are. But you're in pain, aren't you?" She was stroking Mame as she spoke, listening to her body through her fingers.

She said, "I tried to get the Powells to take care of this before they left, but they just couldn't."

"They knew?"

"Mame has several malignant tumors that are growing larger every day. They're pressing on her spine, and now it looks as if they've affected nerves to her legs."

I felt a flash of anger. How dare the Powells go off at a time like this and leave Mame with somebody who wasn't family? After a lifetime of love and devotion, Mame deserved better.

As if she read my mind, the vet said, "No two people handle death the same way. They just couldn't face it."

"It won't be any easier for them when they come back."

Softly, she said, "I'm not sure they're coming back. Before they left, they made a point of telling me they were members of the Hemlock Society, and that they'd always wanted to end their days in Italy. I think they were telling me they'd made plans to die there."

Our eyes met, and then we quickly looked away, both of us too young to want to dwell on the question we would ultimately face. Personally, I plan on dying the way my grandparents did. Both of them dropped dead in the midst of active lives, vital one minute and gone the next. But back in some forbidden recess of my mind is the awful knowledge that not everybody is so lucky. If I'm not one of the lucky ones, will I try to hang on to youth like the man who killed Todd and Christy because he refused to quit driving, or will I take the way of the Powells? I don't know. Like Scarlett O'Hara, I'll think about that tomorrow.

I looked at Mame again. I thought of the fatal drug in Conrad's body. I thought of Mame chewing on Conrad's finger. Guilt tightened its fingers around my throat and made my voice tight.

"Just a few days ago, Mame went for a walk and ran into the woods. She was frisky as a pup."

The vet smiled down at Mame and stroked her neck. "Had a good last run, did you? Good for you."

"Could it have been too much for her?"

She looked up at me and shook her head. "This has been coming for a long time."

"Can I stay with her while . . . ?"

"Of course. You can hold her and talk to her while she goes to sleep."

She unbuckled Mame's collar and handed it to me. I sat on the examining table with Mame cradled in my arms, while the vet slipped a needle into a vein. The vet stepped out of the room, and Mame looked into my face with clear eyes, unafraid and perhaps relieved.

Softly, I sang, "Put the blame on Mame, boys, put the blame on Mame."

I sang the same words over and over until Mame's eyes closed. Then I sang them a few more times just in case her spirit was hovering around listening.

The vet came in and took Mame from me. "The Powells made arrangements before they left," she said. "You don't have to do anything else."

I slid off the table, tears streaming down my face. "She was a sweet little dog."

"She was."

I stopped at the receptionist's counter long enough to fill out one of the blank checks Judge Powell had signed for emergencies. I knew he had loved Mame dearly, and so had Mrs. Powell, but I didn't think they had been fair to her at the end.

I was still leaking tears when I opened the front door and collided blindly with a man coming in with a cat. I muttered a quick apology and slipped past him to the parking lot. As I opened the Bronco's door, Ethan Crane's voice sounded behind me.

"Dixie? Sorry I didn't recognize you back there, I was concentrating on my cat. Had to leave her to get her toenails clipped."

I wiped ineffectually at my streaming eyes. "I didn't recognize you either. Had something in my eye."

He touched my shoulder. "Is something wrong?"

The next thing I knew I was bawling and babbling while Ethan had an arm around my shoulder and was patting me and making soothing noises.

"The vet said she would have died anyway but she doesn't know about her chewing on Conrad's finger . . . it had that drug in it that kills in just seconds, and maybe Mame broke the skin . . . I don't know, she could have . . . I didn't look, I should have looked . . . maybe she got some of the drug in her system, maybe that's what really killed her . . . I shouldn't have left her at home alone . . . the Powells were going to go off and kill themselves anyway . . . I should have paid somebody to stay with her and they would never have known . . . it's just plain mean and selfish to do that, you know?"

Ethan pointed to a Starbucks at the edge of the parking lot. "Dixie, you need coffee."

With his arm still around my shoulders, he guided me across the blacktop and put me at a minuscule table outside the Starbucks front door. He ducked inside, and by the time he came back with two coffees, I had got myself under control. He spilled a handful of cream and sugar containers on the table and took the other chair. For a minute or two we were busy with the coffees, and then we were stuck in one of those awkward moments when nobody can think of what to say next.

I said, "Sorry to disintegrate on you like that."

"No problem. I'm sorry about your dog."

"She wasn't mine, actually. I was taking care of her."

"I'm still sorry."

I looked directly at him for the first time. No doubt about it, he was extraordinarily handsome, but his face wore a new look of tension.

I said, "I guess you've heard about the arrests at Leo Brossi's call center."

He huffed a mirthless laugh. "Brossi's not the big fish. Denton Ferrelli's the one they should be after."

"You didn't say that when we talked before."

Humility obviously wasn't Ethan Crane's long suit. He gave me a long hard look that seemed to be contemplating whether he could get away with lying.

"I didn't know then what I know now."

"Now that you have new information, could you share it with me?"

I thought I did very well to keep the acid off my tongue when I said that. I guess he thought so too, because he gave me a hint of an approving grin.

25

Ethan said, "What I've learned is that Denton Ferrelli has a history of smelly financial deals, and he always has help from organized crime and corrupt politicians. Like he brokered around five billion a year in deposits into savings and loans all over the country. But first he got an agreement that the S and Ls would lend the money to people he named. Every one of them was somebody with the Mafia."

My eyes got big at the word *Mafia*, and Ethan smiled grimly.

"Like they say on the street, Denton has connects. Not just with the mob but with a lot of politicians. Dirty money goes into a bank or a savings and loan, comes out clean through unsecured loans, and goes into the pockets of crooked politicians. Then they use their clout to help the people who bought them."

"What about Leo Brossi?"

Ethan held up two fingers squeezed tightly together. "Denton and Brossi are close. A few years ago, Leo Brossi got a Miami bank to loan him four million dollars with nothing but his personal guarantee as security. On the day the loan was finalized, Brossi loaned the same amount to a real estate company owned by Denton Ferrelli and Wayne Black."

"The same Senator Wayne Black who was playing golf with Denton when Conrad was killed?"

"The same, only he wasn't a senator then. Now get this: Ferrelli and Black used the money to buy a building in Miami's prime financial district. They never paid a dime on their loan from Brossi because their deal with him only required them to repay the loan if the cash flow from the building was sufficient to cover it. They claimed it wasn't, so Brossi then defaulted on his four million bank loan."

"But how—"

"Money talks, Dixie. It speaks in a very loud voice. The bank sued Leo Brossi. It also sued the Ferrelli and Black real estate company. But because of some political maneuvering, the FDIC stepped in and arranged a highly unusual settlement whereby Ferrelli and Black only had to repay half a million and Brossi didn't have to pay anything. To sweeten the settlement, Ferrelli and Black got to keep the building."

My brain cells were groaning from the strain of trying to follow slippery financial deals involving millions and billions. My brain was more acquainted with numbers in the hundreds.

Ethan leaned over the table. "Dixie, you shouldn't be going around asking questions about Denton Ferrelli or Leo Brossi. Those guys play dirty, and they play for keeps. You're nothing but an annoying insect at their picnic, and they'll smash you without a second thought."

"They've already tried to smash me."

"Me too. Now that Stevie Ferrelli won't be taking Conrad's place, Denton is putting pressure on the other board members. He wants to kill the plans for the circus retirement home, and I'm fighting him. That means I might as well have a bull's-eye painted on my back. I'm not a big name in the legal world, but Denton can make it so I won't even get work doing simple wills."

I was sure what he said was true, and there wasn't a thing I could say to make it less depressing. We tossed our empties in an open trash can and ambled back to the vet's parking lot.

As I got into the steamy Bronco, I said, "Thanks for the coffee, Ethan, and for the shoulder."

"Anytime."

"Next time I hope I won't need the shoulder."

Surprise registered in his eyes. "Me too. See you, Dixie."

I had my engine running before he was in his car, and my heart was doing a tango. What the hell was wrong with me? Last night I'd realized I was attracted to Guidry, and now I'd just given a not-so-subtle notice to Ethan Crane that I'd like to get better acquainted.

As I pulled out of the lot, I muttered, "Get a grip, girl. Next thing you'll start having fantasies about cucumbers and zucchini."

Back at Mame's house, I examined the urine-stained rug in the study and decided it had to be cleaned by professionals. I called a company and made arrangements to meet them Monday morning. I washed Mame's food and water bowls and stacked them on a pantry shelf. I put her collar and leash on the top shelf of the hall closet. I vacuumed up russet dog hairs. I took the opened bag of organic senior kibble and a box of Jubilee Wafers to pass along to another elderly dog client. When—or if—the Powells returned, it would be to a house that showed no visible signs that Mame had ever lived there.

I locked the door behind me and headed south on Midnight Pass Road, retracing the zigzag route I'd taken earlier but this time visiting cats and birds. It was after eleven when I finished with the last cat and drove down the tree-lined drive to my apartment. Exhilarated after last night's storm, the treetops were filled with songbirds and parakeets chirping their heads off, and every seabird in the area was drawing exuberant circles and loops in the sky.

When I came around the last bend, I saw Guidry's car parked beside the carport. I pulled the Bronco into its slot and started toward my stairs, then detoured to the wooden deck when I saw Michael and Paco and Guidry sitting at the table. I expected them to be celebrating Paco's success, but all three men wore strained faces. Actually, only Guidry and Paco looked strained. Michael's face was thunderous. Something was up. The air was crackling with it, and whatever it was had made Michael mad as a stuck bull.

I gave Paco a big smile. "Good job this morning."

He took the praise like a dog. A nod, a smile. No preening, no aw-shucks-it-was-nothing silliness.

I said, "Too bad Brossi wasn't there when you made the bust."

"He was supposed to be, but somebody slugged him yesterday and broke his nose. He was home with an ice bag."

I met Guidry's gaze and felt my face grow hot with remorse. My little escapade yesterday had allowed Leo Brossi to escape arrest this morning.

Guidry said, "He'll be taken in, don't worry."

Paco gestured toward their coffee mugs. "Want some coffee?"

"No, I want food."

Like a gladiator hearing the call to battle, Michael was instantly on his feet and headed toward the kitchen.

Paco looked at Guidry and tilted his head toward the back door. "Let's go inside."

I went ahead of them to the kitchen. I was a good hour beyond my limit of going without breakfast. Whatever Paco and Guidry had to tell me would have to wait until I'd had something to eat.

Michael was already slamming food from the refrigerator to the cooktop, laying paper-thin slices of ham on the grill and topping them with Gruyère cheese, grilling a split croissant beside them, and somehow with a few moves putting it all together and flipping it on a plate next to a slice of honeydew melon.

Paco and Guidry cast covetous looks at my plate, so he did the same for them and then for himself. Paco poured a round of coffee for everybody, and we all sat around the butcher-block island and ate like hogs. I was surprised that Guidry knew the trick to eating a sandwich that oozed melted cheese, but then I remembered he was from New Orleans. Probably had a French nanny who made him *croque-monsieurs* when he was still in diapers. Probably wore pure linen diapers too.

Once my stomach was reassured, I said, "You guys have something to tell me?"

Michael's face darkened, and he got up and started putting food away with a vengeance.

Guidry said, "We picked Gabe Marks up for questioning. He said he does odd jobs sometimes for Leo Brossi, but he denied knowing Denton Ferrelli. Also denied trying to run you down with his truck. He said you're a crazy woman who shot at him when he went to his girlfriend's apartment. He didn't deny using Scoline to capture alligators, but he has a valid Florida Alligator Harvest Permit, and, like he said, most everybody who handles alligators has some drugged darts. We couldn't hold him."

Three pairs of eyes were watching me, Michael like a statue by the sink. Nobody asked if it was true that I'd shot at Gabe Marks, just as nobody had asked if I was the person who had caused Leo Brossi to be home with ice on his face last night. I was stuck with being the only one who knew for sure I'd done both those things.

I said, "I can't prove it was Gabe Marks who tried to run me down in the parking lot. I can't prove he put snakes in my apartment. I can't prove he was the one driving Conrad's car or that he shot drugged darts into Conrad and Stevie. But I know Denton hired Gabe to kill them, and I know he wants me dead. Denton is a respected man with important political connections. He has powerful mob connections. If Gabe doesn't kill me, Denton will have somebody else do it."

Nobody spoke. Nobody argued with me.

I said, "It's hopeless, isn't it?"

Guidry said, "Nothing's ever hopeless, Dixie."

That wasn't true, and we all knew it. Some things are flat-out hopeless, and there's nothing anybody can do about it. The kitchen seemed very still and quiet. The clock on the wall made faint clicking noises as the second hand moved. Sunshine streamed through the bay window facing the shore, and dust motes shimmered in the golden light. In that peaceful moment, it seemed incongruous that death could lurk nearby. But death is always lurking. The question isn't if death will ultimately win but how we will face it when it does. I thought about how gracefully Mame had dealt with the hopelessness of her situation, how fearlessly she had gone to her last moment. Perhaps that's why pets exist—to teach humans how to die.

I said, "What would it take to nail Denton Ferrelli for murdering Conrad and Stevie? Or for hiring Gabe Marks to do it?"

"A confession. A detailed account of how they did it. Details we could corroborate."

"What if you caught one of them trying to kill somebody else?"

Guidry narrowed his gray eyes in a suspicious look. "Then we'd arrest him for attempted murder."

"What if the somebody else was wired? What if the somebody else cleverly got a detailed account of how Conrad and Stevie were killed? And what if you rushed in and saved the somebody else before he actually killed her?"

Michael slapped the refrigerator door and glared at me.

Guidry said, "The somebody else would have to be pretty stupid to set herself up like that."

I pushed my coffee mug away and rested my forearms on the butcher block. Everything suddenly seemed crystal clear to me. I just had to explain it so they understood it. Especially so Michael understood.

"If Gabe Marks isn't locked up, and soon, he will kill me. Even if he is locked up, Denton will find somebody to kill me. Or he may do it himself. Denton is a psychopathic monster who enjoys hurting people. Gabe is a dumb thug who enjoys hurting people. Separately or together, they are determined to kill me, and they will. Even if I ran away, Denton has the contacts and the power to track me. He thinks I'm a danger to him, and he's determined to shut me up."

Michael turned away and stood motionless with his hands braced on the countertop, every hard line of his body saying he knew what I was saying was true and that he could not bear it.

I said, "Look, I'm not the shrinking violet you think I

am. I know how to handle a gun, I know how to handle myself in a fight. So why not use me? Why not let Denton get
to me? You have a whole fucking SWAT team that could
swarm him the minute it sounded like things were getting
too hairy. It would work, Guidry. It may be the only way to
keep me alive."

Michael said, "No! Goddamn it, no!"

Paco said, "I don't like it either, Michael, but she's
right. It may be the only way."

Guidry said, "I never thought you were a shrinking violet."

"Well, okay, how about it?"

He looked at Michael. "Michael would have to be okay
with it."

Michael said, "Then it's never happening. Never."

He lasered us all with a look of sheer despair, and I got
up and put my arms around him. Michael has taken care of
me since the first time our mother left us when he was four
and I was two. He kept me safe then, and for the rest of his
life he's felt that was his sacred duty. I could feel his strong
heart pounding under his shirt, and I knew he was feeling
utter anguish at not being able to protect me now.

I said, "I have to do this by myself, hon. It's the only
way. And I won't be alone. Guidry and his guys will be
close by. It will make it a whole lot easier if you have faith
in me, if you believe I can do it."

"Shit, Dixie."

"I know."

He gave a gigantic sigh and squeezed me close. "Guidry,
you son-of-a-bitch, if anything happens to her—"

Guidry got up and rapped his knuckles a couple of times
on the butcher block, like a ritual to ward off bad luck.

"I'll get the stuff you'll need. I'll be back later."

He went out the door without closing it behind him. I
watched him cross the deck to his car and back out. The
world looked different now, because I had moved to a new
place in it.

Good or bad, I had taken a step in a new direction, and
there was no going back.

26

I went up to my apartment, but I was too keyed up to nap. I took a long shower. I dressed in clean shorts and sleeveless top. I put on clean white Keds. I switched on the TV and saw Leo Brossi leaving the police station with his attorney while reporters yelled questions at him. His nose was taped and one eye was swollen almost shut. A newscaster said Brossi claimed he'd banged into a cabinet door the day before, but the newscaster didn't sound as if he believed the story. I felt a little better about punching Brossi.

I entered pet visits in my client notebook. I made invoices. I returned all the calls that had to be returned. I went to the kitchen and looked out the window through the belled iron heart. I went back to the office-closet and looked up Denton Ferrelli's address in the phone book and wrote it down. That made me feel efficient, as if I'd confirmed an important detail.

I still had several hours before I made my afternoon rounds, and I felt like somebody all dressed up with no place to go. I finally couldn't stand it anymore and went downstairs and pulled the Bronco out of the carport. I wanted to see where my enemy lived. One of them, anyway.

Until a few years ago, a drawbridge connected the mainland to Bird Key, Lido Key, Casey Key, St. Armand's Key, and Longboat Key. But people who moved here to escape the fast pace of big cities objected to the slow pace of waiting for the bridge to open, so now we have a span of soaring concrete. Who knows, one day the people who came here to escape concrete wastelands may grow impatient with the water around the keys and demand the waterways be paved over.

I passed the exit to Bird Key, which has the feeling of a tropical gated community, and Lido Key, home of Mote Marine Laboratory and Pelican Man's Bird Sanctuary, both places where dedicated volunteers work to rescue injured wildlife. On St. Armand's Key, I slowed for pedestrians around the fashion circle, then turned onto John Ringling Parkway. The New Pass Bridge spilled me onto Gulf of Mexico Drive and Longboat Key, where buildings that look like public libraries are really the homes of multimillionaires. Longboat Key has a gulfside beach where sea oats wave in the breeze, but it isn't open to the public like Siesta's Crescent Beach. To enjoy the sand on Longboat Key, you have to buy a house or a condo. Otherwise, the Longboat Key Police Department will arrest you for trespassing. At least the people who named the streets had a sense of humor—boat lovers can live on Sloop, Ketch, Schooner, Yawl, or Outrigger. Golfers live on Birdie, Wedge, Chipping, or Putter.

At Harbourside Drive, I turned to skirt the bay, scanning the sleek boats slipped at the Longboat Key Moorings. One of those boats belonged to Denton Ferrelli. The Longboat Key Golf Club has two courses, one harborside, and one inland. The clubhouse of the harborside course was less than a hundred feet away from the dock. I imagined Denton coming into that dock after killing his brother. Perhaps the lipstick he'd used to draw the leering grin on Conrad's face had been tossed into the sea. I imagined him mooring his boat and ambling over to play golf with his friends.

Back on Gulf of Mexico Drive, I began watching for Denton's street. It was one of the older streets edging the bay, where normal people used to live in normal houses. Now those normal houses are being bought up and bulldozed to make room for megamansions in which two or three people count their money or plan where their money will go when they die or whatever really rich people do when they're alone. Denton's three-story gray stucco edifice squatted at the end of the street like a leering gargoyle. A black iron gate spanned a driveway that curved to a garage somewhere behind the house. I could see open air at the back, but tall stucco walls ran along both sides of the lot. Only boats and fish would be looking at them, but Denton and Marian Ferrelli were taking no chance of being seen inside their house.

I drove past the end wall and over the curb to park beside the wall where I thought I would be out of view. The builders had spared an ancient banyan tree there, in a thick green copse of palmetto fronds and potato vines. From the car window, I could see the third-story roof and the side of a second-story deck that was probably above the garage. Part of the deck was covered with a blue canvas awning, and the rest was caged with ribbing that rose to the third-story roof. Too hot now, but probably a pleasant place to sit early in the morning and late in the afternoon and watch sailboats and dolphins on the bay. I got out of the Bronco and eased the door shut, then walked between the stucco wall and the rooting banyan branches toward the back of the lot.

An old mango tree at the far end of the wall emitted a pungent odor of rotten fruit, and I could hear the scurrying of fruit rats as I approached. Careful not to step on any of the mushy mangoes on the ground, I slipped under the overhanging branches and stopped behind the tree's thick trunk. A rat the size of a cat leaped past me with a mango in its mouth, giving me a red-eyed glare as if it thought I had come to steal its booty.

Cautiously, I angled my head so I could see the back of the house, but all I got was a view of a five-car garage and the pavement in front of it. All the garage doors were closed. Above the garage, the deck shimmered in the afternoon sun. A blue-and-white-striped table umbrella made an occasional movement from the sea breeze, but that was the only sign of life. No doors slammed, no car motors started, no music or conversation sounded. With Reggie's keen senses, I was surprised he wasn't barking at the fruit rats. Or at me. But maybe he wasn't here. Maybe Denton had taken him someplace else. I didn't want to think about the someplace else he might have taken him.

After a while I got the prickly, uneasy feeling that happens when somebody is staring, as if eyes were boring into the back of my head. I looked behind me, but all I saw was a screen of palmetto fronds, potato vines, and trailing banyan branches. No-see-ums were beginning to snip at my flesh and get into places no living creature should get into without specific permission. If I ever gave permission to go there, it wouldn't be to an invisible biting insect. Not that anybody was asking.

I looked at my watch. It would soon be time to start on my afternoon pet rounds, and the drive home would take me about forty minutes. I shouldn't have come here. I should have stayed home and taken a nap. What had I expected to see, anyway?

A sound reached me, the mechanical whine of the front gate swinging open, then the sound of a car engine. A shiny red car came to a jerking stop in front of the garage. I squinted through the leaves at it. I knew that car. It was the classic red Honda I'd seen in Birdlegs Stephenson's garage. I knew the man getting out of it too. It was Leo Brossi, still with his nose taped and wearing dark glasses to hide his swollen eye.

One of the garage doors lumbered up, and Denton Ferrelli strolled out to meet Brossi. They stood close together and spoke in low tones for a couple of minutes, then Brossi laughed and stepped back.

He said, "Where you going to kill him?"

Denton said, "I thought I'd take him out to the country where nobody can see."

"That's good. You can throw him in the river for the alligators."

"You want to come watch?"

"Sure. I haven't seen a dog killed in a long time."

Denton went back inside the garage and came out with

Reggie on a leash. My mouth went dry. Now I knew why Reggie hadn't barked. He wore a muzzle buckled around his mouth to keep him quiet. He looked listless too, as if he were drugged or exhausted.

Brossi said, "I don't want that dog in my car. He might shit or throw up or something."

Denton looked down at him with a pouting frown, but went back inside the garage and prodded Reggie into the backseat of a black Land Rover. Denton backed the car out of the garage, and Leo Brossi got in the passenger side. Denton swung the car back and then moved forward toward the front gate. As they drove off, I could see them laughing.

I ran for the Bronco, pulling out my cell phone as I went. I started the motor while I punched in Guidry's number. Something seemed different, and I looked at the phone screen.

"Fuck!"

There was no light on the screen, no nagging little logo of a lone battery trying to get my attention. My phone was dead.

I threw the phone on the passenger seat and waited until I was sure Denton had turned onto Gulf of Mexico Drive before I tore out after him. This wasn't about catching the killer of Conrad and Stevie Ferrelli anymore. This was about preventing Reggie's murder.

At Gulf of Mexico Drive, I looked south and saw Denton's car half a mile ahead. I stayed well back, passing cars that got in my line of vision, but not getting close enough for him to recognize me. At St. Armand's circle, I slowed at every crosswalk to let wilted pedestrians creep across the street, then turned onto John Ringling Boulevard and picked up speed. Denton had had to slow down too, though, so I hadn't lost him. We raced over the new causeway to the mainland, where Denton hung a right along the curve of the bay.

Keeping my eyes on Denton and traffic, I tried the cell phone again, as if it might have resurrected itself. It was still dead. I had the feeling that it was glad I was being punished for not charging it, like its nasty little electric innards were saying, *See what you made me do?*

I sped up to get through a yellow light before it turned red, and got closer to Denton to make sure I hadn't lost him. That was him, all right. That was Leo Brossi in the passenger seat and that was Reggie standing muzzled and forlorn in the backseat. We were going south on Tamiami Trail. At Clark Road, which leads to Interstate 75 or the Myakka River, Denton turned.

I got a sick taste in my mouth. Birdlegs had said Gabe Marks lived in the country near the Myakka River. Now Brossi's crude jibe about throwing Reggie to the alligators seemed even more cruel, because he probably meant it literally. The Myakka River is full of brooding alligators waiting for new flesh to eat.

After a few miles, Denton crossed 75 and continued southeast. Toward the Myakka. Perhaps toward Gabe Marks's place.

I slowed the Bronco and pulled to the shoulder. This was insane. I should turn around now. I should go home and make my afternoon rounds. I should go home and plug in my dead cell phone and recharge its battery. I should wait for Guidry to bring a transmitter for me to wear when I accosted Denton Ferrelli.

But Denton had Reggie with him, and he planned to kill him. Reggie wasn't a fellow human being, but he was a fellow being, and he was a damn sight more deserving of respect than a lot of humans.

While Denton's car got smaller and smaller in the distance, I sat and debated with myself. Then I took my foot off the brake and drove straight ahead. In the end, it all boiled down to one thing—if I didn't try to save Reggie, I would never be able to live with myself.

Out of the city, Clark Road becomes State Highway 72. There was enough traffic to keep me from feeling conspicuous, but I stayed three or four cars behind Denton. After about ten miles of orange groves and vegetable and plant farms, he left the highway, turning right on a side road. To let him get farther ahead, I stopped on the highway shoulder for a couple of minutes before I turned. The new road was a paved farm-to-market that cut between densely wooded pinelands interspersed with occasional cattle farms. The pines had once been farmed for turpentine, but when the turpentine market bottomed out, trees were cut to make way for cows.

Denton's Land Rover was a black dot ahead of me. I imagined him laughing with Leo Brossi as they planned Reggie's murder. The black dot turned left and disappeared, and I stomped on the gas. When I reached the turn, he was already half a mile away. If he had been observant, he might wonder at a car taking the same route. On the other hand, he was headed directly toward the Myakka River and the popular Myakka River State Park. The park comprises almost thirty thousand acres of prairie grasses and wildflowers that have been obliterated in the rest of Florida, so it's a state treasure. The Myakka flows through twelve miles of the park on its way to Charlotte Harbor. Outside the park, a few farmers and ranchers cling to a way of life that in just one generation has become an anachronism.

Denton turned right, bouncing down a sandy road and whipping a high cloud of white dust. I pulled to the side of the road and watched the dust. After about half a mile, the dust cloud stopped, and the black dot that was Denton's Land Rover emerged, going slowly toward a group of frame buildings set far back on the left side of the road. He had reached his destination.

I moved forward, turning at a snail's pace to keep from exciting the dust. Wide ditches lay on each side of the narrow road. On the right was a wilderness of pine, oak, palmetto, and palm above a morass of saw palmetto, wax myrtle, gallberry, fetterbush, and staggerbush teeming with deer and wild hogs. Ospreys perched in the trees, and a red-shouldered hawk watched my passage from the top of a runner oak. On the left, a barbed-wire fence enclosed thick yellow cordgrass, tall as a man. The grass hid the house where Denton and Leo Brossi had taken Reggie. I prayed it hid me too.

27

Well back from the driveway leading to the house, I pulled to the side of the road and got out of the Bronco. I managed to bound across the ditch without getting bitten by any critters hiding in its vines and grasses, and balanced on the ditch's edge while I pushed down the lowest string of barbed wire. Gingerly, I stretched my leg over it, whispering ouches and shits when sharp barbs punctured my flesh. At least I managed to crawl through without snagging my shirt or my hair on the top wire.

I crouched low and began swimming through the cordgrass, parting it with outstretched arms, praying I didn't step on a snake. Swarms of gnats and mosquitoes rose like steam, and a fine mist of pollen covered me from the grass heads. I felt a sneeze coming on and pinched my nose. The sneeze imploded inside my head, causing lightning flashes across my cortex.

Something sticky brushed my bare shoulder. I instinctively slapped it away and then gave an involuntary shriek when I saw it was a furry tarantula. The thing scurried away into the grass, while I rubbed my skin and remembered all the stories I'd heard as a child about how a tarantula's bite will cause your flesh to rot away and leave a big cavity down to your bones. I couldn't see a bite mark, but for all I knew a tarantula's bite might be invisible. Shuddering, I moved on, wanting to get to the end of this teeming field.

I could hear men's voices now, and a heavy laugh floated over the grass. I couldn't see anything except the pale grass stems, but I didn't dare stand up. All I could do was press on, hoping my movement through the sea of grass wasn't an obvious trail the men were watching. With luck, I would come out behind one of the sheds. If I weren't lucky, death might be waiting for me on the other side of this ocean of grass. Oddly enough, it wasn't death that I feared, but turning coward and running away without saving Reggie.

After what seemed an eternity, I got close enough to the end of the field of cordgrass to see a dilapidated shed directly in front of me, one of a number of similar buildings scattered behind and to the side of a battered old house. A wall of stacked lumber stood at the end of the driveway, with logs piled higher than my head. Gabe either sold wood to people nostalgic for fires roaring inside while snow fell outside, or he just kept trim by felling trees and chopping logs. Several snakeskins hung with their top ends nailed to logs in the stack, and a long alligator hide was stretched on a plywood board raised on sawhorses.

The front yard was littered with abandoned furniture, parts of cars that had been there so long that grass grew on them, and rusted pieces of farm equipment. On the far side of the sandy driveway, the weathered frame house had a sagging front porch and a pile of garbage beside the porch steps. Not a compost heap, just a pile of garbage. Eggshells and egg cartons, plastic milk bottles and bread wrappers and greasy KFC boxes, all rotting and stinking in the glaring heat and probably being aerated by roaches the size of small mice. The garbage pile made Gabe seem even more dangerous. He really was as dumb and primitive as he looked, and a violent nature in a stupid man makes a lethal combination.

Gabe himself was apparently having some kind of standoff with Denton and Leo. They were below him next to the car, while Gabe stood on the porch with his hammy arms folded over his chest and his chin defiantly tilted to show he didn't defer to any man. Anybody looking at the three men would immediately have known they came from different worlds. Denton was dressed like a lawyer, dark trousers, white dress shirt with the sleeves rolled partway up his arms. Leo looked like the pimp he had been. A foot shorter than Denton, his pinkish beige pants were too tight and too shiny, and an expensive palm-printed silk shirt still managed to look cheap on him. Gabe wore a dark mesh muscle shirt that emphasized his defined chest, and stained jeans that hugged thighs thick as tree trunks. He stood with legs spread, feet firmly planted in knee-high leather boots. I didn't have to be any closer to know he smelled like the garbage heap below him.

Denton was speaking in a measured monotone, as if he wanted something and was being careful not to rile Gabe in the asking. He pointed toward his Land Rover, where Reggie was standing in the backseat looking out the side window. Then he raised his hands in a gesture of being at his wit's end, as if he didn't know what he would do if Gabe didn't do whatever he was asking.

Gabe gave him a scornful look, dumb rube showing contempt for the helplessness of the city slicker, and unfolded his arms.

"This is the last time! I'm not doing it again!"

He came down the steps, walking with the swaggering strut peculiar to men of small minds and large egos, and Denton permitted himself a quick smile of victory. He had manipulated Gabe, and it didn't look as if it were the first time.

Denton opened the car door and Reggie backed away, whining and uncertain. Denton reached in and grabbed Reggie's leash and jerked him out, while Gabe turned and walked toward the small shed in front of me. I heard the door open, and I imagined sharp hoes and scythes and all kinds of toxic and poisonous farm supplies that would be harmful to a dog. Reggie must have had the same idea, because he struggled and fought, but Denton had him on a choke chain that finally brought him across the driveway to the shed.

Denton said, "Get in there, dammit!"

A moment later the door slammed shut, and I heard a wooden latch drop into place.

At least Reggie was alive. Still muzzled, he was stuck in a good dog's dilemma. Denton had been a guest in Reggie's home, which put him in the category of humans to whom he was supposed to show submission. But Reggie was a smart dog, and I had the feeling that Denton had pushed him beyond his limit.

Leo Brossi's voice carried well enough for me to hear him ask Gabe a question that made my heart clatter.

"How long will it take you to load the darts?"

Gabe said something that was lost, and the three men went inside the house.

As soon as the front door closed behind them, I hunkered over and began moving through the tall grass toward the shed. All the windows on this side of the house had opaque window shades pulled halfway down. To see me, a person would have to raise a shade or stoop to look under it. They could also see me if they were sitting in a chair where they would be at the level of the lower part of the window, but I didn't want to think about that.

I also didn't want to think about how Gabe was loading a dart gun with a deadly poison that would paralyze Reggie within seconds. He would die a horrible death, fully conscious and unable to move.

Getting as close to the edge of the screening cordgrass as I could, I told myself *Go!* and ran like hell around the shed to the door. As I'd expected, it had a simple wooden latch high above my head. I stood on tiptoe and stretched my arm as high as it would go. As I did, I spoke low to Reggie.

"Hey, Reggie, it's me. I'm getting you out. Don't jump when I open the door, okay?"

Inside the shed, Reggie must have recognized my scent because he began to whine eagerly and scratch at the door. My fingertips touched the latch and I jumped to push the wooden bar up from its crude resting place. It went up and then flopped back down. I grunted and jumped at it again, this time sending it farther up before it slid back into its slot. I heaved myself upward and knocked the bar to the very top, where it hung poised at the very edge. Good. It hadn't settled back. Another good jump and I could knock it the rest of the way out.

I stretched my arm up and gathered myself to jump. A large hand suddenly closed on mine, and an arm hard as steel wrapped around my ribs and jerked me backward. A man's triumphant laugh drowned out the sound of my own terror.

Denton Ferrelli said, "Hello, dog-sitter. We've been waiting for you."

The truth hit me all in one gulp. I had been tricked. Denton had known all along that I was following him. The talk about killing Reggie had been a ruse to get me to follow him to this remote place. Nobody would know to look for me here, and nobody would hear me scream. They would kill me here and dump my body in the woods and nobody would ever find it. Animals would eat my flesh and scatter my bones while search parties combed Siesta Key.

I wasn't so different from Gabe after all. Like Gabe, I had thought I was being smart and brave when I was really just being stupid and arrogant.

Denton Ferrelli swung me around while I kicked and flailed and screamed, all my noise and struggle as useless as the squeaks and air-peddling of a mouse about to be dropped in a snake's mouth. My gun was in my shorts pocket, but the armlock Denton had on me made it impossible to reach. While I hung from his forearm, he carried me toward Leo and Gabe, who stood at the bottom of the porch steps. Leo's malicious grin gave his sharp-boned face the look of a demented skeleton. A demented skeleton with a piece of tape stretched over the ridge of its nose.

Gabe was stern and self-righteous as a televangelist. He had put on a straw cowboy hat with the sides curled up like a rodeo rider, and he held a twenty-caliber dart gun pointed down at his side. The hilt of another gun stuck out from a thick leather holster draped around his hips, and a square metal container that I assumed held loaded darts was stuck in his waistband. I felt a little spurt of appreciation for his professionalism. He had backup ready, the same as a law-enforcement officer would.

Behind us, Reggie was scratching and jumping at the shed's door.

I said, "Just so you know, my Bronco has a tracking device on it. If I'm not home soon, people will come looking for me."

Denton laughed again. "You're such a transparent liar. You're a cute little dog-sitter too. Too bad you couldn't mind your own fucking business."

Panting and twisting, I said, "You're cute too, Denton. I love the little ironic twists you give to murder. The kitten with broken legs for Conrad was a real stroke of genius."

He chuckled, and his voice went high as if he were speaking lines on a stage. "Hey, Conrad, come see what I've found. It's beautiful, man, some kind of rare bird I never saw before. Come look, it's back here in the woods."

In his normal voice, he said, "Stupid freak believed every word. Thought I wanted to share the joy I felt with my little brother. Gabe was in the trees waiting. He shot him while he leaned over looking at the damned cat."

Gabe said, "Are you gonna keep holding her?"

Denton's grip loosened a bit, and his voice came out sharp. "Don't be a fool! Of course I'm not."

"Then let her go so I can hit her running."

My mind was whirling. Denton didn't want to hold me while Gabe shot me with that dart gun because the dart might accidentally go into him instead of me. When he let me go, there would be a split second while he jumped out of the way. In that moment, I might be able to scoop my gun out of my pocket and shoot Gabe before he shot me. But I wasn't ready yet. I couldn't face that instant yet.

"Having your mother's horse stomp her to death was clever too. Was your mother the first one, or were you already killing people before her?"

His arm tightened, squeezing my ribs so hard I could barely breathe. "Them and their goddamn animals. Always love for some four-legged beast. Not for me. Never any love for old Denton, not after sweet animal-sucking Conrad was born. Conrad's little narrow head didn't tear her up coming out. He didn't have an ugly purple bruise on his face that never went away. Oh, he was easy to love. They should be grateful to me, I got them all together with their fucking animals. And now the dog-sitter will be joining them."

A final piece of the puzzle fell into place. The reason Denton hated me was because I worked with animals. A mother who trained horses so well they thought with one mind had probably spent more time with them than she did with her little boy. Especially her first little boy, when the act with the horses was new and she was working hard to perfect it. Because I worked with animals, Denton had moved me to the place in his mind where a twisted coil of hatred toward his mother lay.

"What about your father? And Stevie? Why kill them?"

He made a bitter sound that was half laugh. "Conrad was the only one who mattered to him. Conrad and his stupid sissy clothes and his freak circus friends, his freak man-wife. All of them were freaks, and they didn't care how they humiliated me. Never gave it one thought. I made millions with nothing but my brains, all Conrad ever did was give away the money somebody else made. Well, now they can all get together and dress up in their stupid clown outfits, forever and ever, amen."

Self-pity from anybody is annoying. From a murderer, it's downright disgusting.

Gabe must have thought so too, because he yelled, "Let her go, damn it!"

Denton's arm muscles tensed in preparation for flinging them wide, and I braced myself to land on my feet.

28

I was almost surprised that fear didn't buckle my knees when Denton took his arm away and let my feet touch the ground. He crossed the distance between me and the other men and stood beside Leo Brossi.

Little cold fingers climbed my spine, vertebra by vertebra. It was almost a sick joke: woman convinces cops to use her as a lure to catch a killer, woman goes off on her own with dead phone, woman gets killed after all.

He said, "Okay, Gabe, do it."

Leo said, "Not so fast. I'm fucking that bitch first, and then I have some other things planned for her."

Gabe frowned at him. "You didn't say anything about that."

Leo said, "What the hell's the matter with you, boy? You probably fuck rattlesnakes. Denton, take the bitch in the house. I'm not doing her in the yard."

Denton said, "Leo, don't complicate things."

"Look, the bitch hit me. She broke my nose. I've got a fuck coming, and I'm taking it."

Gabe said, "Rape ain't right. I don't care how much of a cunt she is."

It almost sounded as if Gabe might have a thread of decency somewhere in his beetle brain. I suddenly remembered the stuffed toy he'd brought the baby. The memory of it was a little ray of light. Denton Ferrelli had a sick twisted mind, and Leo Brossi was a career criminal, but

Gabe was just a dumb kid living with snakes and alligators and thinking that killing things made him a man.

I said, "Leo will rape your baby girl if he gets a chance, Gabe."

Leo said, "Goddamn it, Denton, get the woman in the house!"

Like a bull pricked by picadors, Gabe glowered at me and then at Leo. "Not in my house."

Leo said, "I'm not asking your permission, boy."

Gabe's lower lip crept forward. "I ain't your boy."

Denton said, "That's enough, both of you!"

I said, "Guess what, Gabe. Leo raped Priscilla before he gave her to you. The baby might even be his."

A dark painful flush spread up Gabe's neck. Denton laughed, and Gabe looked quickly at him.

I said, "They think you're funny, Gabe. They think it's funny to use your woman, your baby, anything they want. And when they're through with you, they'll think it's funny when they kill you."

"Shut up, cunt. Ain't nobody killing me."

"They'll have to. You know too much. You think they're going to let you go around knowing what you know?"

Gabe was dumb, but he wasn't so dumb he didn't know I could be telling the truth. His brow furrowed and he cut his eyes toward Leo and Denton.

Leo said, "Kid, she's fucking with your mind. Now shut up and do as you're told. I want the woman in the house."

Denton said, "Leo, let it go."

Over him, Gabe said, "What the hell you mean, do as I'm told?"

Gabe's face looked like a four-year-old's about to cry or throw a tantrum, and his hand holding the dart gun looked twitchy. He swung angrily toward Denton.

"You was there both times, and if you think I won't tell the cops you was, you better think again."

Denton scowled at him. "Gabe, this isn't the time—"

Reggie slammed himself against the door of the shed with such determined force that it cracked and rattled against the wooden latch. The men all shot a quick look toward the shed, and my hand began to inch toward my shorts pocket where my .38 was making a hard statement on my thigh.

As if the words were wrenched from him, Gabe pulled himself taller and sputtered, "Mr. Brossi, is what she said true? Did you rape Priscilla?"

Leo Brossi grinned and made a lewd jerking motion with his pelvis, looking in his shiny silk like a banty rooster posturing under a bull.

"Wasn't rape, boy. She liked it. Probably never had nothing but boys before."

Denton said, "Leo, that's enough!"

Stung, a small man between two large men, Leo pivoted toward Denton to make himself feel bigger.

"Speak for yourself, Denton. You have your plans, I have mine."

Behind him, Gabe made a strangled sound and whipped the dart gun up to point it at Leo Brossi. Brossi made a quick instinctive movement to the back of his waist, and in the next instant a shimmering knife blade sliced through the air and pierced the side of Gabe's neck.

For a second, time seemed to freeze. Gabe remained standing for what seemed an eternity, staring at Leo with incredulous shock, his face traced by inarticulate runnels of private agony. The geyser of dark blood arching from his neck seemed to move in imperceptible increments. My hand seemed to take eons to creep into my shorts pocket and come out with my .38.

At the same time, Denton shouted "Fool!" and ran to stand behind Gabe and chop his fist down on Gabe's thick forearm holding the gun still pointed toward Leo Brossi.

Perhaps it was the blow that caused Gabe's trigger finger to squeeze instinctively, or perhaps Gabe's final movement was deliberate. The dart left the gun with a sharp *phifftt* and caught Leo square in the shoulder. Leo's other hand swung toward the point of impact as if to pull the dart out, but the drug was faster than his hand. His eyelids fluttered, his face quivered, and he crumpled to the ground and lay motionless, only the horror in his eyes evidence that he was conscious.

Only then did Gabe fall into the pool of his own blood, his sturdy young legs in their tight denim already flaccid in death.

I held my gun extended with both hands, waiting for the moment when I had a clear target. Inside the shed, Reggie was hysterical, banging himself against the shed door so hard it seemed as if the door must surely split from the impact.

As Gabe fell, Denton crouched low and scrambled through the river of blood to grab Gabe's backup dart gun from its leather holster. I gripped my gun and sighted his head, my finger ready on the trigger.

Denton's fear was palpable. Things hadn't gone the way he'd planned. A lifetime of bullying people weaker than himself hadn't prepared him for the moment when one of his thugs lay bleeding out on the sandy ground, another was turning blue from asphyxiation, and a woman he'd planned to feed to the alligators had him in her gunsight.

The shed door slammed open with a loud crack, and Reggie charged out in snarling fury, graceful flanks smoothly churning, wide chest heaving, no confusion in his mind anymore about whether it was right to attack a man who had been welcome in his master's home. Even muzzled, he was a ferocious sight.

Denton jerked to his feet, swerved his eyes once toward Reggie, and aimed the dart gun at me.

I emptied my .38 into Denton's cesspool heart.

29

At the memorial service for Conrad and Stevie, swirling dust motes shimmered like sequins above a large photograph of them at their wedding. In the photo, Stevie was radiant in a traditional bridal gown and veil; Conrad wore a splendid morning coat, a pleated white shirt, modestly patterned skorts, and his signature ear bobs. They looked so vital, so alive, that it was hard to believe they were dead.

Inside the chapel, an organist played softly while the audience sat in silence, still stunned at the ugly violence that had lived among them. Outside, the media slavered over a breaking scandal that involved some of Florida's most prestigious politicians and businessmen. A grand jury had decided that Leo Brossi had killed and been killed by Gabe Marks, and that I had shot Denton Ferrelli in self-defense. Once again, my name had become front-page news. I had actually been turned into something of a heroine, which shows that people who write about killing don't have a clue what it means to do it.

I sat with Josephine and her husband. Josephine kept an arm tight around my shoulders as if she were afraid I might bolt and run. I might have too, if I hadn't known reporters would love to see it.

A moment of quiet fell, and then the organist swung into a loud rendition of "Stars and Stripes Forever," the signal circus bands use to alert performers that a major disas-

ter has struck. At the cue, a line of clowns wearing red
noses and big silly shoes stepped through the side door and
took seats in the front two rows. Pete followed them, also
dressed in full clown, and stepped to the dais to deliver the
eulogy. Now that Denton was no longer a threat to Conrad's plan for a retirement home for circus performers, I
knew there was joy mixed with Pete's sadness.

I looked over my shoulder and saw Guidry a few rows
back and across the aisle. Ethan Crane was almost directly
behind him, and both of them were watching me. Their
eyes held identical questions that I couldn't decipher. Or
maybe I just didn't want to.

I can barely answer my own questions, how could I answer theirs?

There are tears in the very heart of things,
And mortality touches the human mind.

—VIRGIL, THE AENEID

Keep reading for an excerpt from the next
Dixie Hemingway novel

EVEN CAT SITTERS
GET THE BLUES

Coming soon in hardcover from St. Martin's Minotaur

1

hristmas was coming, and I had killed a man.

Either of those facts was enough to make me want to crawl in bed and pull the covers over my head for a long, long time.

Not to mention the fact that I was having feelings for two men, when I'd never expected or wanted to love even one man again, ever.

Not to also mention the fact that I'd agreed to take care of an unknown, free-wheeling iguana today.

It was all too much for any one person, especially this person. I figured I had every right to put the brakes on my life and refuse to go on. To just stand up and yell, "Okay, time out! No more life for me for a while. I'll get back to you when I'm ready."

Instead, I crawled out of bed at four a.m., just like I do every friggin' day, and gutted up to face whatever the day would bring. It's a genetic curse, coming as I do from a long line of people who just keep on keeping on, even when anybody in their right mind would step aside for a while.

I'm Dixie Hemingway, no relation to you know who. I'm a pet-sitter on Siesta Key, which is a semi-tropical barrier island off Sarasota, Florida. Until almost four years ago, I was a deputy with the Sarasota County Sheriff's Department. My husband was a deputy too. His name was Todd. We had a beautiful little girl. Her name was Christy.

We were happy in the way of all young families, aware that bad things happened to other people, but blocking out how exquisitely tenuous life really is. That all changed in a heartbeat. Two heartbeats, actually—the last of Todd's and Christy's.

I've read somewhere that some excavators in Siberia found an intact wooly mammoth that had been entombed in ice for millennia. A butterfly was on the mammoth's tongue. I think about that wooly mammoth a lot, because life's like that. One second you can be blissfully standing in golden sunshine with butterflies flitting around you, and the next second, *whap!* The world goes dark and you're totally alone and frozen.

I went a little bit crazy when that happened to me. To tell the truth, I went more than a little crazy. My rage was so great that the sheriff's department wisely decided that sending me out in public with a gun on my belt was like dropping a piranha in a goldfish bowl. But grief held too long eventually becomes a memorial to yourself, and you have to let it go.

When I was able to function again, I became a pet-sitter. I like pets and they like me, and I'm not often in situations where I might revert to the old fury that buzzed in my veins for so long. I can't say I'm completely free of either the grief or the craziness that goes with it, but I'm a lot better.

At least I was until I killed that man.

Not that he didn't need killing. He did, and the Grand Jury agreed that he did. Actually, they agreed that I had killed him in self-defense and that it was a damn good thing I had, given the awful things he had done and would have done again, but that didn't change the fact that I had to live with knowing I'd killed somebody.

Killing changes a person. Ask any combat veteran responsible for enemy deaths. Ask any cop who's had to take out a criminal. You can justify it, you can know that it was your job, that it was necessary, and that you'd do it again in the same circumstance, but it still changes you, even if nobody else knows it.

That, plus the fact that Christmas would be here in exactly eleven days, was causing me to avoid almost all human contact.

In my line of work, avoiding human contact is actually pretty easy. If a pet client is new, I have one meeting with its humans when we sign a contract and make sure everybody understands exactly what I will and will not do for their pet. I'm pretty much a pushover when it comes to pets, so I'll do whatever they need, but I try not to let the humans know that right up front. They give me a key to their house, a security code number if they have an alarm system, show me their pet's toys and favorite hiding places, and tell me what they want done in the event they both die while they're away. Living in a retirement mecca where the majority of the inhabitants are over the age of sixty-five makes that an issue that comes up more frequently than you'd think. Sometimes it's the other way around; they tell me what they want done with the pet in the event it dies while they're away. That also happens more frequently than you'd think. Once we've all made sure we're in accord about what's best for the pet, they leave and I don't have any more contact with them until they return.

That's my modus operandi and it's practically set in stone. The fact that I'd deviated so much from it when I agreed to take care of an iguana that day was a mystery. His owner had called the night before and talked me into taking the job even though he wasn't one of my regular clients, and even though it is absolutely against my professional standards to take on a pet without first meeting both pet and owner. We'd had a bad connection and I'd had to strain to hear him. To this day, I'm not exactly sure what he said that was so persuasive—his husky Irish accent, maybe, not full-blown faith-and-begorra Irish, but with enough of a lilt to make my mouth want to smile. Or maybe it was just that I have a soft spot in my heart for iguanas because my grandfather had one.

I said, "The iguana is in a cage?"

"No, no, he runs free. I don't fancy cages."

I nodded at the phone. My grandfather had felt the same way.

He said, "Somebody will be there to let you in. All you have to do is put out fresh vegetables. He dotes on yellow squash, and there's some romaine and red chard. I'm forever in your debt for doing this, miss. Leave me a bill and I'll get a check off to you the instant I get home."

"You want me to go just the one time?"

"Yes, that's all. Oh, and this is very important—his name is Ziggy. Zig-ee."

He gave me his address on Midnight Pass Road, and rang off before I could get a phone number. When I looked at the notes I'd scrawled, they were pathetic. I'd written *Ken Curtis (?) Vegs Yellow sqsh Ziggy*.

Except for the address, that was it. I hadn't even verified the caller's name, and he had said it so fast I wasn't sure I'd caught it right. I pride myself on handling my business in a professional manner, but any half-assed amateur could have handled that call better. I consoled myself that it would be an easy twenty bucks. Iguanas don't have to be walked or groomed, so all I'd have to do was put out some veggies for him, and I'd be out in no time.

The weather for the last few days had been what southwest Floridians call cold and wintry, meaning night temperatures had dipped into the high fifties, and the days' highs hovered just below seventy. For tourists and seasonal snow-birds, the cold weather was a major disappointment. For thin-blooded year-round locals like me, it was an aberrant misery.

My apartment is above a four-stall carport, with a long covered porch running its length. The porch faces the Gulf of Mexico, where time and capricious tides have carved a narrow hiccup of beach-front property that shifts and transforms itself every few months, making it an undesirable spot for developers and investors. When I opened the French doors next morning and stepped out on the porch, it was so chilly I could see my breath in the pale light of a co-conut sky. Rain clouds were building purple mountains over the Gulf, but they looked several hours away. At least that's what I told myself when I decided to take my bike instead of the Bronco. The truth is that at that pre-dawn hour, when the birds are still sleeping in the palms, oaks, pines, and sea grape, I feel invincible on my bike, gliding down empty streets and breathing in the salty air as if I were a bird myself.

Siesta Key is eight miles long, north to south, with one main thoroughfare named Midnight Pass Road. Sarasota Bay lies on our east side, and the Gulf of Mexico is on the west. (Two drawbridges connect us to Sarasota, so one of our favorite bitch topics is how long we had to wait for a sailboat to pass when a bridge was up.) About seven thousand permanent people call the key home, but during "the season" from October to May, our population swells to around twenty-four thousand. Except for times when our streets are clogged with sun-bemused snowbirds, tourists, or carousing students on spring break, we're a fairly laid-back bunch.

I live near the south end so I always begin the day working my way north, just taking care of dogs. Dogs can't wait for you the way other pets can. Once all the dogs have been walked and fed and groomed, I retrace my route and call on the pets who don't have to pee outside. Cats and hamsters and rabbits and guinea pigs and birds. Not snakes. I don't take care of snakes. I'm not exactly snakephobic, but it makes me go swimmy-headed to hold a squirming little mouse above a gaping snake's mouth, so I refer those jobs to other pet-sitters.

No matter who else is on my daily list of calls, I always start with Billy Elliott. Billy's a former racing greyhound who lives with Tom Hale in the Sea Breeze condos. Tom's a CPA whose spine was crushed a few years ago when a wall of lumber at a home-improvement store fell on him. Then to make his misery complete, his wife left him and took their children and most of their possessions. Eventually, Tom got his act together, moved into the Sea Breeze and started doing whatever it is that CPAs do at his kitchen table. He and I trade services. I go by twice a day and run with Billy Elliott, and Tom handles anything having to do with me and money.

With all that had happened to him, Tom was about as closed off from the world as I was, but when I got to his condo that morning, there was a big Christmas wreath on his door. It wasn't just a generic wreath, either, but a customized affair with a sassy red velvet bow and a toy greyhound perched above a nest of gilded pine cones. I stood a moment gaping at the thing before I unlocked the door and let myself into the dark foyer where Billy Elliott was nervously prancing on the tile floor. We kissed hello, I clipped the leash on his collar, and we slipped out of the apartment as quietly as thieves. On the ride down in the elevator, I considered asking him what had possessed Tom to have such a fancy wreath made for his door, but I thought it might hurt Billy Elliott's feelings, seeing as his facsimile was the focal point of the wreath.

We ran tippy-toe across the downstairs lobby and went outside to the parking lot for our run. Billy Elliott knew the routine—run fairly slowly and pee on selected bushes until we came to the oval track encircled by parked cars, and then stretch out and run like hell, full out, galloping like crazy, just like when he was a young dog chasing a mechanical rabbit while crowds cheered and bet money on him. Except this time he had a wheezing blonde human slowing him down because her thigh muscles weren't nearly as strong as his. When he had finally run out all his nervous energy and I was about to fall over from breathing so hard, we ran at a slower pace back to the Sea Breeze's front door.

A woman with a Corgi on a short leash was just coming out, and we stood aside while they passed. The woman nodded, but the Corgi was embarrassed on account of wearing a pair of miniature deer antlers and an ermine-trimmed red velvet jacket, so he kept his head averted. Billy Elliott and I exchanged a *can-you-believe-that?* look, but we didn't let on how dorky we thought it was.

Upstairs, I could smell coffee brewing in the kitchen, and the lights we re on in Tom's living room. I hadn't noticed it before, but there was a lavishly decorated Christmas tree in the corner. Now that I knew it was there, I could smell it, too, a pleasant balsam odor. My gosh, not only a wreath, but a real Christmas tree! Tom and I don't always talk when I pop in and out of his apartment, but you'd think something like plans to buy a Christmas tree would have come up at least once. I wondered how he'd managed to get the top ornaments on. To tell the truth, I felt a little put out that he hadn't asked me to help him. I mean, I didn't want a tree of my own, but if he wanted to have one I would have been happy to help him with it.

I yelled toward the kitchen. "Morning, Tom! Nice tree!"

He wheeled into the living room with a curious grin on his face and his mop of curly black hair looking slept on. Instead of his usual sloppy sweats, he wore a snazzy red velour bathrobe. He looked a little bit like the Corgi.

I said, "Wow, you've really got the Christmas spirit, don't you?" I could hear the little defensive whine in my voice, but I couldn't do anything about it.

He grinned even wider and made some inarticulate sounds that sounded like he was trying to deny it and claim it at the same time. Clinking sounds came from the kitchen, the sounds of mugs being removed from a cupboard, and a silky woman's voice called, "Darlin', did you ask me something?"

Oh. Now I understood. Tom hadn't been hit by the Christmas spirit, he'd been hit by romance. And he hadn't told me. He hadn't said, "Hey, Dixie, I've got a woman in my life now, so when you come to run with Billy Elliott, you may meet her."

For some reason, that made me vaguely angry, which was stupid, because Tom's personal life wasn't any of my business, and I was actually glad that he had a girlfriend after being alone for so long. But I was still sulky at the change in him.

I said, "Oh, excuse me," and beat a fast retreat, knowing

all the time that Tom would feel bad at the way I acted, but not able to do anything about that, either. I didn't even hang Billy Elliott's leash in the hall closet before I left, just left it sloppily looped over the arm of a chair.

The nasty truth was that I was jealous. Not like a woman jealous that another woman is with a man she wants, but jealous that Tom had found the strength to let his old love go and be happy with somebody new. I wasn't sure I'd ever be able to do that, and I was afraid I would self-destruct if I didn't, and soon.